PLAIN TRUTH

Plainly Maryland—Book 3

SUSAN LANTZ SIMPSON

Martha

Thanks to your support

Susan Lantz Simpson

Vinspire Publishing
www.vinspirepublishing.com

For my sister, Carol,
and sisters everywhere!

PROLOGUE

A shadowy figure crept into the employees' room and slipped close to the brass coat tree laden with heavy, black, wool capes. Shaky hands fumbled beneath the garments. Where was that bag? It should be there. It was always there. It had to be there today. The exploring fingers shook a little more, making the search more difficult.

Aha! There. The quilted bag. Quickly, quietly, the fingers drew a bulging zippered deposit bag from a large pocket. Yesterday must have been a very prosperous day if the weight of the bag was any indication. The hand thrust the fat bag deep into the plethora of yarn and crochet hooks. Next a gold and diamond watch found a burial place within the skeins of yarn.

Now make sure the capes are hanging straight, that the quilted bag is safely hidden beneath its owner's cape, and escape.

CHAPTER ONE

"I'll not kneel and confess to a sin I did not commit!"

KatieAnn Mast's adamant cry echoed in the small room. Heat rushed into her cheeks and burned her eyes. *Great! Blazing red cheeks and eyes that spark fire. That'll make a good impression.* Not stomping her foot required a strong, concentrated effort. She looked from Bishop John to her *mamm* and then down at her sturdy, black shoes.

"KatieAnn, all things can be forgiven, you know," Bishop John began. "The Bible says if we confess our sins, the Lord is faithful and will forgive our sins."

"You believe that, *jah*?" Mamm practically whispered.

"Of course I believe that, but Mamm, I didn't do anything wrong."

"The money and watch were found in your bag. Deborah, of course, will not press charges. It's not our way. She's happy everything was returned." The bishop stroked his beard.

"I did not take the money or the watch. I do not steal."

"KatieAnn, the money and watch were found in your bag."

Did the man think she hadn't heard him the first time?

"If you just ask for forgiveness, all will be well, and there will be no danger of the *bann*." Mamm's eyes pleaded with her as they filled with tears.

"I'll be shunned for something I didn't even do?" KatieAnn was horrified. This was her family. These were her people. Wouldn't they give her the benefit of the doubt? They had known her all her life. "I thought we were innocent until proven guilty."

"The evidence is pretty strong." Bishop John yanked at the hairs of his beard.

KatieAnn expected him to pluck his chin bald. "I'll tell you like I told Deborah." She forced herself to stay calm when she wanted to shout. "I don't know how the deposit bag and watch got into my bag. I did not put them there. I've taken the deposit to the bank for Deborah many times and never stole the money. And what would I want with an *Englischer's* watch?"

"You did like pretty jewelry during your *rumspringa*."

KatieAnn couldn't believe her *mamm* brought that up. "That was two years ago, Mamm. I've been a baptized church member for two years now. Besides, liking jewelry doesn't mean I'd steal it!"

"Please, KatieAnn, I don't want to lose you." Mamm was on the verge of an all-out crying jag.

"The Lord Gott wants you to do the right thing." The bishop focused a stern gaze on her.

"Does the Lord Gott want me to lie? That's what I would be doing if I said I stole those things. Then I'd have to kneel before the church to ask forgiveness for lying." She hoped she didn't sound too disrespectful. That would not help her case in the least.

"Think on these things, KatieAnn." The bishop's admonishing frown drew his dark, bushy eyebrows together in a unibrow. Like a wooly worm had crawled across his forehead and died there. KatieAnn stifled a laugh that would surely *kumm* out as hysterical. That would never do at such a time as this.

"This week is an off Sunday, so you have until next Sunday's church meeting to make a decision. Maybe you can talk some sense into her, Ida." With that the bishop turned and strode from the kitchen.

Mamm sank onto a sturdy oak chair and dropped her head into rough, work-worn hands. "This can't be." The sobs began.

KatieAnn knelt and wrapped her arms around her *mamm's* shaking shoulders. "It will be all right, Mamm. Somehow this will all work out."

She would try to comfort her *mamm,* but who would comfort her and help her out of this mess?

∽

KatieAnn ate little supper and contributed only a few obligatory grunts to the table-time conversation. She wanted only to get the meal over with, clean the kitchen, and escape to her room so she could mull things over yet again. Some clue must have escaped her, some tiniest speck of information that would absolve her of any blame or suspicion.

Mamm ate only slightly more of the ham, cabbage, and potatoes than KatieAnn, but did make an effort to converse with her husband and sons. Thomas and Eli wolfed down their food as though they hadn't eaten in a week — same as always. Daed ate more slowly and kept throwing surreptitious glances in KatieAnn's direction. Supper dragged on forever.

Finally her *bruders* had eaten everything except for the plates and were ready to leave the table. Eli would find some errand to run so he could stop by the Beachy house to visit Sarah. Thomas would probably sit on the front porch and whittle until the late-November air rendered his hands too cold and stiff to wield the knife.

KatieAnn and her *mudder* cleared the table in silence. "I can clean up the kitchen, Mamm. Why don't you go sit with Daed?" Her *mamm* looked ready to burst into tears again, and she simply couldn't deal with that right now. She also didn't want to hear how she should confess and be done with this whole ugly business.

"*Danki*, KatieAnn. Maybe I will." Mamm reached a shaky hand up to push a piece of dark golden hair back into her bun.

When did that silver creep into Mamm's hair? KatieAnn hugged the older woman and blew out the breath she'd been holding. Now she'd make quick work of the dishes and sneak upstairs, if all went according to her plan.

~

KatieAnn pulled on a long, flannel nightgown and brushed her waist-length auburn hair. She gently massaged her scalp with her fingertips. She would have to pin her hair and *kapp* more loosely tomorrow, though she doubted too-tight hair pins were the source of her pounding headache. She rolled her shoulders forward and back and then tilted her head from side to side in a vain attempt to release the knots of tension.

On her knees beside her bed for her evening prayers, the only word she could utter was, "help." Gott knew her heart and mind so the actual words weren't necessary. She sighed and blew out the oil lamp before diving beneath the blanket and quilt. Perhaps, in the silent darkness, she could make some sense of the last fifteen or so hours of her life.

Just this morning, she'd arrived at Deborah's Old Time Bake Shop before the first rooster even thought of crowing. The pink and purple fingers of dawn had barely begun to scribble across the sky. Using the key Deborah gave her more than a year ago, she let herself in the back door. After a couple hours of baking, she would unlock the front door. Customers often wanted to grab a home-made muffin or pastry on their way to work.

She hung her navy quilted bag on the empty coat tree in the employees' room. Her *bruder* James' *fraa*, Mary, was expecting their third child. KatieAnn usually spent her lunch break knitting a blanket for the *boppli* while nibbling at a sandwich or leftover muffin from the morning's baking. Her black cape and bonnet went over the bag on the same hook so there would be plenty of room for the rest of the staff to hang their outer garments. In the big kitchen, she turned on the lights and ovens, and scrubbed her hands at the sink. Just like always.

KatieAnn liked getting to work early to mix the dough for the goodies they would sell. Later, after the breakfast rush, she'd prepare her original "knots" —just the twisted portion of pretzels in various flavors. After two years at the bake shop, she'd found that, while she liked baking the old favorites, she most enjoyed developing her own concoctions. Deborah trusted her and let her experiment with new ideas. Correction. Deborah *used* to trust her. KatieAnn wasn't exactly sure how Deborah felt now.

All right, KatieAnn. Think!

Deborah entered the shop about a half hour later. KatieAnn already had *kaffi* brewing. From the big commercial ovens, the delicious aromas of muffins and Danish filled the shop. She had just started on the doughnuts.

"Mmm! Smells *gut* in here." Deborah said the same thing every morning on her way into the office to work on the bank deposit before customers began streaming in. Yesterday had been extremely busy, so Deborah had told her she might take longer than usual to prepare the deposit. She said she should be available to help in the shop by the time it opened for business. KatieAnn wasn't worried since the rest of the staff was due in soon.

Frannie Kauffman arrived first. She was a widow in her forties. All her *kinner* were grown, so she put in a lot of time at the shop. KatieAnn's *gut freind* Grace Hershberger was next to open the door. As usual, eighteen-year-old Lizzie Graber crept in as the customers entered. That girl! Even though she was the bishop's niece, she was not terribly reliable. She was nice enough, for sure, but mostly interested in finding a husband.

Lizzie tried to sneak in amongst the customers waiting for Deborah to unlock the door, but as always, her fellow employees and boss saw her. "Sorry I'm late." Lizzie sailed past Deborah on her way to the employees' room at the back of the store.

Deborah shook her head and rolled her eyes. She greeted Mrs. Sampson who purchased her usual blueberry muffin and *kaffi* and made small talk with each of the other customers. When the first onslaught of customers had been waited on, Deborah headed back to her office. She poked her head in the kitchen and held up a hand. "Girls!"

KatieAnn turned from her mixing bowl to look at Deborah. Light glinted off a shiny object dangling from Deborah's fingers. What on earth was she holding?

"This belongs to Mrs. Sampson, ain't so?" Deborah shook the object in her hand.

KatieAnn wiped her hands on a checked dish towel and scooted over to get a closer look. The rather large gold-and-diamond watch sparkled as it twirled in Deborah's fingers. The piece was a bit too fancy, as far as KatieAnn was concerned. She used to like pretty jewelry back before she joined the church, but this watch was downright gaudy. "I believe that does belong to Mrs. Sampson."

"I'll drop it off to her on the way to the bank. I'm

leaving in a few minutes."

"Okay." KatieAnn and Frannie went back to work. Up front, Grace laughed with a customer. This would be another busy day, for sure and certain.

Deborah rushed from the office. Her hands were full with the deposit bag, watch, and books. "These books are due at the library today. I might as well drop them off while I'm out. *Ach*! I have to mail some bills too. Where did I leave them?" She dropped everything on a counter and scampered off in search of the mail.

"Whew!" Frannie sighed when the last of the doughnuts had been arranged on the big silver trays.

"I'll take them out." Frannie's arthritis sometimes gave her fits. Though the older woman never complained, KatieAnn could tell the trays were sometimes hard for her to carry.

A sudden influx of customers kept KatieAnn, Grace, and Lizzie scurrying about. Frannie refilled the empty *kaffi* maker several times to keep it perking.

"Everyone must have smelled fresh doughnuts this morning," Grace called as she whizzed past KatieAnn.

"Well, we did have the sign posted about the new cookies-and-cream doughnut debuting today." KatieAnn turned back to wait on a customer.

"I think you scored a winner with this one." Grace laughed. "You may sell out in record time."

They bantered back and forth and chatted with the customers until Deborah appeared, pale and shaking. Conversation died as all the workers stared at their boss. KatieAnn gave voice to their question. "Deborah, *was ist letz?*"

Deborah's voice came out in a hoarse whisper. "Th-the deposit and th-the watch. I can't find them."

"You dropped them down on the kitchen counter," Frannie reminded her. "They must have fallen."

Deborah shook her head. "*Nee*. I looked."

"Well, they couldn't have just walked off," Grace said. "We'll help you look."

"Maybe you took them into the employees' room when you got your cape," Lizzie suggested.

"I don't think so."

"I'll double check." Lizzie raced away, bumping into the front counter and almost toppling a display of muffins on a stand beneath a glass dome.

"That girl!" Deborah muttered. "A regular bull in a china shop."

A loud crash sent everyone running to the back of the shop.

"Someone stay out front, please." Deborah scurried around the counter as quickly as her plump legs could carry her.

KatieAnn and Grace reached the employees' room first. "*Ach*, Lizzie! Are you all right?" KatieAnn reached out for the girl. Lizzie leaned against the wall gasping for breath. The coat tree lay on the floor with capes, bonnets, and tote bags scattered around it.

"What happened?" Deborah panted as she entered the room. "Lizzie?"

"I-I'm okay. I'm sorry. I was rushing and bumped into the coat tree."

"Are you sure you're okay?" KatieAnn let go of Lizzie's arm when she saw the girl was steady on her feet.

"I'm fine. Let me just pick up this stuff."

KatieAnn righted the coat tree while Grace picked up and shook off the capes and bonnets before rehanging them. Deborah turned away to continue her search.

Lizzie reached for KatieAnn's bag, but she grabbed the wrong end. Knitting needles clanged on the floor as a ball of green yarn rolled out. Then, with a thud and a clink, out plopped the bulging vinyl deposit bag and the gold-

and-diamond watch. Lizzie gasped.

"*Ach*! How did those get in my bag?" All the strength left KatieAnn's legs. Her hands shook, and her knees threatened to buckle. She crouched on the floor beside Lizzie. "I-I did not put those there." She looked up into Deborah's horrified face. Grace stared, open-mouthed. "H-honest, Deborah. I didn't put those in my bag." Tears threatened to pour.

Only Lizzie seemed unaffected and continued to chatter. "Well, maybe you just wanted to get them out of the way and brought them to a safe place."

"I never came into this room after I started baking."

"*Nee*?" Deborah stared at her.

"You know me, Deborah. I would never take something that didn't belong to me. I've even taken your deposits to the bank before with *nee* problems."

"Of course you wouldn't steal!" Grace was quick to defend her. "Anyway, Frannie can vouch for you. She was with you in the kitchen the whole time, ain't so?"

"*Jah*. Well, she went out front once to take some muffins."

"Could a customer have slipped back here?" Grace looked from KatieAnn to Deborah.

"I suppose it's possible," Deborah conceded.

"But why would they put these things in KatieAnn's bag that was under her cape?" Lizzie voiced what the others most likely were thinking.

"Who knows?" Deborah pulled the bag and watch from Lizzie's hands. "I'm just glad they've been found. Let me recount and get this out of here. Back to work, girls."

KatieAnn jumped up and trailed behind Deborah. "You do believe me, don't you, Deborah?"

Deborah turned. She patted KatieAnn's arm but her tight smile was obviously forced. "Of course. I've always trusted you." She turned and marched into the office to recount the deposit.

KatieAnn struggled to swallow the boulder-sized lump clogging her throat. Did Deborah and the others think she'd taken the money and the watch?

CHAPTER TWO

"Apparently they do," KatieAnn whispered into the darkness of her room.

Deborah had pulled her aside and asked her not to *kumm* into work the next day or the rest of the week. Or ever again? Now she didn't have a job, and once news of the incident at the bake shop hit the grapevine—and it most likely had spread far and wide, since the bishop had already been by—not a single person would hire her. She'd be labeled an unrepentant thief.

She punched her pillow and turned over. The blanket and quilt twisted around to further aggravate her. What did it matter if she was labeled a thief? If she didn't kneel in front of the church and confess, she'd be shunned. So not only would nobody hire her, they couldn't even eat with or talk to her.

"But I'm innocent!" She bolted up in bed and pounded the mattress with her fist. "Lord Gott, You know I'm innocent. I can't confess to a sin I didn't commit." Why, oh why, did this happen to her? She flopped back down, rolled onto her stomach, and buried her face in the pillow. The storm of sobs she'd held back all day finally drenched her pillow. "What am I going to do?" she moaned with each shuddering gulp of air.

To say she slept fitfully would be a huge understatement. KatieAnn doubted she closed her eyes for more than thirty consecutive minutes the whole miserable night. Even before Old Benny the rooster crowed, she dragged her weary body out of bed. She might as well help prepare breakfast while she was still allowed to communicate with her family.

She wouldn't be heading out to work, so she pulled on an old dress. Her head still ached, so she pinned her long hair loosely and positioned her *kapp*. The cold water she splashed on her face did nothing to reduce the swelling of her eyelids or erase the red lines most likely streaking her eyes. "It can't be helped," she muttered and shuffled to the kitchen.

Mamm already stood at the stove frying bacon, her back to the kitchen doorway. Slumped shoulders and a loud sigh told KatieAnn her *mamm* had had a restless night, too.

"*Gut mariye*, Mamm."

Ida nodded. She turned, tears shimmering in her eyes.

"*Ach,* Mamm! I'm so sorry. I can't understand why all this happened."

"KatieAnn, please," Ida choked out. "I can't lose you, too. Rebecca has been in Maryland so long, and I hardly see her or her *kinner*. You're my *boppli*." Her voice caught. She grabbed KatieAnn in a tight hug.

"I know, Mamm. I know you miss Rebecca and her family. I do, too."

"Can you, uh, can you confess?"

"Mamm, do you want me to lie?"

"*Nee*, but I don't want you placed under the *bann*."

"I don't want that either, but I can't lie. That's a sin, just like stealing. I won't let them put me under the *bann*.

I-I'll leave first."

"Leave?" Ida gasped and clapped her hand over her mouth.

"I don't want to, Mamm. I love my family and community. Paradise has always been my home. I don't want to leave." Tears spilled down her cheeks.

Ida hugged her *dochder* tighter. "We will talk of this later. Let's get breakfast on the table before Daed and the *buwe* get inside."

"Okay." KatieAnn swiped at her moist eyes and began cracking eggs for her *mudder* to fry in the pan of bacon grease.

A cloud of gloom hung over the breakfast table. Even Eli's and Thomas' half-hearted attempts to lighten the mood fell flat. They soon abandoned their efforts and concentrated on consuming eggs, bacon, and biscuits as quickly as they could swallow them. Joshua pretty much stuck with grunting any replies required of him.

It's all my fault. Everyone is miserable because of me, and I didn't do anything wrong! Did her *bruders* and parents truly believe she stole the money and watch? Didn't they know her at all?

How she longed for the big *schweschder* who protected and defended her when she was a little girl. Maybe she should write a letter to Rebecca before her beloved *schweschder* heard any rumors from someone else. Rebecca would believe her.

KatieAnn discarded her mostly uneaten breakfast and filled the kitchen sink with soapy water. Her *daed* and *bruders* had gulped the last crumbs of their meal, jammed hats on their heads, and made a beeline for the door. They couldn't seem to escape the solemn atmosphere of the kitchen fast enough. Too bad she couldn't escape too.

She was so accustomed to being at work and baking way before this time of the morning. Being at loose ends left her completely discombobulated. She missed the bake shop already. She had forgotten to give Deborah her shop key, but she was sure her former boss would be by later to fetch it.

KatieAnn sighed, not for the first time this morning. She hung up the blue-checked dish cloth and slipped upstairs to compose a letter. How could she tell her *schweschder* she'd been accused of stealing and everyone here believed it to be true? *Ach*! It hurt that her own *freinden* and family thought so little of her. What had she ever done to arouse any doubts about her character?

Sure, she'd been a mischievous little girl. She had liked to run and climb and do daring stunts like her older *bruders*. But she'd been obedient. One trip to the woodshed back when she was seven and had ignored her chores had seen to that! During her *rumspringa*, she hadn't done anything outlandish. She'd had one of those prepaid cell phones. She wore jeans to a movie and bought lots of pretty jewelry—all inexpensive costume stuff. But when she took her instruction classes for baptism and joined the church, she had forsaken all those things. She'd never had any intention of leaving her faith during her running around time. She had adhered to the Ordnung the best she knew how.

Why did everyone think ill of her? How that money and watch got in her bag was as big a mystery to her as it was to everyone else. After grabbing a writing tablet and pen from her top dresser drawer, she sat on the bed and poured her heart out to Rebecca. She had to keep wiping away tears so they wouldn't drip onto her letter and smudge the ink.

At last she replaced the cap on the pen and folded the paper in thirds. She stuffed it into an envelope, sealed the flap and pressed a stamp to the corner. Maybe a brisk stroll to the mailbox would help clear her mind.

KatieAnn pulled her cape a little tighter against the crisp air as she ambled down the gravel lane. This kind of cold would bring snow before too long. She shivered at the thought. The snow-covered fields were beautiful, for sure, but she'd never enjoyed icy winds and frigid temperatures. Better enjoy the outdoors while she could.

She placed her letter in the silver metal box and raised the red flag to alert the mailman. The clip clop of a horse's hooves drew closer as she resisted the urge to flee into the woods so she wouldn't have to face anyone. Maybe if she ignored the approaching horse, the driver would pass on by. She could only hope so.

"KatieAnn!"

No such luck. She couldn't pretend she didn't hear her name shouted out loud enough to wake the dead. She hesitated but then turned to face the driver. "*Ach*, Timothy. *Wie bist du heit*?"

"I'm fine." To her dismay, he pulled up alongside her. "More importantly, how are you holding up?"

"So you've heard. I guess the grapevine has really been buzzing. Everyone in the state must know by now that KatieAnn Mast tried to steal from her employer."

"I don't believe that for a minute. I've known you all my life, and I know for certain you'd never do such a thing."

"*Danki*, Timothy. You're a *gut freind*." KatieAnn blinked back tears before looking into Timothy's concerned green eyes.

"Do you want to go for a ride?"

"Don't you have to go to work?"

"I have been working. I have to deliver some supplies." Timothy nodded to his wagon. "You could ride along."

"I'd better see if my *mamm* needs help with something." She paused for a minute. "*Ach*, Timothy, I'm feeling so lost, not working."

"I'm sure this will blow over and Deborah will have you back soon. You're the best baker around."

"You're a bit prejudiced." KatieAnn attempted a smile.

"*Nee*, I just know *gut* food."

"Timothy Yoder, you'd eat anything that didn't eat you first!"

"Probably. But your treats are the best around." He licked his lips and patted his stomach.

KatieAnn laughed out loud.

"See, at least I got you to laugh."

"*Danki*, Timothy. You brightened my day. Now you'd better deliver your supplies before *you* get fired."

Timothy continued on his way as KatieAnn resumed her stroll back to the house. Timothy had been a *gut freind* since they were scholars. Timothy believed in her. Knowing that soothed her heart.

If only her family offered her the same support.

The day seemed a week long for KatieAnn, even though she tried to busy her hands and brain with chores, most of which didn't really need to be done. She dusted furniture and shelves, swept wood floors, and shook out braided rugs. Hard as she worked to divert her attention, her thoughts kept returning to the bake shop. Who could have put the money and watch into her bag. And why *her* bag?

Needing to bake, KatieAnn kneaded bread dough and set it aside to rise while she stirred together ingredients for a recipe she had devised for cinnamon caramel apple muffins. This was going to be her next debut at the bake shop. Was. Her muffins would never get their debut now, except with her family.

Female voices penetrated KatieAnn's continuous mental replay of the bake shop fiasco. She focused her attention on them. Who was speaking? Mamm, for one. Grace? It sounded like Grace Hershberger. Maybe Grace had *kumm* to tell her the mystery had been solved and she could return to work! A surge of hope swept through her as she wiped her hands on a dish towel. But hope vanished as quickly as it came. Deborah would be the one visiting if KatieAnn would be allowed to return to the bake shop.

Grace rushed into the kitchen and pulled KatieAnn into a brief hug before she could ponder the situation any further. "I missed you today. It's not the same at the shop without you."

"It's only been one day."

"*Jah*, but you belong at the bake shop."

"Who did the baking today?"

"Frannie. Deborah helped her some. I offered but was needed to wait on customers."

"Lizzie?"

"Pretty much just got in the way. Frannie shooed her out of the kitchen like she'd shoo a dog away from a piece of meat. I was waiting for her to swat Lizzie with a rolled up newspaper."

KatieAnn laughed. "Lizzie tries."

"More like Lizzie is trying. She tries our patience daily!"

"She does all right with the customers, ain't so?"

"I guess. She hasn't scalded anyone by spilling hot *kaffi* on them lately or dropped anyone's doughnuts on the floor and offered to wipe them off." Grace lowered her voice to a near whisper. "I heard her tell Deborah you did leave the kitchen a couple times yesterday."

"Really?" KatieAnn frowned. "Let me think. I carried a heavy tray of doughnuts out front so Frannie wouldn't aggravate her arthritis. Hmm. I don't remember leaving any other time."

"Don't worry about it. *I* know you didn't do anything wrong."

"Is Lizzie trying to make it sound like I might have had the opportunity to hide the money and watch in my bag?"

Grace shrugged. "Planting seeds of doubt, I guess."

"Why would she do that? *Ach!* I do remember. I opened the back door when Jeremiah Kauffman came by with his egg delivery. That's it, though. I would hardly have had time to go hide the money and watch. Does Deborah still have doubts?"

Grace nodded. "I guess."

"She doesn't want me to *kumm* back?"

Grace remained silent.

"She sent you for the shop key?"

Grace stared at the floor. "She didn't exactly send me for the key, but said for me to get it if I visited you. I-I'm sorry." Grace couldn't seem to bring herself to look KatieAnn in the eye.

KatieAnn bit her bottom lip to still the trembling. She expected to taste blood any second. Her shoulders slumped in total dejection. "It isn't your fault. I'll go get the key."

CHAPTER THREE

Two days later, KatieAnn answered a knock at the front door and discovered Timothy Yoder standing on the porch. His huge grin lightened her somber mood. She couldn't help but return his smile.

Timothy held out a sheet of paper. "I stopped by the phone shanty and noticed the red light flashing. The message was for you. Here. I wrote it down so I wouldn't forget anything."

She skimmed the note. Her *schweschder*, Rebecca, wanted her to call the very next day.

KatieAnn received the news with a mixture of excitement and trepidation. She longed to hear her big *schweschder*'s voice, but would Rebecca believe in her innocence or would she think the worst? Wringing her hands, KatieAnn thanked Timothy for his prompt delivery of the message.

"It will be all right," he assured her. "All things work for *gut*..."

"To them that love Gott, to them who are called according to His purpose." KatieAnn finished the verse.

"That's right."

"I'll try to remember that."

"*Gut*. Now smile."

KatieAnn offered a weak smile.

"I think you can do better, but I'll take that." Timothy winked and turned to head home. "Let me know what Rebecca says," he called over his shoulder.

"I will."

Timothy would make some girl a great husband. He was so kind and considerate. Too bad she thought of him as another *bruder*.

The next day KatieAnn helped Mamm clean and hang laundry out in the brisk wind. With that finished, she busied herself with baking. Staying busy helped keep her nerves in check, somewhat.

"More baking?" Her *mudder* stood in the kitchen doorway and took in the flurry of activity. "Don't you think we have enough baked goods to last us quite a while?"

KatieAnn looked at the assorted pies and muffins crowding the counter. "I suppose so. I'm making cookies this time. My *bruders* can scarf down a lot of cookies."

Mamm nodded. She seemed to understand her *dochder*'s need to stay busy.

By two-thirty KatieAnn could not stand to fidget in the house a minute longer. "I'm going to walk down to the phone."

Mamm dropped her mending into the basket. "It's a little early, ain't so?"

"I'll walk slow."

"Can I walk along with you?"

"Sure, Mamm. You can keep me company while I wait for the phone to ring." KatieAnn fetched their cloaks and bonnets. Her nerves had tied her intestines in huge knots that threatened to force the little food she had choked down at noon back up her esophagus. Maybe the cool air would help calm her down and settle her stomach. She was a little afraid to find out what Rebecca had to say.

The old-fashioned, black push-button phone mounted in the phone shanty barely finished its first ring before KatieAnn snatched the receiver from the hook. "Hello?"

"KatieAnn, is that you?"

"Rebecca? It's so *gut* to hear your voice. I've missed you."

"I've missed you, too, little *schweschder*. What in the world is going on there?"

"*Ach*, Rebecca, nobody believes me. They all think I stole—or was trying to steal—from my boss. Now I don't have a job, and the bishop is going to put me under the *bann* if I don't seek forgiveness for a sin I didn't commit." KatieAnn rushed to get her words out before bursting into tears.

"KatieAnn? Are you listening? I'm so sorry. KatieAnn?"

She struggled to pull herself together to utter some type of ungarbled sound. Rebecca's sweet, soothing voice filled her with longing for the relationship they had as *kinner*. Despite their nine-year age difference, they had been close. Rebecca had never treated KatieAnn as a pesky little girl. She had loved her and protected her as fiercely as a *mudder* lion defends her cubs. KatieAnn couldn't bear it if Rebecca doubted her innocence. She sniffed hard. "I-I'm here."

"KatieAnn, I know you. I haven't lived with you for years, but I know you are the same sweet, honest girl. You would not take something that didn't belong to you. Ever!"

Silence.

"KatieAnn, did you hear me?"

Relief flooded KatieAnn's entire being. Rebecca believed her. She sniffed again. "I heard you."

"I want you to *kumm* to Maryland. Stay with me for a

while. Stay forever, if you want. Please say you'll *kumm*. We haven't seen each other in ever so long."

"I-I'd like that."

"KatieAnn, let me talk." Ida reached for the phone.

"Is Mamm there?" KatieAnn heard Rebecca's question even though the receiver was on its way to Mamm's ear. She leaned against her *mudder* so she could hear the conversation too.

"Rebecca? It's *wunderbaar* to hear your voice."

"Mamm, I've missed you. Surely you don't believe our KatieAnn stole anything, do you?"

"I-I can't believe she would…" Mamm's voice trailed off.

"But?"

Mamm kept silent.

"What does Daed say?"

Their *mudder* heaved a great sigh. "He doesn't want to believe KatieAnn did anything wrong either, but the items were in her bag. They didn't get in there by themselves."

"Mamm! You believe your own *dochder*, don't you?" Rebecca's voice came through so loud KatieAnn pulled back a bit.

"I…"

"Mamm, I've asked KatieAnn to visit me."

KatieAnn gently pried the phone from the older woman's hand as tears flooded her *mamm*'s eyes. "I will visit you, Rebecca. Can I *kumm* before next Sunday?"

"For sure. Hannah is getting married this Thursday. I'll have her room ready for you."

"I'll make arrangements and be there Saturday." Then she wouldn't have to kneel before the whole church to confess to a crime she didn't commit or hear the verdict that she was shunned. "Will it be okay with Samuel?"

"Of course. And the *kinner* will be so happy to see

you."

"*Danki*, Rebecca. I'll let you know the final arrangements. Just tell me how you want me to reach you."

Rebecca rattled off the phone number for Beilers' Furniture store, owned by Hannah's soon-to-be husband, Jacob Beiler and his family. They would get the message to her.

"I love you, KatieAnn. I can't wait to see you."

"Me, too. *Danki* so much, Rebecca." KatieAnn hung up the phone and turned to her weeping *mamm*.

Mamm wrapped her arms around her in a fierce hug. Her tears drizzled onto KatieAnn's shoulder. "I can't stand to lose another *dochder*."

"You aren't losing me, Mamm, but you surely will if I stay here and don't make a kneeling confession, ain't so?"

"Y-You're sure you won't confess?"

"It would be a lie."

Mamm nodded.

"This will work out for the best, won't it, Mamm?"

"I hope so."

Saturday's gray sky perfectly matched KatieAnn's mood. Just before dawn, she stuffed the last of her essential toiletry items in the large suitcase she'd purchased from the discount store. She glanced around her room a final time—which could truly be the final time if the bishop kept insisting she confess to her supposed crime. She hauled the heavy suitcase, another large, stuffed-full quilted bag, and her purse down the stairs to say goodbye to her family.

"*Kumm* have some breakfast," Mamm urged.

"I don't think I can." She couldn't project her voice any louder than a whisper. The very thought of eggs or oatmeal made her stomach churn.

"You have a long drive ahead. You should eat some-thing."

"Maybe I'll just take some fruit with me."

"I've packed you a lunch already and some snacks."

"You didn't have to do that, Mamm. I would have done it, but I appreciate it."

"Set your things down. You have time for a cup of *kaffi* or juice, ain't so?"

"Maybe a little juice." She really didn't want any juice either, but to mollify her *mamm*, she'd try to get some ap-ple juice to slide past the lump in her throat. Before she could wiggle into her chair to sit with her family as they ate breakfast, a car horn beeped in the driveway.

"*Ach*! They're early!" KatieAnn was catching a ride with a van load of folks from a neighboring district who were heading to the farmers' market in Annapolis, Mary-land. For an extra fee, the driver would then transport her to Southern Maryland where Rebecca lived. Thank Gott she wouldn't have to take a bus and then have to find some other connection to get her to Rebecca's house.

Eli and Thomas rose from the table to hug their little *schweschder* and to carry her bags outside. Daed wrapped KatieAnn in a bear hug. "Take care, Dochder," he whis-pered.

Mamm sniffed but could no more stop her tears than she could stop the hands of the clock from inching for-ward. "*Ach*, KatieAnn." She pulled her *dochder* into a hug and clung for dear life. "I'll miss you so. Please write. Please *kumm* back to us." Her voice broke, and her shoul-ders shook with silent sobs.

KatieAnn patted her *mamm*'s back. "I'll miss you, too. I love you." She had to wipe a tear from her own eye.

"I-I'm sending a few things for Rebecca, Samuel and the *kinner*."

KatieAnn nodded but didn't trust her voice just yet.

The horn tooted again. "I'd better go, Mamm."

"You take care of yourself, you hear?"

"I will." KatieAnn picked up her purse to leave. She glanced back into Mamm's tear-streaked face. "Please believe me, Mamm. I didn't put those things in my bag. You raised a *gut* girl."

Mamm nodded as tears flowed unchecked from her eyes.

Outside, Thomas and Eli had stowed KatieAnn's bags in the far-back compartment of the extended-size van. The front passenger seat and the second seat were already full. She would have to squeeze into the only vacant spot in the van's back seat. At least the present occupants slid over so she didn't have to trample over their feet.

"*Danki,*" she whispered to her *bruders,* and then climbed aboard.

KatieAnn greeted her fellow passengers as the driver started the engine and turned the van toward the road. The gray clouds, pregnant with rain, mirrored her heavy heart that was ready to burst from sorrow and disappointment. She leaned her head against the cool window and let her mind wander as they bounced along.

She was determined to search for the bright side of this situation. Just as sure as there was a sunny sky waiting to shrug free of the clouds, there was something *gut* to *kumm* from this whole mess her life had become. There had to be! For one thing, she would get to see Rebecca.

Rain pummeled the van. The wipers swished across the windshield with a soft, screeching sound, and she dozed.

In her dream, she soared above the earth, far above her problems and cares, far above the frothy white clouds. KatieAnn parted the clouds with her hands whenever she wanted to peer at the world below. She was free. She was happy. Little gold wings kept her aloft so she could use her hands to brush at the clouds when she wanted to see mountains or rivers far beneath her.

The shuffling of bodies and increased murmurings pulled KatieAnn out of her dreamland oasis. She slammed back to earth with a thud, reality settling heavily upon her. She'd so enjoyed that brief respite. Always a light sleeper, she was surprised she had drifted off with all the various conversations buzzing around her like swarms of bees. Her many nights of tossing and turning must've rendered her sleep deprived so her body could more easily succumb to slumber. An elbow to her ribs made her gasp.

"*Ach*. I'm sorry, dear. I was trying to reach my crochet hook." The older woman next to her pointed near KatieAnn's foot. She retrieved the hook and handed it to the woman. "*Danki*, dear. We'll be getting out in a few minutes." She plunged the crochet hook into a ball of sky blue yarn.

KatieAnn squinted in the glare. "The sun. When did it *kumm* out?" What a drastic change!

"As soon as we came into Maryland, the sky cleared. *Gut* thing, too. Now we won't get all wet." The van pulled into the parking lot of a shopping center and squealed to a stop in front of the Amish Market. "You have a *gut* trip, dear."

"*Danki*."

Everyone piled out of the van and headed for the market. That left KatieAnn alone with the driver. She moved up to the middle seat so she could get out more easily once she reached her destination, and then looked around at the shopping center. The stores weren't open at this early hour, so the cars dotting the parking lot must belong to employees.

Once they got underway again, she settled back in the seat and watched the scenery whizzing by her window.

Thank the Lord Gott for the sun. Maybe it was a sign that everything would be all right after all.

A hint of a smile touched her lips as a song popped into KatieAnn's mind. One evening during her *rumspringa*, she and Grace had attended a production of the musical "Annie" at the local public high school. She had thoroughly enjoyed the story of the little orphan girl and had been held spellbound by all the music. One song, about the sun *kumming* out tomorrow, stuck in her head. Even though she didn't remember all the words, her brain sang the parts she knew and made up words to fill in the blank spots.

A few red, orange, and yellow leaves still clung to many of the trees lining the roads. Back home, bare limbs already scratched the sky. The remaining dew — or maybe it was frost — sparkled like fields of diamonds beneath the sun. The blue sky held not even a trace of the grayness that presided when she left home.

Home. Would Maryland be her home now? Would she like it here well enough to stay? Rebecca lived in a much smaller, more isolated community. Would that be a *gut* thing? The brilliant sunshine warming the interior of the van had to be a positive sign. She would take it as such anyway.

One thing was certain. She couldn't return home unless the real thief confessed or unless she confessed to a crime she would never have dreamed of committing. Perhaps Grace could find out what really happened. And she hoped sweet Timothy found the right girl. She abandoned all hope that Micah Kinsinger would ever inquire about her or care about her. KatieAnn pushed aside the pain caused by the condemnation of her family and *freinden*.

If she planned to make Maryland her home, even if only temporarily, she would have to force herself not to think of what she left behind. She would look forward to seeing Rebecca and her family, and she would make herself useful. Surely with six young *kinner* Rebecca could use her help.

The sun has kumm out, and this is the day the Lord Gott has made. I will rejoice. Please help me, Gott.

CHAPTER FOUR

Now that she was awake and alert, the drive seemed to drag on forever. KatieAnn was anxious to reach her destination and to get out of the van. Her numb backside might have grown to the seat. It didn't matter how many times she wiggled within the confines of the seatbelt, she couldn't find an entirely comfortable position. She tried to force herself to sit still and enjoy the scenery.

The hustle and busyness in Annapolis, even so early in the morning, gradually gave way to a more serene setting. Huge, lush horse farms with mansion-like houses lined either side of the road for a time. Trees and fields and an occasional house or business made up the scenery until they reached the next town.

KatieAnn's stomach emitted a loud grumble. No wonder. She'd put nothing at all in her stomach this day. "Do you mind if I eat a snack in the van?" she asked the driver.

"Not at all. You go right ahead."

"Would you like some fruit or crackers? I have plenty."

"No, thanks. I'm so full of coffee I'm about to burst."

KatieAnn pulled two plastic baggies from her bag.

One contained cheese and crackers, and the other held red, seedless grapes. She munched as quietly as she could and took care not to drop crumbs on the seat or floor.

"It shouldn't be too much longer now." The driver looked at her in the rearview mirror. "We'll reach St. Mary's County in about ten minutes. The address you gave me isn't too far over the county line."

KatieAnn nodded and then realized the driver probably couldn't see her movement. "Okay." She answered around a mouthful of grapes.

Shortly after the van crossed into St. Mary's County, KatieAnn spied several horse-drawn buggies heading toward an Amish market. *Just like home. Sort of.* The van stopped at another red light and then turned onto a different road. KatieAnn vaguely remembered this part of the journey from a long-ago visit to her sister. She stuffed everything back into her bag. Oh, how she'd love to tidy up a bit! She must look wrinkled and travel-worn, but that couldn't be helped.

The van bumped along a gravel driveway and stopped before a white, two-story farmhouse. KatieAnn unclipped her seatbelt and pulled on the door handle as soon as the van braked. Stretching her legs would feel *wunderbaar*.

She hopped from the van and twisted from side to side, and then shook each leg in an effort to stretch. The driver removed her bags and set them on the ground so he could close the rear door. KatieAnn held out an envelope containing her payment.

"I'll carry your things up for you." He took the envelope and stuffed it into a pocket.

"*Danki*, but I'm sure I can manage. I appreciate your driving me all the way here."

"No problem. You have a good visit."

"*Danki*." *I hope I will.*

The driver turned back to the van as KatieAnn bent to lift her bags. She took a deep breath and headed up the walkway. "This is it," she said under her breath.

Before she got halfway to the front porch, the door flew open and Rebecca burst out with little ones of assorted sizes trailing behind her.

"KatieAnn! I am so glad you're here. It's been so long." Rebecca wrapped her in a big hug, which nearly caused her to drop her bags. "Jonas, Eli, *kumm* get your *aenti's* things!"

"It's all right, Rebecca. The bags are pretty heavy."

"The *buwe* can handle it. They help Samuel with the wood and chores. They're big and strong, ain't so?"

"*Jah*, Mamm." Jonas, the taller *bu*, stepped forward and reached for a bag.

"*Jah*, Mamm," Eli echoed. He gave a little grunt but lifted another bag.

"*Danki*, Jonas and Eli. You were both so little when I saw you last. My, how you've grown."

The little *buwe* puffed out their chests and straightened to be taller. KatieAnn smiled at them.

"Put them in Hannah's room—KatieAnn's room now," Rebecca instructed.

"Is this Emma? She's practically a lady."

The five-year-old smiled shyly and emerged from behind Rebecca, dragging her *schweschder* with her.

"Me lady too," Elizabeth said.

"You certainly are." KatieAnn stooped down to the girls' level. They were miniatures of their *mamm* with the same bright green eyes and dark honey-gold hair. Elizabeth's dimples grew until she broke out in giggles.

"Your *kinner* are precious."

"Two more," Emma whispered.

"What?"

"She means there are two more *kinner*," Rebecca

clarified.

"Of course. The twins. Where are they?"

"Napping, thankfully. They got up too early so they are taking an early nap." Rebecca sighed.

"I guess I'll meet them in a little while then."

"*Kumm*. How about something to eat or drink? It's getting a bit nippy out here."

"Can we have cocoa, Mamm?" Emma asked.

"Maybe we can."

Jonas and Eli galloped down the stairs as the women and girls entered the big house. They halted abruptly at their *mamm*'s expression and her posture.

Rebecca stared at the *buwe* with hands on her hips. "Is that the way you walk down steps?"

Both of them hung their heads. "Sorry, Mamm."

"Does your *daed* need you back outside with him?"

"He said we could wait until after the noon meal," Jonas replied.

"All right. I guess we'd better see to that."

"I can help you," KatieAnn offered. "Just let me wash up."

"Everything is almost ready. Emma, can you show your *aenti* where the bathroom is, please? We aren't doing anything elaborate, I'm afraid. I have homemade chicken noodle soup and sandwiches today. Since tomorrow is a church Sunday, I need to prepare for the meal. Church is at the Zooks' place. Do you remember them, KatieAnn? Barbara Zook has the quilt shop."

"I remember Barbara's shop and her lovely quilts."

"Everyone will be so glad to see you again."

"You may have to re-introduce me to folks. I don't remember which names go with which faces."

"For sure."

After washing up, KatieAnn hurried back to help out in
the kitchen. She couldn't imagine how Rebecca managed
everything on her own. She watched her *schweschder* settle the twins, still with pillow marks creasing their rosy
cheeks, in their highchairs and pull them close to the big
oak table. KatieAnn handed Emma and Elizabeth napkins and silverware to set at each blue-checked placemat.
Then she carried glasses of milk to the table for all the
children.

"*Wilkom*, KatieAnn!" Samuel's voice boomed as soon
as he stomped into the house.

She smiled at her sister's husband. "I appreciate your
having me. I'll try not to interrupt your life too much."

"With six lively *kinner*, I doubt you will be any interruption at all." Samuel laughed.

"I will gladly help however I can." KatieAnn wanted
to be sure Samuel knew she planned to pull her own
weight.

"We know you will, Schweschder." Rebecca squeezed
KatieAnn's arm.

"Let's sit and get ready for prayer." Samuel led the
way to the table.

The four older *kinner* scrambled to get situated at their
accustomed spots at the table. KatieAnn took the vacant
chair between Emma and Elizabeth.

"Hannah sat there too," Emma whispered. A sad look
crossed her little face.

"You miss Hannah, ain't so?"

Emma nodded. Little wisps of honey-gold hair curled
at the nape of the little girl's neck.

KatieAnn patted Emma's knee. She followed Samuel's
lead and bowed her head for silent prayer.

In between bites of her ham and cheese sandwich, she
helped two-year-old Elizabeth maneuver spoonsful of

soup to her mouth. The little girl wanted to do everything herself, but KatieAnn devised a spur-of-the moment game so some soup would actually go into the little girl instead of onto her.

Rebecca nodded and smiled. She offered food to Grace and Benjamin on their highchair trays in between glances at Elizabeth.

"No wonder you're still so skinny," KatieAnn observed. "I don't think I've seen you take a bite of food for yourself yet."

Rebecca laughed. "I eat whenever I can."

"I hope I can spell you sometimes while I'm here so you can get a break."

"That would be nice. With preparing for Hannah's wedding this past Thursday and Esther's wedding this week, I've been pretty busy."

"'Tis the season, I guess." KatieAnn would probably never find that out for herself. What man would want a *fraa* he couldn't trust? If her reputation as a thief continued, she'd die an old *maedel*.

After lunch, Jonas and Eli followed Samuel outside. Emma was assigned the task of entertaining her three younger siblings—quite a task for a five-year-old, KatieAnn thought. But then she was the youngest in her family and had never watched over anyone. Instead, everyone hovered over her.

As soon as Rebecca and KatieAnn cleared away the mess from lunch, they began working on food for tomorrow's common meal, thereby creating a new mess. They also prepared a few dishes that would serve as tomorrow evening's supper since cooking was not usually done on Sundays.

KatieAnn spent what remained of the day performing odd chores and reacquainting herself with her nieces and nephews. Fatigue loomed large by sundown, so she was eager to bid everyone *gut nacht* and crawl into bed. Despite the strange bed in a strange room in a strange house, she dropped off to sleep the instant she turned onto her right side and pulled the covers up to her chin. Thoughts and dreams of vinyl money bags and fancy watches did not plague her tonight.

CHAPTER FIVE

KatieAnn opened one eye to peer into the darkness. For a moment she was confused. Her other eye popped open, and she jerked her head off the pillow. Something wasn't right. "*Ach*! I'm at Rebecca's house. No wonder I felt so disoriented." Her whisper practically echoed in the stillness. Suddenly chilled, she shivered and pulled at the blanket and quilt. She considered flopping back onto her side and covering her head. But *nee*. There was that clinking sound that must have awakened her. It must be Rebecca pulling out pans or dishes. That meant it was time to crawl out of bed.

She dressed quickly, coiled her long hair into a bun, and secured her *kapp*. For some reason, butterflies flapped their wings in her stomach. She had met a lot of folks from Rebecca's community, but that was a long time ago. Still, she was certain they would be nice people. Surely her tainted reputation had not preceded her here.

"You should have gotten me up sooner to help, Rebecca."

"I thought you might be extra tired after your long drive yesterday and being badgered by the *kinner* ever since you got here. I can handle breakfast just fine. Besides we're only having cold cereal, bread and jam and maybe some of the apple butter Mamm sent. Hers is always the best."

"I'm sure you can handle things fine, but I want to help. Please don't treat me as a guest."

"In that case, would you see that Emma and Elizabeth are dressed for church? I'll get the twins as soon as we're ready to eat. They're dressed, but I don't want them getting messed up before we even leave!"

KatieAnn headed back up to her nieces' room to hurry them along. Emma tried so hard to do things for herself and to be a little *mudder* to Elizabeth, but the little girls would need help with their hair.

After the hurry and scurry of getting ready, everyone was finally fed, cleaned up, and loaded into the buggy — although KatieAnn thought packed like brown sugar firmly pressed in a measuring cup might be a better description. She smiled to herself. Funny how her analogies so often centered around baking. How she missed the bake shop and concocting new recipes! Maybe Rebecca would let her use her family as guinea pigs to try out her original treats. *Kinner* ate anything sweet, didn't they?

The little ones chattered until Samuel told them to hush and prepare their minds and hearts for church. They quieted instantly. If only KatieAnn's nerves would settle down on command, too. Any newcomer always stood out, even in a crowd of people clothed in the same colors and style of dress.

Gray buggies already dotted the Zooks' property by the time the Hertzler buggy rolled in. *Gut.* There wouldn't be time to socialize beforehand. They would simply file into the building and take their seats. Jonas and Eli, not yet ready to sit with the older *buwe*, trotted along behind Samuel. Rebecca had her hands full with the twins, so KatieAnn took charge of Emma and Elizabeth.

"*Danki*," Rebecca said. "They usually have to walk in on their own. They will like having their *aenti*'s attention."

KatieAnn smiled down at her two precious little nieces and led them to a backless wooden bench on the women's side in the Zooks' big barn. She tried hard to concentrate on the ministers' sermons, but fatigue threatened to slam her eyelids shut. She forced them open, lifted her gaze to the men's side of the barn, and barely suppressed a gasp. A big, blond man sat there, looking right at her.

A little older than herself, the young man didn't wear a beard, which indicated his single status. He appeared quite tall…his shoulders an inch or two higher than those of the men on either side of him. Not hard to look at either. In fact, KatieAnn admitted to herself that he was actually downright handsome. Such amazing eyes! Sapphire blue, like her favorite gemstone.

His lips curved into a smile.

Totally embarrassed, face on fire, KatieAnn dropped her gaze to her lap. She'd risk falling asleep rather than look into those eyes again. She jumped, startled out of her self-absorption, when Elizabeth leaned her head against her arm. KatieAnn shifted to drape that arm around the little girl so they would both be a bit more comfortable. Then she compelled herself to tune back into Bishop Sol who was delivering the final sermon of the morning.

Finally the service was over and KatieAnn shook Elizabeth awake. Still mortified that the young man across the way had caught her staring at him, she looked for a way to escape unnoticed. Could she hoist Elizabeth into her arms and hide behind her? At a mere five feet nothing, she shouldn't have a terribly difficult time hiding behind anything. She hoped to make a beeline for the kitchen.

To her relief, a groggy Elizabeth asked to be carried. KatieAnn gratefully obliged. She settled the little girl on her hip and reached for Emma's hand. The twins, having napped through the entire service, were now wide awake and eager to be active. Rebecca quickly ushered them outside. KatieAnn followed close on her heels.

Before they reached the house, some of the not-yet-teenage girls took charge of entertaining the younger *kinner,* freeing the women to prepare the meal. Food would be taken out as soon as the benches were converted to tables. Rebecca handed off the twins to one of the girls. KatieAnn deposited Elizabeth on the ground beside Emma. Hand-in-hand, the two ran off to play.

"Whew!" Rebecca tucked a few errant strands of hair back where they belonged. "*Kumm* on in the kitchen. I'll re-introduce you to the women."

KatieAnn nodded and followed her *schweschder.* With any luck she'd be able to stay in the kitchen until Rebecca and Samuel were ready to head home.

"Here is the new bride!" Rebecca exclaimed as soon as the door closed behind them. "And the bride-to-be. You all remember my little *schweschder,* don't you? KatieAnn, this is Hannah, who just married Jacob Beiler." Rebecca paused long enough for KatieAnn to mumble a greeting. "This is Esther Stauffer, soon to be married to Andrew Fisher."

KatieAnn barely got an acknowledgement past her lips before Esther began chattering. "I remember you, KatieAnn. You probably remember me as the one they whispered about as likely to be an old *maedel.*"

"You're definitely going to prove that wrong." Hannah squeezed Esther's arm.

That will be my title now, KatieAnn lamented silently.

"You'll be at the wedding, won't you? I'd really like

you to."

"Of course. *Danki.*"

"I'm planning to bake for the dessert table," Rebecca told them.

"You don't have to," Esther replied. "You're still recuperating from Hannah's wedding."

"I'll do the baking." KatieAnn heard herself volunteer for the job.

"Great idea!" Rebecca sounded relieved. "Esther, my *schweschder* is a *wunderbaar* baker. "She worked in a bake shop back home."

"That sounds fine to me. I can't wait to taste your treats." Esther winked at KatieAnn.

"We'd better get this food out to a bunch of hungry men." Barbara Zook interrupted the wedding talk. "I'm Barbara Zook, in case you don't remember me. *Wilkom*, KatieAnn. We're glad to have you here."

"*Danki.* And I do remember your shop and lovely quilts."

"Do you like to quilt, KatieAnn?"

"I do. Baking is my favorite thing, but I do like to quilt."

"Maybe we'll have a quilting while you're here."

"*Ach*! It's little KatieAnn all grown up." Miriam Esh offered a broad smile as she bustled over to join the group. "You didn't get a whole lot taller, but you certainly turned into a lovely young woman."

A warm flush crept up KatieAnn's neck and headed for her scalp. She tried to busy herself removing lids and aluminum foil from bowls of potato salad and coleslaw and platters of sliced ham and beef.

"Here, you bring these cups, and I'll bring the tea." Esther thrust a package of Styrofoam cups into her hands. "I'll introduce you to everyone."

Exactly what KatieAnn did not want to happen. How

could she politely refuse to help? Something akin to horror must have passed across her face, as Esther quickly added, "I promise I won't let anyone bite you."

She forced a weak smile and looked around. She hoped Rebecca would intervene and get her out of this, but her *schweschder* stood across the kitchen stirring something in a big green plastic bowl while conversing with an older woman whose name KatieAnn couldn't recall.

"Scoot, you two." Barbara shooed them toward the door. "Bishop Sol was a little long-winded today. Those men will be ready for food and drink. I know I am."

"*Jah.* The sooner they eat, the sooner we can eat." Esther headed out.

KatieAnn had no choice but to follow the dark-haired young woman with the big, chocolate eyes. She drew a quivering breath, pulled herself as tall as possible, and marched in the direction of the door. After all, she wasn't going to her execution. And since she'd probably be in Maryland for a while, she'd have to meet everyone some time. Even the young man with the sapphire eyes.

"That's my *schweschder*, Lydia, over there." Esther nodded toward the refrigerator as they left the kitchen. "She moved back here with her *kinner*, David and Ella, who are no doubt running around outside while it's still not terribly cold out." Esther lowered her voice. "Lydia's husband was killed in a logging accident."

"I'm so sorry. It must have been awful for her."

"*Jah.* She's doing pretty *gut* now. And the woman she's talking to is my *mamm*, Leah. That's Sarah Esh over there with her new baby. She was Sarah Fisher, our school teacher, before she married Zeke, Miriam's son." Esther paused to take a breath.

Barbara opened her mouth to speak, but Esther cut her off. "We're going, Barbara." She pushed open the door and led the way back to the barn where tables and benches had been arranged. "Here, let's put these on the end of this table. The other women will bring out the food. We can start filling cups."

Almost before Esther finished speaking, bowls, plates, and utensils appeared on the table. Esther and KatieAnn filled cups with tea and water in rapid succession. Esther introduced KatieAnn to Bishop Sol and the other men, some of whom she remembered from years ago. Esther's face broke into a big smile as the next man stepped up to the table.

"I bet I know who this is." KatieAnn smiled.

"This is Andrew Fisher."

"The soon-to-be groom, ain't so?"

Andrew grinned. "That's right. That is, if this temperamental woman will still have me."

"Temperamental? Me? You must have me confused with someone else."

"I don't think so."

Andrew reached for Esther's hand, but she drew it back. "You're holding up the line."

He shrugged and winked but moved on down the table.

"This is Luke Troyer," Esther announced. "He's Mose and Martha's son."

KatieAnn looked up from the cup she was filling into a pair of laughing sapphire eyes. Her cheeks grew warm. They'd probably turned as red as the sliced tomatoes on the plate farther down the table. She lowered her eyes fast.

"Nice to meet you, KatieAnn." Luke's voice was deep and rich. "Will you be staying a while?"

She made herself look up and up until her gaze locked with Luke's. She felt like a dwarf next to this huge young man.

"Probably." She managed the one word, but it wasn't easy.

"That's *gut*. I guess I'll be seeing you, then."

"There's a young people's gathering tonight, ain't so, Luke?" Esther feigned innocence. She would certainly know the goings on of the community.

"For sure," Luke answered.

"Maybe KatieAnn could go."

KatieAnn's flush must have passed from tomato red to pickled beet purple, judging by the gigantic wave of heat that washed up her neck and into her face. If only the earth would open and swallow her!

"That would be great." Luke nodded at the two women and moved along after being elbowed by Jacob.

"This impatient man is Jacob Beiler, Hannah's new husband." Esther continued on with introductions, apparently oblivious to her helper's discomfiture.

KatieAnn hardly heard anything else, though. Her mind was still on Luke Troyer.

CHAPTER SIX

KatieAnn pleaded fatigue and got out of attending the young people's gathering on Sunday, but she did have to attend Esther's wedding.

Avoiding contact with people was not her goal. Everyone in Southern Maryland had been nice and friendly. But what if, somehow, someone found out about the accusations made against her at home? That fear consumed her. The whole community would ostracize her, and she would embarrass Rebecca and Samuel. She didn't know where she would go if Bishop Sol and the ministers asked her to leave. So it simply seemed better to lie low and avoid calling any attention to herself.

Thursday turned out to be a brisk, sunny November day. Red, gold, and orange leaves danced in the cool breeze. Esther looked radiant in her new purple dress and white apron. Earlier, Rebecca had whispered her fear that Esther would change her mind at the last minute after her previous misgivings concerning Andrew's sincerity. Apparently Andrew had been quite a mischievous little *bu*, and Esther had some trouble believing he'd really changed into a kind, caring man.

Obviously, Esther had set aside those doubts and truly trusted Andrew now. The bride sat calmly throughout the entire three-hour service with her hands clasped in her lap—although she did occasionally look across the way to lock gazes with her husband-to-be. KatieAnn watched in amusement. She'd most likely never experience marriage firsthand.

Near the conclusion of the service, Esther's vows to care for Andrew and to love him until death were spoken clear and strong, without any wavering. Happy tears shimmered in her brown eyes. Andrew's eyes got a little misty too. How sweet.

To KatieAnn's surprise, tears threatened to spill down her own cheeks. She didn't know if it was because she was so moved by the obvious love between the marrying couple or because she was unlikely to know such love and devotion. She clenched her hands as if that could hold back her tears. She had to maintain her composure. After all, Esther's *mamm*, Leah, only sniffed once or twice so why should KatieAnn, practically a stranger, start bawling like a *boppli*?

Her gaze wandered the room until it landed on Luke Troyer, only to find his attention fixed on her. Her breath caught, and her heart performed a crazy little dance. How long had he been watching her? She forced her breathing into a more normal pattern and lowered her lashes until her heart settled down. She didn't look up again until the wedding service concluded.

Now she had to get through the meals and activities.

She scanned the wedding guests and sighed in relief when she didn't spot a single soul from home. As far as she could tell from snippets of overheard conversations, most of the out-of-town guests came from Ohio, not Pennsylvania. Perhaps she could let down her guard a teensy bit and actually enjoy the day.

Busying herself with the other women in the kitchen, she made sure platters and bowls of ham, roast beef, potatoes, green beans, creamed celery, and breads were kept full. She hoped her specialty desserts would be well received.

"Have you eaten yet?" Barbara Zook entered the kitchen with two empty bowls.

"*Nee*. I've been so busy I hadn't given thought to eating yet."

"You'd best give it some thought. Little thing like you will blow away in a strong wind. My, I thought Hannah was tiny, but you've got her beat. You go ahead and eat before some of these young men who act like they haven't eaten since last winter gobble up everything in sight."

KatieAnn laughed. She liked Barbara's straightforward manner and sense of humor. "I'm fine. I'll keep things going here so everyone else can visit."

"Nothing doing. You can visit, too. Maybe you'll like it well enough here to stay. We need more young people. We'd love for you to join us permanently."

"That's nice of you to say." A little voice in her brain threatened to tattle on her. It wanted to tell Barbara she wouldn't be so eager for KatieAnn to stay if she knew she'd been branded a thief back home.

Reluctantly, she emerged from the kitchen to join the other guests. Barbara was right, from the look of the buffet table. Some bowls were empty, and mere traces of food adhered to the sides of others. She put a spoonful each of coleslaw, bean salad, and creamed celery on a plate, added a sliver of roast beef, and then scanned the room. At Rebecca's beckon, she headed in that direction.

"Is that all you're eating?" Rebecca looked at KatieAnn's plate.

"I'm saving plenty of room for dessert."

"You still have that sweet tooth?"

"I do. How about you?" KatieAnn remembered how she and Rebecca used to try to outdo each other in cookie eating.

"Unfortunately, but I'm trying to do better." Rebecca patted her stomach.

"Your belly is as flat as ever."

"Not quite, but it's not too bad for having six *kinner*."

"I should say not. You don't look like you've had any."

Rebecca lowered her voice. "You'll join the young people in a bit, won't you?"

"I-I don't know."

"It will be *gut* for you. You'll get to know some people your age." Rebecca's voice dropped to whisper level. "Don't worry. Your secret is safe as far as I can tell."

"Maybe." She didn't want to make a definite commitment.

A hand clamped down on her shoulder and she jumped.

"Did you get something?" Barbara leaned over her to peer at the table.

"I did."

"Not enough to keep a bird alive. You'd better hit that dessert table while there are a few crumbs left."

KatieAnn nodded while chewing a forkful of coleslaw.

"Those squiggly brownies were delicious. Make sure you get one—if there are any more on the plate." Barbara stood on tiptoe to try to see the dessert table better.

"KatieAnn made those," Rebecca said.

"Really?" Barbara looked at KatieAnn. "What else did you bake?"

"Just some cookies," KatieAnn began.

"She made surprise cookies!" Rebecca announced.

Miriam joined the group and heard only the last few words. "What's the surprise?"

"It's a surprise." KatieAnn giggled.

"I'll have to try those. Which ones are they?" Miriam acted like she was about to make a mad dash for the desserts.

"On the end beside the brownies, if they haven't been moved."

"Be right back!"

"Grab me one, Miriam," Barbara called after the other woman.

Rebecca and KatieAnn laughed. Rebecca elbowed her *schweschder* playfully. "I have a hunch your baked treats will be in high demand."

Later, when the young unmarried people gathered for games and singing, the married women shooed KatieAnn out of the kitchen to join them. She found herself suddenly overcome by shyness since she didn't know anyone very well. Maybe she could find a secluded corner and observe the activities unnoticed.

She slipped into the swept-clean barn and located the perfect corner. The antics of some of the young men made her smile. One of the games totally captivated her, and unconsciously, she let down her guard. When someone touched her arm, she gasped and nearly jumped to the rafters.

"*Ach*! I'm so sorry I scared you."

KatieAnn patted her thumping chest and nodded. She couldn't catch her breath enough to speak.

"You probably don't remember me. I'm Rosanna, Jeremiah and Nancy Yoder's *dochder*."

KatieAnn turned to face the girl squarely. Because Rosanna stood several inches taller, she had to look up to do so. The hair swept back beneath the other girl's *kapp* was so brown it was almost black. Raven colored, KatieAnn decided. The blue-gray eyes stroked her memory. When she'd visited Maryland years ago, she had been fascinated by one little girl's blue-gray eyes. This was the same little girl, all grown up.

KatieAnn smiled. "Actually, I believe I do remember you—or at least your unusual but beautiful eyes."

Rosanna laughed, a merry, tinkling sound. "I guess they are different." Her voice came out silky, soothing. "Will you be staying here long?"

She hesitated for a fraction of a second. "I-I'm not sure, but probably."

"*Gut.* I'm sure Rebecca will be glad to have your help, not that she doesn't seem to have everything under control. It's just, well, I mean, I'm sure an extra pair of hands is always nice."

"Rebecca does seem very organized and is a *gut mamm*, but I'm hoping I can help her out or at least give her a break once in a while." She paused, her attention caught by a young man who had been playing but now ambled toward her secluded corner.

"That's Luke Troyer headed this way."

"Is he your beau?"

"Pshaw!" Rosanna shook her head. "Not at all. He works for my *daed* in the machine shop. He's like a big *bruder* to me."

"I wonder what he—" KatieAnn didn't get to finish her thought.

"Hello, ladies." He greeted them with an exaggerated bow. "I'm glad you joined us, KatieAnn. Don't you two want to play?"

"I'm okay watching," KatieAnn answered.

"Me, too," Rosanna concurred.

"Well, *kumm* on over. We're going to sing in a couple minutes. You can do that, ain't so?"

"We can." Rosanna answered for both girls.

At Rosanna's urging, KatieAnn joined the group.

Rosanna had just finished introducing her to the others when the song leader began. KatieAnn lost herself in the songs. Music always had a way of calming her and transporting her away from the cares of the world.

At the end of the singing, the young folks mingled. Some couples paired off to talk privately. To her surprise, KatieAnn actually enjoyed the singing. She liked talking to Rosanna and the other girls, but she still feared getting too close to anyone. What if they found out about her? What if she had to leave? She didn't want to cause anyone undue pain. "I think I'll see if Rebecca is ready to leave," she whispered to Rosanna.

"Don't you want to stay longer? We can take you home, if you like."

"*Danki*, but I am a bit tired."

"I guess you are. You just got to Maryland and have been busy ever since, I'm sure. We'll have lots of other singings. Do you suppose I could drop by to visit?"

"Sure. I'd like that."

Rosanna linked her arm with KatieAnn's. "I'll walk back to the house with you."

"I don't want to keep you from the fun."

"I'm a bit tired myself."

They walked in companionable silence. When they reached the house, KatieAnn found Rebecca trying to prepare the four youngest children for the trip home. She quickly stepped in to lend a hand. Being with the young people was fun, but keeping her distance still seemed like the best plan to her.

CHAPTER SEVEN

"Mail!" Samuel tossed a couple of envelopes onto the kitchen counter when he came in for the noon meal the next day. Meal time was slightly quieter on days that Eli and Jonas were in school.

"Junk mail, *jah*?" Rebecca set a steaming bowl of homemade chicken noodle soup on the table at Samuel's usual place.

"Looks like it, except for a letter for KatieAnn."

"Already? Mamm must be lonely." KatieAnn laughed.

"It didn't look like your *mamm*'s address."

"Really? I'll look at it later." KatieAnn tied bibs around Grace's and Benjamin's necks. They kicked their feet in their highchairs but had already learned they had to wait until after the silent prayer to eat. KatieAnn doubted they understood about prayer, but they definitely knew Samuel's signal that the prayer was over and the meal could begin!

"This soup hits the spot." Samuel licked his lips. "It's blustery and cold out there."

"I'm thankful yesterday was nice for Esther's wedding."

"It was a nice day," KatieAnn murmured. "Esther looked so happy."

"She did indeed. She didn't think she'd ever find someone, and Andrew would have been her last choice. I'm glad she realized people can completely change." Rebecca raised a spoonful of soup to her mouth.

Samuel grunted and took a big bite of a fat buttermilk biscuit oozing melted butter.

"You changed, Samuel," Rebecca teased. "You turned into a *wunderbaar daed* and husband. You aren't the *bu* I first married."

"*Bu*, was I?"

"We both grew up, ain't so?"

"For sure." Samuel sent a lopsided buttery smile to his *fraa*.

After Samuel returned to his outside work, with the kitchen set to rights, and all four little ones tucked in for naps, Rebecca and KatieAnn finally had a chance to sit for a few minutes and give attention to the overflowing mending basket. With two rough-and-tumble little *buwe*, two active little girls, two babies, and a man who worked with animals and farm equipment, the bottom of the mending basket rarely showed itself. Rebecca seemed to be the only one not to make regular contributions to the contents.

Rebecca pulled out one of many *buwe's* socks. "I think my family's toes have teeth." She wiggled her finger through a hole in the toe of the sock.

"It seems so." KatieAnn smiled and plucked another sock from the basket.

"Don't forget your letter."

"*Ach*! I did. Let me see who wrote already. Samuel didn't think it was Mamm." She popped up from her chair and sped off to the kitchen, and then returned to the living room at a slower pace, turning the envelope over and over in her hands. "It's from Grace."

"Your *freind*?"

"*Jah*. Grace Hershberger has been my *freind* forever. She works, uh, worked at the bakery with me."

"She probably misses you."

"Maybe. She must have written this as soon as I left." She withdrew the single sheet of paper from the envelope and smiled as she read. "Grace says the customers have been asking about me and my specials. I always tried to think up new treats." Her smile wilted and was replaced by a wide-eyed fearful expression. Her grip on the paper loosened. It fluttered to the floor between her and Rebecca.

"*Was ist letz?*" Rebecca dropped the sock she had been mending and stared at her *schweschder*.

"Grace asked..." KatieAnn cleared her throat, but her voice still came out not much louder than a squeak. "She asked if I have Deborah's recipe book." Tears rushed to her eyes. "Rebecca, I never used Deborah's recipe book. I never used her recipes—only my own."

"You've been here. How could you possibly be suspected of taking it?"

"Deborah told Grace she hadn't used the book since before I left." KatieAnn covered her face with her hands and moaned softly.

Rebecca snatched the letter from its resting place on the floor. She scanned the lines of small, neat handwriting. "She said Deborah will probably contact you."

"I don't have anything to tell her. I did *not* take her book." Tears spilled over and rolled down KatieAnn's cheeks.

Rebecca slid from her chair. She knelt beside KatieAnn and pulled her into a hug. "I believe you. Truly, I do."

KatieAnn nodded against her *schweschder's* shoulder, unable to form any words. Rebecca's tenderness and loyalty so touched her that she released all the pent-up pain and sadness in great, gulping sobs. Rebecca swayed with her in a rocking motion and rhythmically patted her back.

"*Danki*." KatieAnn sniffed and pulled back slightly. "I'm so sorry to act like such a *boppli*."

"You haven't been at all. You've been very brave."

"I just can't figure out who keeps taking things and blaming me."

"Let's think about this." Rebecca returned to her chair. "Who does the baking at Deborah's shop?"

"I did most of it. Deborah did some."

"Did Deborah use her recipe book?"

"Sometimes."

"Did you use any books?"

"*Nee*, not usually. I sort of make up my recipes as I go and write them down later."

"Have you seen her book before?"

"Sure, but I never used it."

"Where did she keep it?"

"On or in her desk, I suppose."

"Who else works at the bake shop?"

"Grace, Lizzie, and Frannie."

"Do they bake?"

"Rarely." KatieAnn smiled. She couldn't imagine Lizzie baking without injuring herself or burning down the building. Frannie and Grace stayed busy waiting on customers and keeping the display cases filled.

"I'm thinking Deborah just mislaid the book, and it will probably turn up soon, if it hasn't already."

"I hope you're right."

Rebecca and KatieAnn darned socks in silence for a while, each lost in thought, until a knock at the back door startled them. Before either could get out of their chairs, the door flew open and a woman's voice called out,

"Anyone home?"

"Miriam? Is that you?" Rebecca looked toward the door.

"It is."

"We're in the living room. *Kumm* on in." Rebecca cut a dark thread, plunged her needle into the little red tomato pin cushion, and laid the mended sock aside. *"Wie bist du heit?"*

"I'm fine." Miriam pointed at the overflowing basket. "I'm sure it's *gut* to have some help with all that mending."

"It surely is. I'm very happy KatieAnn is here—and not just to help with chores." As inconspicuously as possible, Rebecca transferred the letter from the little table where it lay for the world to see to the chair right beneath her dress.

"We're glad you're here, too, KatieAnn."

"Danki." Thank Gott Rebecca moved the letter! She doubted Miriam would be nosey, but she'd rather not take the chance that other eyes would read the words Grace had written. "I've missed Rebecca and her family, so I'm glad for this chance to visit." She tried to keep her face averted so Miriam couldn't see her puffy eyes.

"Have a seat, Miriam. We won't make you mend." Rebecca laughed. "Would you like something to drink?"

Miriam dropped into the closest chair. "I'm fine. I can't stay very long. Levi is minding the store and Grossmammi Sallie for a few minutes."

"How is Levi's *grossmammi*?"

"She has her *gut* days and her bad days. On her *gut* days, she's about as spry as ever. On her bad days, she's so forgetful she's almost helpless."

"I'm so sorry. I'll pray she has mostly *gut* days."

"Danki, Rebecca. We can all use prayers. What I really stopped by for was to ask KatieAnn if she'd like a job

while she's here. Actually, it would be more like doing me a huge favor."

Startled, KatieAnn pricked her thumb with the needle. She dropped her mending in her lap and braved a look at Miriam. "A job?"

"*Jah*. In my store. My *dochder*-in-law, Sarah, worked for me sometimes before the *boppli* came. Now she's too busy."

"Uh, I'm not sure." KatieAnn looked helplessly at Rebecca.

"I think it might be a *gut* idea."

"Really?" KatieAnn couldn't believe her ears. They had just been talking about the problems at her last job, and Rebecca thought she should work at another store?

"Of course it's up to you, but it may give you something to do besides chase after little ones."

"You can think about it," Miriam assured her. "You wouldn't have to work every day. Wednesdays and Saturdays are my busiest days."

KatieAnn nodded. "I'll definitely think about it."

"Great. I've got to get back. If you want, you can drop by tomorrow."

"Okay."

Miriam disappeared as quickly as she had appeared. The *schweschders* exchanged shocked looks as the kitchen door slammed closed behind Miriam.

"Do you really think I should do it?"

"Why not? It will get you out of the house and away from noisy *kinner* for a couple days and give you a little spending money, too."

"What if they find out about my reputation as a thief?"

"KatieAnn, you are not a thief! I don't see how anyone at home can possibly believe that about you. Anyway, nobody here knows about that."

"I don't remember where Miriam's store is."

"It isn't far. Samuel or I can take you over tomorrow. She opens at eight in the morning."

"Should I do it?" KatieAnn chewed on a fingernail.

"Why not go check it out tomorrow and see if it suits you?"

"I guess that wouldn't hurt. Is it okay if I bake a treat to take to Grossmammi Sallie?"

"Why, I think that would be *wunderbaar*. I'm sure she would enjoy anything you take."

Until they all learn I'm a suspected criminal!

⌒

Fear snaked its tentacles around KatieAnn's body and squeezed her intestines, making it impossible to eat breakfast on Saturday morning. She chided herself over such foolishness. She had worked in a bakery for years and that was a store, so she should definitely not be so nervous. She sipped a little hot tea in an effort to calm the beast that had taken up residence in her stomach.

"I can take you over right after breakfast." Samuel laid down his fork and chewed his last bite of sausage.

"*Danki*. I'll just help Rebecca clean up."

"*Nee*. You go on. Emma will help me tidy up. Just don't forget your treat for Grossmammi Sallie."

⌒

KatieAnn approached the front door of Eshs' store slowly. She thought about hurrying back to the buggy and begging Samuel to take her with him, but he had headed the buggy for home practically before she had both feet on the ground. She could do this. It was a small store, after all. She *would* do this.

She took a deep breath and continued her internal chant. She turned the door knob, pasted a tremulous smile on her face, and pushed the door. A little bell jangled above her head alerting the world that she had just entered the store.

KatieAnn was pleasantly surprised. The store wasn't as small as it appeared. She sniffed in an effort to identify the pleasant aroma that greeted her—a combination of cinnamon or some other spice and apples with a little hickory smoke thrown in.

Her gaze took in the aisles of housewares, grooming items, bolts of black, blue, purple, and green fabric, and even toys and games. Bins of old-fashioned penny candy lined the check-out counter. A display case with baked treats sat beside the cash register. Miriam Esh's attention was focused on the blue cloth she was measuring and cutting for a customer, so KatieAnn's entrance wasn't terribly noticeable.

Motion beside the wood stove at the back of the store captured her attention. A thin, frail, elderly woman rocked in a heavy oak chair in time to some internal rhythm. Her white head, with the scalp showing through the hair at the center part from all the years of being pulled into a severe bun, bobbed with the chair's to-and-fro movement. *Kapp* strings danced around the wizened face. A memory of those dried apple dolls she'd seen in a craft store flitted across her brain, and KatieAnn smiled. This must be Grossmammi Sallie.

The old woman stopped rocking abruptly and beckoned. KatieAnn looked right, left and behind her to make sure she was the recipient of the summons. The woman's puckered lips widened into a smile that lit up her entire, wrinkled face. KatieAnn smiled back—a genuine smile this time. She crossed the room and squatted beside the well-used rocking chair.

"What a pretty girl." The woman reached out a gnarled hand to touch her hair and cheek.

"You must be Grossmammi Sallie." KatieAnn took the wrinkled hand with paper-thin skin into her own hand.

"That's me."

"I'm KatieAnn Mast. I'm going to help Miriam in the store sometimes." Now that she'd said the words, she guessed she was committed to working here.

"*Gut.* Miriam works too hard."

"I brought you something." KatieAnn pulled out her tin of soft oatmeal cookies. She wondered if she should have cleared this idea with Miriam in case Sallie wasn't supposed to have sweets, but the joy shining in Sallie's crinkled eyes made KatieAnn feel she had done the right thing. "Would you like one?" She opened the lid, letting Sallie peek into the tin and the sweet smell of cookies waft out.

Sallie bobbed her head and giggled like one of Rebecca's *kinner.* She snatched two cookies from the tin and laughed with glee. "*Danki.*" She barely got the word out before taking a huge bite of one of the cookies. "Mmmm. *Appeditlich!*" Her tongue snaked out to ensnare any crumbs adhering to her lips.

KatieAnn smiled and patted the old woman's arm. "I'm glad you like them. I'll set the tin behind the counter so you can have more cookies later."

Sallie nodded and kept chewing.

"*Ach*, KatieAnn. I thought I saw you *kumm* in. I see you've met Grossmammi Sallie."

"I have indeed."

"I like this girl. She brought cookies." Sallie's words came out slightly garbled around the treat she still chewed.

"I hope it was all right to bring the cookies."

"It's fine. Grossmammi loves her sweets. So have you decided to take me up on my offer?"

"I-I'll try. You'll have to show me how things are done. I worked in a bake shop. I waited on customers sometimes, but usually I stayed busy with the baking."

"There's nothing to it. You'll be fine. I'll show you around."

KatieAnn stood and shook her tingling legs that had cramped from crouching. She patted Sallie's hand and promised to visit with her again later. Then she followed Miriam around from aisle to aisle, making mental notes she hoped she would be able to recall when necessary.

She waited on a few customers, cut fabric for several others, and persuaded Sallie to eat half of a ham and cheese sandwich and a few apple slices for lunch.

"*Gut*, you're getting her to eat." Miriam made the casual comment as she passed by. "I think you could both use some fattening up."

KatieAnn simply nodded. She'd heard that remark all her life. She had too much nervous energy to gain weight. She could never be still. Even if she sat, she tapped her toes or drummed her fingers. Sometimes she had to tuck her hands under her legs during the three-hour church services to keep them still.

Samuel returned to fetch KatieAnn late in the afternoon so she could help Rebecca with any last-minute meal preparations or chores. Tomorrow was an off Sunday, so there would be no church services, but there would be no unnecessary chores either. A day of rest would be welcome. KatieAnn felt she'd been on the go ever since she arrived in Maryland, and she was emotionally spent.

"You'll *kumm* back, *jah*?" Sallie tugged on KatieAnn's hand when she bid the old woman farewell.

"For sure. And I'll bring you another treat."

Sallie's face crinkled into a huge smile.

KatieAnn shivered when she walked out into the brisk November air. The store had been a bit overheated, probably to keep Sallie warm. The flurry of activity also helped generate heat. Now gray clouds masked the sun and a cool breeze slapped her in the face. She quickly climbed into the buggy beside Samuel.

They rode the short distance home in silence. Maybe next time she'd walk to the store unless it was too cold. Samuel stopped at the end of the driveway and handed the reins to KatieAnn. He hopped out to pull mail from the metal mailbox. Twenty seconds later, he slid back inside the buggy. KatieAnn didn't miss the frown that wrinkled his brow when he tossed the only piece of mail into her lap.

She looked up at Samuel in surprise. Turning the envelope over, she read the return address that Samuel had no doubt already read. Deborah. KatieAnn's heart plummeted to her toes.

CHAPTER EIGHT

KatieAnn stuffed the envelope into her purse. She hopped out of the buggy as soon as the wheels stopped turning, thanked Samuel for the ride and ignored the questioning look he shot in her direction. After rushing up the steps, she yanked open the back door. She'd read whatever Deborah had to say later when she could be alone and could cry in private.

"I'm home, Rebecca. I'll help as soon as I wash up."

"How was the store?" Rebecca clanged a spoon against a pot she'd been stirring on the stove.

"Fairly busy. I enjoyed spending some time with Grossmammi Sallie."

"I'm sure she enjoyed the company."

"What can I do to help you?"

"This stew is for tomorrow. There's a meatloaf in the oven for tonight. If you like, you can mash the potatoes. They should be ready."

"Okay."

Dinner time passed in a blur. Her mind kept traveling to the unopened letter buried in her purse. Would Deborah accuse her of taking something else?

"I think your *aenti* is tired," Rebecca said.

"What?"

"Emma has been talking to you."

"*Ach!* I'm so sorry, Emma. My mind wandered. What did you say?" KatieAnn made a concerted effort to focus her attention on her little niece.

A short time later, she and Rebecca stowed food away and cleaned the kitchen in silence. KatieAnn could tell her big *schewschder* struggled to keep quiet. She should have told Rebecca about the letter but couldn't bring herself to do so. Ignoring it would not make it go away, though.

Finally Rebecca spoke. "Samuel said you got mail. Did Mamm write?"

When did Samuel have a chance to tell Rebecca about her letter? Maybe the two had some kind of secret language. "*Nee*, it wasn't from Mamm. It was from Deborah Miller."

"Did you read the letter?"

"Not yet."

"Do you want to go get it or do you want to read it in private?"

"I-I'll get it when we're finished here. I'm afraid to read what she wrote."

"We'll deal with it—whatever it is."

"*Jah.*" That was easy for Rebecca to say. Her reputation wasn't at stake. Still, KatieAnn held her tongue. Rebecca was trying to be encouraging and helpful. She stacked the last plate in the cabinet and hung up the red-and-white-checked dish towel.

She dragged her feet on the way to retrieve her purse, not at all eager to read the contents of the letter. Since Samuel and the *kinner* were in the living room, she carried the bag back to the kitchen and plunked it down on the table. After yanking out the letter, she took a deep breath to brace herself for whatever accusations it might contain.

Gathering her courage, she slid her finger beneath the envelope's flap and extracted the single sheet of note paper.

KatieAnn scanned the brief letter. She felt the color drain from her face like life draining from her body. Tears pricked her eyes, and she wasn't sure if they were tears of sadness, anger, or both.

"KatieAnn?" Rebecca's voice came out whisper soft. "What does it say?"

"It says...it says..." KatieAnn gulped and tried to get control of her anger. "I'll read it."

KatieAnn,

My recipe book is missing. It really isn't valuable except to me. It was my grossmammi's and then my mamm's. I would like to have it back. If you have taken it, please mail it back to me right away.

Deborah Miller

Rebecca gasped and wrung her hands.

"She naturally assumes I stole her book! I wonder if she even asked Frannie or Grace or Lizzie about it. I never used her book anyway. I have my own recipes. I don't need hers!" KatieAnn's anger gave way to hurt and humiliation. Her bravado evaporated like air from a pin-pricked balloon. "They all think I'm a thief." Hot tears spilled down her cheeks. "They don't trust me. I-I'll never be able to go h-home."

Once again, Rebecca pulled her into a hug. "This will work out. Somehow it will work out. Have faith, dear. Remember all things work for *gut* to those who love Gott."

"Where's the *gut* in this?" KatieAnn sniffed and swiped at her eyes.

"We'll find it. If not today, then tomorrow or the next

day."

Tomorrow. That song played in KatieAnn's brain again. Would the sun *kumm* out? Would things be better? She felt like Annie from the play. She had red hair and felt like an orphan, too. All she needed was a red dress and a scruffy little dog.

After Sunday's noon meal, KatieAnn donned her warm outerwear and bonnet to take the *kinner* outside for a little playtime. Thank Gott it was an off Sunday so there wasn't any church service! After a night spent tossing and turning and alternately crying and praying, her face must be blotchy and swollen. Both Rebecca and Samuel politely avoided commenting on her sad appearance. The little ones were just happy she would go out to play with them.

The day was raw for November in Southern Maryland. The sun struggled to warm the air, and the blustery wind made that task even harder. To KatieAnn, who had lived in Pennsylvania all her life, cold Novembers were the norm. Today's weather was apparently a bit unusual for St. Mary's County. Rebecca said last winter had been unusually cold and snowy, and she hoped they didn't have a repeat this year.

"Ready?" KatieAnn turned to her nieces and nephews who looked like they were ready to explore the North Pole.

"*Jah!*" four voices answered in unison. The twins would *kumm* out with Rebecca for a few minutes after they awoke from their naps.

"Let's go then!"

KatieAnn pushed first one girl and then the other on the wooden swing suspended by ropes from a solid limb of the big oak tree in the front yard. She tossed a ball with the *buwe* and chased all four in a game of tag.

Rosy-cheeked and breathless, they all stopped at the sound of a buggy driving up the long gravel driveway. Who could be visiting?

"Do you recognize the buggy?" KatieAnn asked Jonas and Eli. It would take her a while to distinguish which horse belonged to which family.

"It looks like Jeremiah Yoders'," Eli answered.

"That's Rosanna's *daed*, ain't so?"

"*Jah*. And Caleb's and Nathan's and Adam's and Mary's and Martha's too." Jonas clearly felt important that he could add to the conversation.

"I didn't know there were so many *kinner*. Is Rosanna the oldest?"

"*Jah*," Eli replied.

The buggy drew closer. Excited little faces peered out the back. KatieAnn guessed the *buwe* were slightly older than Eli and Jonas. The little girls looked about Emma's age. *Gut*. The *kinner* would have others to play with for a while so she could rest.

"*Wie bist du heit*," Nancy Yoder called as she exited the buggy. Little ones of various sizes hopped out after their *mamm*.

"*Gut*," KatieAnn replied. At least for the moment she was *gut*.

"*Wilkom*," Rebecca called from the doorway. "*Kumm* on inside."

Eli, Jonas, and Emma ran to greet the new arrivals and immediately began playing a game. Elizabeth, tired of trying to keep up with the older *kinner*, begged to be held. KatieAnn obliged and hoisted the little girl up to settle on her hip. Elizabeth's legs dangled halfway down KatieAnn's body.

"The *kinner* are about as big as you are," Rosanna teased.

"I suppose they are. It's great to see you again,

Rosanna."

"Are you too cold to stay outside a while longer?"

"I'm fine. We can sit on the porch if you like. This one is getting heavy." KatieAnn bounced Elizabeth, eliciting giggles from her little niece.

"How are things with you?" Rosanna dropped onto a wooden rocking chair.

"Okay." KatieAnn sat on the porch swing and settled Elizabeth on her lap. Elizabeth snuggled close and rested her head against KatieAnn's shoulder.

"You seem a little sad. Are you missing your home?"

"Uh, I miss my *mamm*, but I'm happy to be here with Rebecca. Even though she's older, we've always been close. I've missed her, and I love her *kinner*." She gave Elizabeth a little hug and gazed out at the yard where the others squealed and laughed with their friends.

"Rebecca's *kinner* are sweet, and the twins are precious. I'm glad you're here, and I hope you'll stay a *gut* long while."

"*Danki*." She didn't mention she might be here forever unless the people in this community heard about the bakery shop mess.

"Someone else asked about you, too."

"Who?"

"Do you remember Luke Troyer?"

"Luke with the sapphire blue eyes."

Rosanna laughed. "I guess Luke's eyes are blue. I hadn't really noticed particularly."

How did she not notice those startlingly blue eyes? They made KatieAnn forget all about Micah Kinsinger. Besides when she ran into Micah in town before she left, he had scowled and then pretended he didn't seen her. He, too, must believe the worst about her.

Rosanna's eyes twinkled. "Anyway, Luke asked if I knew how long you were staying here. I said I hoped for a long time. I'm pretty sure he didn't mean for me to hear him, but I did. I heard him mumble, 'me too.'"

"He was probably just clearing his throat or something."

"*Nee*. I distinctly heard those two words. I think he's definitely interested in you."

"Rosanna, he's only seen me maybe twice."

"Don't you believe in love at first sight?" Rosanna sighed and a dreamy, faraway expression overtook her face.

This time KatieAnn laughed. "Love? You must read a lot of romance novels. Love takes time."

"Not always." She lowered her voice. "I confess I do read romance novels, but only Christian ones. And I believe some people know as soon as they meet that they were meant to be together."

"That's very rare, I'm thinking."

"I don't know. It seems Jake and Hannah were destined to be together."

"I thought they had lots of obstacles to overcome."

"I guess so, but they did. Something was there from the beginning that kept pulling them back to each other."

"Hmmm. And who do you feel 'destined' to be with?"

"I, well, I sort of have my eye on someone. He lives in another district, though. I see him sometimes when I take candles over for one of the shops to sell."

"And does he share your sentiments?"

"I-I'm not sure...yet."

"Do you make those lovely, fragrant candles that Miriam sells in her store?" KatieAnn repositioned Elizabeth who had nodded off to sleep and become dead weight in her arms.

"If you mean the votives she has near the check-out counter, then *jah*, I made them."

"They smell *wunderbaar*. How do you make them?"

"You'll have to *kumm* over one day and I'll show you how. So you've been to Esh's store?"

"I was there yesterday. I told Miriam I would help out at the store on Wednesdays and Saturdays. She said Sarah helped before her *boppli* was born. With Christmas only a few weeks away, Miriam needs some extra hands. I suspect she needs help with Grossmammi Sallie, too."

"Did you meet her?"

"I did. She's such a sweet lady."

"She was having a *gut* day then?"

"I believe so. She'd get a little forgetful sometimes, but at her age, I'm sure that's to be expected."

"I think Miriam is afraid Sallie will wander off somewhere since she can still get around quite well."

"Oooh. I wouldn't want that to happen. I'll try to keep an eye on her when I'm there." KatieAnn placed a hand on one of Elizabeth's cheeks. "This little one is getting pretty cold. I think we'd better go inside."

"Okay. It is nippy today."

"Maybe if we make some hot cocoa, we can get the others to *kumm* inside, too. Rebecca's little ones have been outside for quite a while now."

"Great idea. I'll help."

With a little grunt, KatieAnn pushed to her feet. "Maybe I can ease this one down for a nap, but I have a feeling she'll wake up as soon as we get inside, especially if she smells cocoa."

Rosanna held the door so KatieAnn could maneuver herself and Elizabeth inside. "Ah, the heat feels *gut*."

"You should have told me you were cold. We could have *kumm* in sooner. I'm probably a little more used to the cold."

"That's okay. I was really only starting to get cold."

As if on some silent cue, Elizabeth pulled her head away from KatieAnn's shoulder and blinked her eyes twice.

"What did I tell you?" KatieAnn mouthed to Rosanna. "Well, hello, sleepyhead. Would you like to lie down to nap a little longer?"

The little head shook vehemently.

"Okay. You can help us make hot cocoa. Let's get our bonnets and cloaks off and wash our hands, *jah*?"

Elizabeth's chin bobbed up and down. KatieAnn set her on her feet and began removing outerwear.

"So what do you think of Luke?" Rosanna waited until Elizabeth carried napkins to the table to ask her question.

"I really don't know him. We only met him briefly. He seems nice enough. He didn't send you on a fishing expedition, did he?"

"Of course not. He'd probably be totally mortified if he knew I asked you about him. You did notice his eyes, though."

"They are beautiful. I can't believe you never noticed."

"Luke is Luke. He's always been around. He's like a *bruder*. Now, Matthew Zimmerman, on the other hand…" Rosanna clapped her hand over her mouth.

Both girls giggled. KatieAnn thought perhaps she had met a *freind* and kindred spirit…if her past didn't catch up with her and spoil things, that is.

CHAPTER NINE

Hoping the sun would eventually appear to warm the cold, gray Wednesday morning, KatieAnn set out at a brisk pace toward Esh's store. She didn't want to disturb Samuel's work again to have him drive her, so she'd dressed warmly and assured Rebecca she could make the trek on foot.

My, but it was cold! Her breath came out in little clouds around her head. If today was any indication, Southern Maryland's fall and winter would be similar to Pennsylvania's. KatieAnn ducked her head momentarily to avoid the full force of the wind. She'd *wilkom* the overly warm temperature inside the store today.

"I didn't even hear the buggy." Miriam looked up from her work when the bell over the door chimed, heralding KatieAnn's arrival.

"I walked."

"Brave girl! It's pretty cold out."

"It certainly is." After stuffing her gloves into the pockets of her cloak, she pulled her big quilted bag off her shoulder and opened it to remove a sealed plastic bag filled with her orange dream muffins. She crossed the room to greet Grossmammi Sallie, who sat contentedly rocking by the wood stove.

"I brought you a treat." KatieAnn bent to hug the old woman.

"*Jah?*" Dry, thin lips curved upward into a smile.

"Muffins. Would you like one now?"

The woman's head bobbed up and down.

"Let me get this cloak and bonnet off and find you a napkin." KatieAnn raised her voice so Miriam could hear her. "I have extra muffins."

"*Gut.* I'll have one directly."

KatieAnn dusted and straightened shelves and waited on an occasional customer when Miriam was otherwise occupied. She made sure to visit with Sallie every now and then.

"These muffins are *wunderbaar,*" Miriam announced when she took a midmorning break. "You should sell your baked goods — even open a bakery."

"*Danki,* but you've only tried my oatmeal cookies and these muffins."

"I have a feeling all your baked treats are *appeditlich.*"

Heat rushed to KatieAnn's cheeks. She prayed Miriam always thought highly of her, that no one here ever had a reason to doubt her trustworthiness.

The sky grew darker as the afternoon wore on, yet customers continued to visit the store. The approaching holidays ensured steady business. A blast of cold air entered with each new arrival. KatieAnn shivered each time the door opened. Periodically, she checked to make sure Sallie was warm.

Each time she asked, Sallie gave the same answer. "Snug as a bug." Every time the old woman got out of her rocking chair for a stroll around the store, she returned to wrap herself in her cocoon of shawls and afghans.

"Have you seen my calculator?" Miriam called out

from the fabric cutting area.

"*Nee*, I haven't." KatieAnn fretted. *Will I be accused of taking it?* "I'll look around for it, Miriam." Fear held her in an icy grip. This couldn't be happening again. She scrutinized every bin and shelf in every aisle. *Relax. Breathe. Miriam probably misplaced it. She hasn't accused you of taking it.*

"*Ach*, I can't believe it!" Miriam slapped her own forehead. "I'm such a scatterbrain. The calculator is in my pocket. I appreciate you looking for it, though." She began to punch in numbers. "I must be getting forgetful in my old age."

KatieAnn let out the breath she'd been holding. Relief flooded her. Her pounding heart slowed to its normal rhythm. Maybe she shouldn't work in any kind of store.

By the time she left in late afternoon, she wished she had asked Samuel to pick her up. The relentless wind seemed determined to blow any remaining leaves from the trees and pulled KatieAnn's breath from her in ragged gasps. Gray clouds threatened to spill their contents at any moment. As the wind tried to rip her cloak from her body, she clutched the garment at the throat. She struggled to make forward progress but found herself pushed back a step for every step forward. With each brief respite from the wind, she increased her pace. *I'll be frozen before I get to Rebecca's house.* She scarcely heard the clip clop and rattle of an approaching buggy.

"Hey!" A deep male voice called.

Startled, KatieAnn turned just as icy pellets of sleet began dropping from the sky. She squinted in an effort to identify the owner of the voice.

"KatieAnn, is that you?" The buggy pulled alongside her.

She looked up and straight into the sapphire eyes of Luke Troyer. "*Jah*, it's me."

"Get in the buggy before you freeze."

KatieAnn hesitated. For her to be alone with Luke, just the two of them in an enclosed buggy, wouldn't be considered proper. But sleet pummeled her and stung her exposed cheeks. Her fingers tingled with cold even inside her knit gloves. Did she choose impropriety or hypothermia?

"*Kumm,* get out of this nasty weather." Luke's voice sounded encouraging.

"Okay." KatieAnn's teeth chattered. If she didn't get inside that buggy, she'd surely freeze. The horse pranced in place, obviously eager to start trotting again. She climbed inside and situated herself as far from the driver as possible.

"Here." Luke tossed her a blanket he'd pulled from under the seat. "You must be about frozen."

"Just about." KatieAnn had to force the two words out between shivers.

"Why are you out walking? It isn't exactly a balmy day for a stroll."

"That's for sure." Free of the wind and sleet, her chill began to dissipate. "I helped out at Esh's store today. I walked there this morning so I wouldn't have to bother Samuel. For sure and certain, I did not expect the weather would turn so mean." She shivered again.

"One thing you can always count on with Southern Maryland weather is that you can't count on Southern Maryland weather!"

She laughed. "I'll remember that."

They rode in silence for a few moments as KatieAnn continued to thaw. Out of the corner of her eye, she caught Luke squirming. Why was he so antsy, all of a sudden?

"Say, KatieAnn, are you planning to go to the singing on Sunday evening?"

"Uh, I hadn't really thought about it."

"It might be fun. You'd get to know some other young folks and maybe make some new *freinden* for however long you're here." His voice rose at the end as if he wanted to ask how long she would be in the community.

"Uh, I, uh…"

"I'm sure Rosanne will go. I know you know her."

"*Jah*, we've talked a few times."

"We're really all nice folks."

KatieAnn had to smile. Luke looked like a puppy eager to please. "I'm sure you're all nice. I-I'll think about it."

"*Gut*." After a moment's pause, he added, "How long did you say you'd be here?"

"I didn't say."

"Oh."

"I think it will probably be a while, though."

"Through the holidays, at least?"

"At least."

"*Gut*."

Luke turned those sapphire eyes on KatieAnn. His smile warmed her from her heart down to her toes. It might even melt the ice crystals clinging to the brown and green grass. She couldn't help but smile back.

"I appreciate the ride home, Luke," she said as they bumped along the Hertzlers' driveway. "I'd have frozen for sure if you hadn't offered a ride."

"I'm glad I happened along."

"Me, too." She opened the buggy door and hopped out.

"See you Sunday."

She smiled before turning toward the house. Wood smoke billowed from the brick chimney, promising warmth within. A sudden reality check stole the smile from her face. If Luke found out about her supposed crime, he'd want nothing to do with her. Getting to know the other young people, particularly Luke Troyer, would most likely only bring heartache.

Saturday morning's clear, blue sky boasted a sun that shone bright enough to cause blindness. The wind of the previous few days had fizzled to an occasional breeze. Temperatures soared to a balmy fifty degrees. Luke had certainly been right about Southern Maryland's unpredictable weather.

"I think I'm safe to walk today," KatieAnn told Rebeca and Samuel at breakfast. "I don't see a cloud in the sky anywhere."

"*Jah*, it looks like a right nice day ahead, even warm to be nearly Thanksgiving."

Thanksgiving. This would be the first year KatieAnn didn't share Thanksgiving with her parents and *bruders*. She probably wouldn't be in Pennsylvania for Christmas, either. A wave of sadness washed over her. She missed Mamm, Daed, Thomas, Eli, James and Mary, Caleb and Eliza, and all her nieces and nephews. Holidays were family times, and she loved her big, boisterous family.

But she had to look on the bright side. At least she had Rebecca. These would be the first holidays she'd shared with her *schweschder* in a long time. And she was certain Rebecca's six *kinner* would keep things lively. Subconsciously, she heaved a sigh.

Rebecca turned sympathetic eyes on her. "I know it will be hard for you being away from home on the holidays, but we're very happy to have you here with us."

"I'm glad to be here with you. I've missed you."

"I'm glad you're here, *aenti*." Little Emma's grin spread across her entire face.

"Me, too," three other young voices echoed. Even the

twins' heads bobbed up and down as though their toddler minds understood the conversation.

"*Danki*." KatieAnn smiled into each little face. "Now, I'd better help clean up and start walking."

Her walk to Esh's store was brisk but invigorating, nothing at all like Wednesday's frigid trek battling a ferocious wind. She arrived early, rosy-cheeked but energized, and called out a greeting as she pushed open the front door.

"There's my girl." Grossmammi Sallie's voice carried across the store. "Did you bring me a treat?"

KatieAnn burst out laughing at the shriveled, cotton-haired woman who sounded more like a spoiled little girl than a *grossmammi*. "Now whatever makes you think I'd do that?" She held her bag behind her.

"What are you hiding?"

"Probably nothing you'd like. It's just my special cookies 'n cream doughnuts."

The old woman cackled with glee and held out her hands.

"You're spoiling her something fierce." Miriam shook her head and made a clucking sound with her tongue.

"Leave her alone, Miriam." Sallie's voice boomed surprisingly strong. "At my age, spoiling is a *gut* thing."

Miriam produced paper napkins while KatieAnn opened her bag and removed a fat doughnut for Sallie and another one for Miriam. She closed the bag and set the extra doughnuts on the counter.

"Ahhh!" Sallie mumbled around the wad of doughnut in her mouth.

"These are absolutely *wunderbaar!*" Miriam proclaimed. "Maybe I should have a case just for your baked treats. I could serve *kaffi*, and we could have a little breakfast nook." She licked powdered sugar off her lips.

KatieAnn smiled and blushed. "I like to bake and

make up new recipes. I'm happy you enjoy them."

"You've got a natural talent, I'm thinking. What do you think, Grossmammi?"

"Mmmm!" Sallie licked each finger before wiping her hands and mouth on the napkin. "*Gut. Ser gut.*"

"So you think we should keep this girl around?" Miriam draped an arm across KatieAnn's shoulders.

"For sure and for certain!" Sallie licked her lips as if her tongue searched for one stray crumb.

Miriam laughed. "It looks like you're a keeper." When the little bell above the door jangled, all three women looked in that direction.

"*Gude mariye*, Clara and Noah," Miriam called to the couple entering the store.

"*Wie bist du heit?*" the woman asked.

"Fine. And you?"

"*Gut.*"

"Levi is out at the barn, if you have time to say 'hello.'" Miriam addressed the tall, thin man with the salt-and-pepper beard. "*Ach*, let me introduce you. This is KatieAnn Mast, Rebecca Hertzler's *schweschder* who has *kumm* for a visit." Miriam nodded. "And KatieAnn, this is Noah and Clara Schwartz."

A bit unnerved by the woman's close scrutiny, KatieAnn had to clear her throat to summon a voice that had gone into hiding.

Clara was a little shorter than her husband, and stockier. Her sharp, thin nose gave her a haughty appearance. Small brown eyes studied KatieAnn from head to heel without a single blink. Dark hair streaked with gray had been pulled back so tightly that the center part had already widened. KatieAnn made a mental note to make sure she pinned her hair more loosely. She certainly didn't want to be bald when she grew older. She forced her lips to smile at Clara.

"Nice to meet you." Noah's smile seemed genuine and lit his whole face. Despite his scraggly beard and bushy eyebrows, his expression was much more pleasant than his wife's sour countenance. "What's this?" He pointed to the doughnuts peeking out of the bag on the counter.

"KatieAnn has been helping me at the store. She always brings a treat for Grossmammi Sallie." At Miriam's words, they all looked at Sallie who, with her chin tucked into her chest, snored softly in the rocking chair beside the stove.

"Are they for sale?" Noah reached into his pocket.

KatieAnn looked at Miriam, unsure what she should say.

"Help yourself, Noah," Miriam answered. "The doughnuts are on the house today, but I might try to talk KatieAnn into baking enough to sell."

Noah extracted a doughnut from the bag and bit off a hefty chunk. "*Appeditlich*! You've got to try one, Clara."

"Maybe later."

"I'll head out to find Levi. *Kumm* on out to the buggy when you're done."

"*Jah, jah.*" Clara spun about and walked up the next aisle as her husband slipped out the door.

"Can I help you find anything in particular, Clara?" Miriam rolled her eyes at KatieAnn.

"Just cut me some fabric, I guess. I want to make a new dress before we head north."

"Clara's son and his wife are expecting their first *boppli* any day now," Miriam explained.

"How nice," KatieAnn replied. "Do they live far away?"

"Pennsylvania. Close to Persimmon Creek." Clara looked up from the bolts of fabric to stare at KatieAnn. "That's where you're from, ain't so? We're going right after Thanksgiving. Maybe I can look up your folks while

I'm there, if I have time."

Ice ran through KatieAnn's veins. She couldn't force a smile or an answer, even if she wanted to. Somehow she managed a slight nod. She doubted Clara saw, though, since she had already turned to haul out a bolt of dark blue fabric.

KatieAnn had a feeling this woman was the last person she would want to visit anywhere remotely near her hometown.

CHAPTER TEN

"I have a bad feeling about this," KatieAnn stood with Rebecca as they washed and dried the supper dishes that evening and made sure all preparations had been completed for the Lord's day. Even though Samuel and the *kinner* had left the kitchen, KatieAnn kept her voice low. "That Clara woman seemed to look right through me, like she could see into my soul."

"I don't want to sound unkind, but Clara can be a busybody." Rebecca paused to dry her hands on a dish towel. "Noah tries to keep her in check."

"That must be a full-time job. Oops! Sorry! That sort of slipped out." KatieAnn bit her lip.

Rebecca laughed. "I'm sure poor Noah has his hands full. He is a very nice, gentle man. Clara can be a bit...uh...prickly. A bit snappish."

"So I gathered."

"I don't think she's a hateful or spiteful person or anything like that. She just likes to—how do I tactfully say this?—pass on any information she hears."

"Gossip, you mean?"

"Well, um, I suppose so. But I don't think you should

worry. She will probably be so busy with the new *boppli* that she never makes it to Persimmon Creek or even talks to anyone who would know what happened at the bake shop. Don't go borrowing trouble. You know, the Lord Jesus tells us not to take any thought for the morrow, for the morrow shall take thought of the things of itself. Sufficient unto the day—"

"Is the evil thereof," KatieAnn finished. "Rebecca, am I evil?"

"Of course not! I believe the verse means each day has enough cares of its own so don't worry about tomorrow's possible troubles."

KatieAnn exhaled audibly in relief. "That makes sense. I'll pray Clara Schwartz has a *gut* visit with her family and *only* visits her family."

∞

Somehow KatieAnn made it through the three-hour church service and the meal afterwards on Sunday. If anyone asked her to recap the sermons, she would be unable to give any kind of detailed summary. Her mind continually travelled to Clara Schwartz and the woman's upcoming trip to Pennsylvania. She did pray, but mainly that Clara would not visit Persimmon Creek and would not ask anyone about her.

KatieAnn tried to focus on the Bible verse Rebecca recited last night. Gott didn't want them to worry but to trust instead. She sincerely wanted to trust, but how was she to turn off the worry? She had yet to figure that out.

When she glanced across the way to the men's side of the room, she found Luke Troyer's sapphire gaze fastened on her. He smiled and nodded ever so slightly. A hint of a smile tugged at her lips before she jerked her attention back to Bishop Sol who was delivering the final, longest sermon.

She stared at the man and caught a few of his words before her mind took off in a new direction. How could she get out of going to the singing tonight? She truly did like the young people she had met here, but if she grew closer to them and Clara came back spreading gossip from home, KatieAnn would have to sever any newfound relationships she'd forged. *Ach!* She must learn to give her worries over to the Lord Gott.

"Cast your cares upon Him…" Bishop Sol was saying.

She jumped. The bishop was talking about giving fears and worries over to the Lord. Was the man a mind reader? From that point on she listened raptly and prayed the bishop's words would calm her troubled spirit.

During the meal and social time following church, Rosanna begged KatieAnn to attend the singing. She promised they would have fun. Her blue-gray eyes expressed so much hope and excitement that KatieAnn could not refuse the invitation. Besides she had already baked some treats to take along just in case she decided to attend. She might as well enjoy at least one more singing with the young people—unless Clara stayed away several weeks, thereby giving her a longer period of freedom.

KatieAnn did enjoy the singing, just as Rosanna had promised. Her strong, clear soprano voice quickly got caught up in the familiar songs from the Ausbund. As the notes of the last song died away, Rosanna latched onto her arm as if afraid she would slip away into the night.

"*Kumm* get something to eat and drink." Rosanna tugged her in the direction of the refreshment table.

"My throat *is* rather dry. A drink would be great."

They wandered over to the table. Each filled a cup with ice and poured soda out of the big liter bottle. KatieAnn took a big gulp. "Ah! That's *gut*. Even though it's cold outside, this feels great on a dry throat."

"For sure." Rosanna passed her a napkin and nudged her toward the treats and chips. "Which items did you make?"

KatieAnn pointed to a plate of brownies and another of cookies.

"Now I know which ones to get." A male voice spoke softly behind them.

She whirled to find Luke Troyer behind her. Thank Gott for the dim lighting! A burning heat in her face told her a blush stained her cheeks. "I'm sure everything is *gut*."

"Probably, but I want to start with yours."

They made their selections and retreated to a stack of hay bales at the back of the barn. The three were just getting settled when they were joined by three other young people—a girl and two young men.

"You remember Micah Beiler, *jah*?" Rosanna asked.

"Your *bruder* recently married Hannah, ain't so?" KatieAnn faced the young man.

"*Jah*, my little *bruder*, Jake." Tall and broad-shouldered like Jacob, Micah sported the same blond hair, but his eyes were brown instead of jade green like his *bruder*'s.

"Micah, you're only a year older than Jacob. Don't make it sound like you're so ancient." Rosanna gave him a playful punch to the upper arm before completing her introductions. "And this is Nancy Swarey and her *bruder* Thomas. They joined the church with me a year ago."

Nancy and Thomas looked a lot alike. Both were slender, with medium brown hair and brown eyes, but Thomas was at least a head taller than Nancy. Both were outgoing with quick smiles.

KatieAnn relaxed as conversation and laughter flowed among the young people. "I know Micah works in his family's furniture business and Luke works for Jeremiah

Yoder, but what do you do?" she asked Thomas.

"I stay busy with my *daed*'s dairy farm. Samuel probably told you that he is going to join us in starting up a cheese factory. We've both been sending our milk out for processing, but once the factory is up and running, we can keep our milk here and make our own cheeses."

"That would be *wunderbaar!*" Samuel had mentioned something about the new venture. "How long have you worked for Jeremiah?" She turned her attention to Luke. That's who she really wanted to talk to, but she didn't want to make it obvious.

"Since I was seventeen, so that's five years now. I've always been curious about how things work ever since I was seven and dismantled my *mamm*'s kitchen clock. Mamm wasn't too happy about that."

KatieAnn laughed. "I guess not."

"I did get it put back together—even if the hands did point the wrong way. It worked."

"You mean it ticked but didn't have the correct time?" Rosanna laughed so hard she nearly spilled her drink.

"Something like that." Luke hung his head and pretended to be contrite. Strands of spun-gold hair fell across his face. "Hey, I've gotten better." He looked up at KatieAnn. "I put things back together the right way now."

She smiled. "Jeremiah must be glad of that."

"These brownies are the best I've ever eaten!" Nancy licked her lips after her last bite. "How long have you been baking?"

"Ever since I tried baking a mud pie in my *mamm*'s oven." KatieAnn grinned. "Of course she wasn't happy either. And I had to scrub the oven."

"These aren't made of mud, are they?" Thomas pretended he was about to spit out his mouthful.

"Of course not. I was six when I tried that recipe."

Thomas swallowed.

"I don't use mud anymore." KatieAnn couldn't resist teasing. "Potting soil has a nicer consistency and doesn't usually contain worms." She and the others burst out laughing at Thomas' shocked expression and the greenish hue that tinted his skin. "I'm only kidding, Thomas. My food is perfectly safe to eat. I promise."

Thomas picked up the half brownie he had laid on a napkin. He turned it every which way as if he expected a worm to poke its head out. "Honest?"

"Honest." KatieAnn laughed again.

"Say, Thomas, if you don't want that brownie, I'd be happy to take it off your hands." Luke reached for the napkin.

"That's okay. I was rather enjoying it before—oh well." He took another bite. "It *is* tasty."

"Don't talk with your mouth full." Nancy elbowed her *bruder*.

"Well, aren't you all prim and proper." Thomas elbowed her in return.

Rosanna nibbled a cookie and scanned the crowd of young people, her head turning one direction and then another.

"Are you looking for anyone in particular?" Micah asked.

"*Nee*, I'm just checking to see who's here."

"It's the same people as at the singing, I suspect," Micah replied. "I didn't feel any cold air from the door opening. I didn't see anyone from any neighboring districts arrive."

"I know. I just thought, uh, never mind." A flush bloomed on Rosanna's face.

"When are you making candles again?" KatieAnn hurried to change the subject, rescuing Rosanna from Micah's teasing.

"I'll probably make some the day after Thanksgiving so I'll have some to sell at the market and at Esh's store." Rosanna's words spilled out fast. She was obviously relieved to talk about her candles. Her eyes brightened and the crimson color faded from her cheeks. "Would you like to watch?"

"I would like very much to watch."

"We'll plan on it then. How about right after the noon meal?"

"That sounds fine with me. I'll be there." KatieAnn looked forward to the new experience.

"Am I invited, too? I might learn something new." Micah returned to his teasing.

"You need to learn some manners!" Rosanna quipped.

"What did I do? I haven't been rude."

"That's debatable. I'm sure you will be needed to fill holiday orders at the furniture shop."

Micah heaved an exaggerated sigh. "I suppose you are right."

The bantering and laughter continued until the hour grew late. Courting couples had slipped away, and the hosts had begun to clean up.

"Are you ready to leave?" Rosanna turned to KatieAnn. Samuel had dropped KatieAnn off with the understanding that Rosanna would drive her home.

"*Jah*. It's getting late." The evening had been loads of fun, but the night was advancing. Tomorrow would be a work day for all of them, either at home or at a job.

Luke fixed KatieAnn with a lingering gaze that made her heart do flips. She had a feeling he wanted to ask to take her home, but she wouldn't give him that opportunity—though she did give him a little smile before wiggling into her cloak and tying on her black bonnet. Best not to let any courting rumors get started. Besides, Clara Schwartz might be home from Pennsylvania soon with her own whopper of a rumor.

~~~

Monday's wash finally flapped in the brisk November wind. If the sun didn't put in an appearance and warm the air a bit, KatieAnn expected to snap frozen pants and dresses off the line later. Overnight, the weather had changed from cool to downright cold. She furiously rubbed her hands together to warm them when she came inside after hanging out the last load of clothes. "Brr! Your weather here is certainly changeable."

"That it is," Rebecca agreed. "Don't you think this would be a perfect day to prepare a big pot of stew for supper?"

"It sure sounds great to me. I'll peel and cut up vegetables when you're ready."

Rebecca tapped her chin. "I guess we can wait until Wednesday to do our Thanksgiving baking."

"Okay." KatieAnn sighed.

"You're missing home for the holidays, ain't so?" Rebecca reached out to tilt up her little *schweschder*'s chin so that they looked into each other's eyes.

"A bit. I am glad to be here with you and your family, though. Really, I am. I've missed you all."

"I know. I also know it's hard being away from home, especially at holidays. My first Thanksgiving and Christmas here were hard even though I had Samuel. I remember well."

"But you adjusted."

"I did. Samuel tried hard to make those first holidays special. And then the next year we had Jonas."

"Is this home to you now?"

"*Jah.* I'm happy here. It's different from Pennsylvania, much quieter, a much smaller community, but I do love it."

"That's *gut.* I hope I'm not too much of a burden for you and Samuel."

"You're not a burden at all. We are glad to have you. You don't know how much I've missed my little *schweschder.* And you're such a big help." Rebecca wrapped her arms around her in a brief hug, making KatieAnn sniff and swipe at a tear that strayed down her cheek. "Let's feed the *kinner* and then start on that stew."

The next few days passed in a whirl of activity with preparations for Thanksgiving. KatieAnn and Rebecca baked apple and pumpkin pies, sweetbreads, and rolls. They chopped cabbage and carrots for coleslaw, peeled a mountain of potatoes and yams to mash, and cooked home-canned green beans and stewed tomatoes. This year Rebecca was excited to roast a fat turkey.

"We don't always have turkey on Thanksgiving," she explained. "Sometimes we'll just do chicken or even ham. But this year we have turkey."

"Well, I feel honored." KatieAnn laughed as she chopped onions and celery for stuffing.

She stayed so busy cooking, cleaning, and entertaining the little ones that she hardly had time to miss her parents and the rest of the family. They usually had at least a skim of snow on the ground at Thanksgiving in Persimmon Creek. Here in Maryland, the air definitely had a bite, but snow had not yet fallen.

"We had so much snow last year, I'd just as soon not see any for a while!" Rebecca declared when KatieAnn mentioned snow to her.

"*Ach,* you've gotten soft after living south for so long, *schweschder.* It would be nice to have a little white on the ground for Christmas, wouldn't it?"

"I suppose so. Maybe by Christmas I'll be ready to see

snow again."

KatieAnn felt like she hadn't slowed down all week, but at last she sat between her nieces at the Thanksgiving table. After a silent prayer, they took turns sharing things they were thankful for. Eli and Jonas were thankful to be off from school for two days. Elizabeth said she was thankful for pumpkin pie, a portion of which smeared her face.

"I'm thankful my *aenti* is here." Emma spoke so softly she practically whispered.

"*Danki.*" KatieAnn gave her precious niece a hug. Emma was such a sensitive, thoughtful girl. Would Grace be tender-hearted like Emma or bolder and more mischievous like Elizabeth? "I am thankful to be here with my *wunderbaar* family."

Another mountain of dishes waited to be washed following the meal. Even Samuel and the *buwe* helped carry dishes from the table to the sink before taking Grace and Benjamin into the living room to play. Emma and Elizabeth were given the task of drying dishes and putting away the ones that belonged in the lower cabinets. Together the two little girls carried the tablecloth outside to shake off the crumbs. Elizabeth's shrieks and giggles reached Rebecca and KatieAnn in the kitchen.

"I shouldn't have sent them out to do that." Rebecca peeked out the window.

KatieAnn joined her to see what the shrieking was about. The tablecloth flew like a parachute and dropped to swallow Elizabeth. She squealed as she attempted to claw her way from underneath. Emma laughed so hard she wasn't much help to the younger girl. "They're having fun."

"*Jah*, but with my *gut* tablecloth!"

"I'll help them." Before she could get outside, the girls dragged the cloth into the kitchen. KatieAnn quickly took it from the four little hands before Rebecca caught sight of it trailing on the floor behind them. "*Danki*, girls." She rolled the cloth into a ball that would be tossed into the gas-powered washing machine on the next laundry day.

Late afternoon and evening were times the two women could relax by the wood stove in the living room. Thoughts of home then stole across KatieAnn's mind. Was her family doing well? Did they miss her as much as she missed them? Oh, how she hoped they did not still hold her responsible for the theft, or near theft, at the bakery! But they must, since she hadn't received any communication to make her believe otherwise.

KatieAnn reached into a wicker basket on the floor beside her chair and pulled out a ball of forest green yarn and a pair of knitting needles. Maybe she would knit mittens or scarves for the *kinner*. The boys were always reaching into their pockets and finding only a single mitten, its mate long gone. Knitting always relaxed her. Something about the repetitive motion and the clacking of the needles soothed her troubled brain. And it had been troubled!

CHAPTER ELEVEN

Neither Samuel nor Rebecca needed the buggy Friday morning, so after chores were done, KatieAnn drove to Rosanna Yoder's house instead of walking in the cold. The horse trotted at a brisk pace. He, too, was probably trying to adjust to the cold weather.

Smoke billowed from the chimney of the Yoders' house and from Jeremiah's shop. Although she had been shielded from the wind, KatieAnn still felt cold. She was always cold if the temperature didn't rise above sixty-five degrees. Her *bruders* used to tell her it was because she was so small. Mamm, too, always tried to fatten her up. She just couldn't seem to grow any taller or heavier. She had accepted that was simply the way the Lord made her.

Of all people to observe her approach, Luke Troyer flew out of Jeremiah's machine shop. "Hey, KatieAnn, if you're going to be here for a while, I'll unhitch for you."

"*Danki*, Luke. I'll probably be a while, so that would be right nice of you—if you can spare a minute."'

"I sure can. I've been here a couple hours already, so I can take a quick break." Luke began unhitching the horse. "It's *gut* to see you again." He spoke quietly for only her ears to hear.

She felt a blush travel all the way up the part in the middle of her scalp. It was the curse of fair skin and auburn hair to blush easily and thoroughly. "Rosanna is going to show me how she makes candles." She spoke to cover her unease.

"She mentioned that at the singing." The horse stepped away from the buggy. "There. I'll take care of this fellow. If you *kumm* to the shop when you're ready to leave, I'll be happy to hitch him back up for you."

"I can probably do it. I don't want to bother you while you're working. I wouldn't want to get you into trouble or anything."

"It wouldn't be a bother at all. Jeremiah won't mind, so just give me a holler when you're ready."

"*Danki*."

"Have fun!" Luke's smile reached his beautiful eyes.

I should not be noticing those eyes. She turned toward the house as the front door opened.

"Hi!" Rosanna's head popped out the door. "I'm so glad you could make it."

"Hi." KatieAnn climbed the steps leading to the front porch of the big, two-story white house.

"It looks like you had some help there." Rosanna's eyes sparkled with mischief. "Maybe a possible suitor, *jah*?"

"Go on with you! You know I'm a visitor here."

"Visitors have been known to stay. Okay, I won't tease anymore. Are you ready to make candles?"

KatieAnn hung her cloak and bonnet on a peg before following her friend into the kitchen. Rosanna tossed her a large, dark green apron and tied a similar one around herself. "Use this old apron to protect your clothes from wax. It's ever so hard to get wax off of things."

The apron practically swallowed KatieAnn as she tied

it over her dress.

"Mamm isn't doing any baking today. We've got plenty of leftovers from Thanksgiving, so we can have the kitchen to ourselves." Rosanna nodded toward an array of glass jars and candle molds. "I've got all my molds out and ready to go. I like to make a variety. Some people like big candles, so I use the jars. Others like the little votives they can put in small candle holders."

"You've got a lot." KatieAnn surveyed the collection of jars.

"I want to make as many as I can today. Candles sell well during the holiday season." Rosanna had already covered the countertops with old copies of the *Budget* to protect them from wax drips. A double boiler waited by the stove. "Don't worry." She chuckled as she followed KatieAnn's gaze. "I have my own pans and utensils for candle making. I don't use any of Mamm's cooking things. She'd have a fit if she found wax stuck in her pans."

Rosanna filled the larger pot about halfway full of water and set it on a stove burner to boil. She set another pot inside the big one. "You can't just put the candle wax directly over the heat. It has to melt slowly or it will evaporate, or worse, catch fire."

KatieAnn nodded her understanding.

"I'm using paraffin wax today, but sometimes I use soy wax. I have even used beeswax, but most folks like the paraffin just fine. In a pinch, old candles can be recycled. I just melt them down and make new ones."

Rosanna put KatieAnn to work cutting the wax into small chunks that would melt more evenly than large chunks. Then she scooped up the chunks and dropped them into the smaller pots. "You know, since there are two of us, I can get two batches going. I have plenty of wax, jars, and molds."

"I don't know, Rosanna. I don't want to mess anything up."

"You won't. I have faith in you." Rosanna quickly got another pot of water on to boil.

KatieAnn wondered what would happen to Rosanna's faith in her once she knew about the accusations against her. She shrugged off that thought and turned her attention back to candle making.

The boiling water slowly melted the chunks of wax. Rosanna kept a candy thermometer nearby to check the temperature of the wax. "The paraffin wax should reach 122 to 140 degrees. It's different for other waxes."

"You just remember all of this without looking it up?"

"I've been making candles for ages. I have the steps memorized. Of course, I use instructions if I want to try something new." Rosanna inserted the thermometer into the melting wax in each pot. "It's getting there."

"What are these little bottles?" KatieAnn picked up small vials lined up on the counter and read the small print on the labels. Lavender. Rose. Cinnamon. Strawberry. Vanilla.

"Those are some of the scents I use. I used to buy oils from Sophie. Now Esther has taken over Sophie's business, so I buy from her." A brief, sad expression crossed Rosanna's face before she continued her explanation. "I also buy some scents from the craft store whenever I can get there. You can decide which ones to use for this batch."

"Can we use vanilla? I love vanilla candles."

"For sure. I think vanilla is my favorite, too. Which other one?"

"How about strawberry? Or would a cinnamon scent be better for the Christmas season?"

"Maybe cinnamon since that makes people think of cookies and apple pie and cider."

"Cinnamon kind of gives you a warm, cozy feeling, ain't so?"

"Exactly. I'll add cinnamon to my wax, and you can add vanilla to yours." Rosanna trickled drops of cinnamon oil into her pot and instructed KatieAnn on the amount of vanilla oil to add to her wax. "Now we'll stir the wax well before adding color."

"Do you just use food coloring?"

"*Nee*. Those don't work too well on candles because they are water based. I've bought a right big selection of oil-based dyes from the craft store. We can each do a different color."

"I don't know why, but I always associate white or pale yellow with vanilla," KatieAnn said.

"I think most people do. You can make your batch pale yellow, and I'll make mine red. I guess people think of red or brown for cinnamon. I'll do the red to go with the season."

"Ah! This is beginning to smell *wunderbaar*." KatieAnn inhaled deeply.

"You're right about that. I think we're about ready to pour. We need to put wicks into the jars and molds we plan to use."

"How do you get them to stay?"

"There are different ways. I just use this double-stick adhesive. We want the wicks to be in the center of the molds, and we'll need to leave about two inches sticking out at the top. Like this." Rosanna demonstrated her technique.

KatieAnn felt clumsy fumbling with the adhesive and skinny wicks. "This is harder than it sounded."

"You'll get the hang of it after the first couple. Can you reach one of those pencils for me?"

"Sure. What are all the pencils for?"

"We wrap this end sticking up around the pencil and

then rest the pencil across the top of the mold. This will keep the wick in place when we pour in the wax. We just want to make sure the wick is going down into the center of the mold."

"I'm not sure I can do this, Rosanna."

"Of course you can. I felt all thumbs when I was learning, too. That's normal."

"If you say so."

"Here. You try putting a wick in. Start with one of the bigger jars. It might be a little easier. Just measure out a length for the wick and stick it in the jar." Rosanna handed KatieAnn the roll of wicking and supervised the measuring, cutting, and placing. "There! It wasn't so hard, was it?"

"Not really, but I'm going to slow you down."

"I'm not in any rush. Just take your time. We'll work together to get all the wicks positioned."

When each jar and mold had a wick situated to meet Rosanna's standards, they got ready to pour the wax. Rosanna only had to reposition a few of KatieAnn's wicks.

"You'd better pour, Rosanna. I don't want to get nervous and spill wax everywhere."

"I don't think you'll do that, but I'll start pouring. You can pour when the pot isn't so full. How does that sound?"

"Okay." KatieAnn still had doubts but would try her best.

"You've got to have confidence in yourself, girl."

"I do if I'm baking, but this is a whole different story."

Rosanna began pouring the light yellow, vanilla-scented wax into the waiting jars and molds. KatieAnn poured the last few candles, and she did so without spilling a single drop.

When all the red, cinnamon-scented wax had been poured, Rosanna set the pots in the sink. She made sure all jars and molds were safe from getting bumped or knocked over. "They have to cool at least twenty-four hours for paraffin candles. Soy and beeswax cool faster. So tomorrow I can move remove the candles from the molds and trim the wicks. I'll probably leave some in jars and decorate the jars for Christmas. Do you want to help with that?"

"I'd like to, but I help Miriam out in the store on Saturdays."

"There will be another time."

"I've seen some of your decorated candles in the store. They're so pretty. The votives are big sellers, too."

"People seem to like homemade candles, which is a *gut* thing because I like making them. How about a snack while the pans soak a bit?"

"Sure."

KatieAnn took a big gulp of cold milk before nibbling at a chocolate chip cookie. She looked in amazement at all the candles cooling on the counter. Candle making took time and effort, but it was fun.

"So tell me. Is St. Mary's County so bad that you can't wait to get home?" Rosanna broke into KatieAnn's thoughts.

"Not at all. It's much quieter here, of course, but I actually like the peacefulness. Everyone stays busy, for sure, but you don't have all the tourists and traffic and the problems they bring."

"That's for certain. We get tourists but mainly through word of mouth. Local *Englischers* tell others about our products. You're staying busy, then, not bored?"

"I couldn't be bored at Rebecca's house with all those little ones running about. I'm so glad to spend time with them all."

"How about spending time with Luke Troyer, too?"

"Huh?"

"I've known Luke forever. He's practically one of the family. I can tell he's interested in you."

"It's just because I'm new."

"I don't think so. Luke isn't like that. He doesn't chase after the first new face he sees. He's a very nice *bu* — uh, man."

"He does indeed seem nice and very thoughtful." At Rosanna's smile and glowing eyes, KatieAnn quickly added, "Don't go playing matchmaker, Rosanna Yoder. I don't know how long I'll be staying."

"It could be a real long time, ain't so?"

CHAPTER TWELVE

Snow threatened to erupt from the heavy, gray clouds on the first Saturday in December. After her run-in with sleet and wind a few weeks ago, KatieAnn didn't dare risk walking to Esh's store. Rebecca assured her she would not be taking the *kinner* out anywhere, so KatieAnn was free to take Brownie and the buggy. Still, she hoped any snow would wait until she had safely returned home before it made an appearance.

As soon as she stopped the buggy near the store, Levi ran out of the barn to help her unhitch. "Here," he said. "I'll take care of the horse. You go on inside. It's a cold one today."

"That's for sure. I appreciate your help, Levi." KatieAnn grabbed her bag and her treats for Sallie and hurried to the store. A glance toward the road alerted her to customers approaching—a buggy and a car. Another buggy was already parked at the hitching post near the front door of the store. As of yet, she was unable to determine who owned which buggy.

The door made no noise when KatieAnn pushed it open. She started to look up to see why the little bell didn't jingle but was immediately distracted by a voice speaking none too softly near the counter. The women's backs were to the door. One was Miriam, but KatieAnn wasn't yet sure who the other woman was.

"I'm telling you, Miriam. You'd better keep an eye on that girl." Now KatieAnn recognized the voice. Clara Schwartz. KatieAnn gasped. What was the woman telling Miriam? Her heart thundered in her ears.

"Pshaw!" Miriam sputtered as Grossmammi Sallie, who sat near the stove, clucked her tongue and wagged her head.

"Really, Miriam. I'd hate to see you fall prey to an innocent-looking thief."

"Honestly, Clara. You know you can't believe everything you hear."

"I heard this from reputable sources. People in her own community."

"Judge not lest ye be judged." Sallie spoke up quite loudly as she shook her finger in Clara's direction. The old rocking chair creaked in protest as an obviously agitated Sallie rocked faster.

Clara ignored the old woman. "I'm just trying to look out for you, Miriam."

"I appreciate your concern, but even in the *Englisch* courts a person is innocent until proven guilty, you know."

KatieAnn's cheeks burned as hot as the embers in Miriam's stove. Should she leave and re-enter, pretending she had just arrived and hadn't heard a word of their conversation? Should she confront the women and offer her defense? Clara had sown seeds of doubt. Would Miriam trust her or ask her not to return to work?

She had to do something. Standing there rooted to the spot would accomplish nothing. She spied the bell a few feet from where she stood and banged against the door as if she had just closed it. "*Ach*, your little bell is on the floor." Thank Gott! It gave her something to say to ease some of the tension in the room.

Miriam seemed flustered. Her voice came out a bit too loud. "Anything else for you today, Clara?"

"*Nee*. I'll just pay for my thread and things and be on my way."

KatieAnn summoned up every ounce of confidence she possessed and crossed the room with false bravado. "*Gude mariye*." She forced as much cheerfulness into those two words as possible, and then bent to hug Sallie.

"*Gut* to see you, dearie." Sallie stopped rocking long enough to return KatieAnn's hug.

"I brought you something."

"Did you now?"

"Of course." KatieAnn felt her lips trembling but coaxed them into a smile for Sallie. "Do you want your treat now or later?"

"Now, please. What did you bring today?"

KatieAnn did not need to look up to know Clara stared at her. She felt it as distinctly as if the woman had plunged a dagger into her back and twisted it for *gut* measure. "Let's see what's in my bag today." She reached into her quilted tote to pull out a sealed plastic bag filled with her jammie surprise muffins. She opened the bag and held it out to Sallie. "Pick one."

"What kind are they?"

"I call them jammie surprise muffins. Try one and tell me if you know what kind of jam is inside."

Sallie's wrinkled face crinkled into a smile. She closed her eyes as a child would do and reached into the bag, wrapped her fingers around a plump muffin and pulled it out. She took a big bite. "Mmm! Raspberry. Right?"

"You guessed it. I'll find you a napkin."

"Here's a paper towel." Miriam fluttered a paper

towel in KatieAnn's direction and handed Clara her bag of purchases. "You should try a muffin, Clara. KatieAnn is a *wunderbaar* baker."

"Maybe another time." Clara picked up her little brown bag of sewing items.

"More for me," Sallie mumbled between bites.

"Just think about what I said, Miriam." Clara turned toward the door.

Miriam ignored the comment. "Have a nice day, Clara. I hope you beat the snow home."

"Whew!" Sallie exclaimed when the door had closed behind Clara. "That woman can talk."

"I'll put your bell back up as soon as I hang up my things," KatieAnn offered. "I believe I saw some customers heading this way when I came in."

"Great." Miriam busied herself straightening the already neat counter.

KatieAnn pretended she didn't see Miriam shake her head at Grossmammi Sallie as though to warn her not to divulge any secrets. Uneasiness plagued her the whole day. She had the urge to tiptoe around the store to make herself as inconspicuous as possible. Aside from assisting customers and dusting shelves, she kept pretty much to herself. Should she let Miriam know she'd overheard the conversation with Clara, or simply act as if nothing was amiss?

Why did Clara have to go to Persimmon Creek? Did she specifically ask about KatieAnn or were the townspeople still talking about the Amish girl who tried to steal from her employer? Maybe she should have fled to someplace farther away than Maryland.

"*Kumm* sit with me a bit, dearie. You've been too quiet today." Sallie reached out to snag KatieAnn's hand when she moved closer to straighten a shelf near the old woman's chair.

"I'm sorry, Grossmammi. I guess I've been busy."

"Too busy to talk to an old woman for a minute?"

"Never." KatieAnn glanced around to make sure she wasn't needed elsewhere. Then she dropped onto a low stool beside Sallie's rocking chair.

Sallie began rubbing one of KatieAnn's cold hands between her own wrinkled palms. "So, what's bothering you today?"

"N-nothing. Why do you ask?"

"You usually smile more. And you don't usually try to disappear into the woodwork."

Nothing seemed wrong with Sallie's mind today. This had to be one of her best days in quite a while. Ordinarily she snoozed off and on, or concentrated on some knitting project.

KatieAnn forced her brow to relax its hold on the wrinkles that had most likely been present all morning. She turned on a smile. "I guess I'm just thinking." That was all she could think to say.

"About anything in particular?"

"N-not really."

Sallie gave KatieAnn's hand a surprisingly strong squeeze. "I don't believe Clara's tale one whit, you know."

KatieAnn drew in a sharp breath. Sallie knew she'd overheard Clara's remarks. "Y-you...she... What do you mean?"

"You could no more steal anything than that horse out there could fly."

Tears sprang up and threatened to fall. She blinked hard and turned her head away. Did Miriam share Sallie's opinion?

"Look at me, girlie."

Compelled to obey, KatieAnn lifted her gaze to search the brown eyes that were bright spots in the withered face.

"I am a *gut* judge of character." Sallie's voice was low but strong. "I may not always remember things. And I know I have *gut* days and bad days, but I know people. I also know in here." She tapped her chest. "My heart says you are a *gut* person. Anyone who knows you would know that. I don't know what happened in Pennsylvania, and I don't have to know. What I do know is that you are not a thief."

"*Danki*, Grossmammi Sallie. That means a lot to me." KatieAnn swiped at her eyes. She raised up from the stool to kiss the wrinkled cheek.

"Now you wipe those tears, and hand me another muffin!"

"Honestly, Rebecca, I didn't know what to do or what to say," KatieAnn said as they cleaned the kitchen after supper. "I wanted to back right out the door and run home. I should have known Clara Schwartz would find out about me on her trip to Pennsylvania. I had so hoped she wouldn't go to Persimmon Creek, that she'd just stay with the new *boppli* and…"

"And mind her own business."

"Exactly."

"Miriam never said anything?"

"Not all day long. Of course, I kind of kept to myself."

"You hid?"

"I did my work, but I tried to stay out of sight. You know out of sight, out of mind? Should I have tried to defend myself?"

"I don't know."

"Grossmammi Sallie knows I overheard Clara. She said she knew I was a *gut* person and not a thief."

"There you go. People aren't going to believe Clara."

"Sallie isn't always, uh, reliable."

"I believe Miriam is a fair person, Schweschder. I think if she had any doubts about you, she would have spoken to you."

"Maybe she just hadn't figured out what to say yet."

"Try not to worry." Rebecca squeezed KatieAnn's arm. A frown wrinkled her forehead. She turned away to hang up the damp dish towel.

"What is it, Rebecca? I saw that frown."

"I-I got a letter from Mamm today."

KatieAnn sank down on the nearest oak chair.

"What did she say?"

"She misses you and wants you to *kumm* home."

"If I confess, you mean."

"*Jah.*" Rebecca's voice came out in a whisper. "I'm afraid so. I really don't think she or Daed or our *bruders* believe you did anything wrong. They just want peace and harmony."

"How can there be peace and harmony if I confess to something I didn't do?" KatieAnn jumped up from the chair so abruptly she almost sent it toppling over. She drew herself up to her full height which still barely reached Rebecca's chin. "*I* won't have peace inside if I lie."

"I know, Schweschder."

"Are you and Samuel tired of having me here? I can find someplace else to go."

"Don't even think such a thing! You are *wilkom* here for as long as you want to stay. Forever, if you like."

"*Danki,* Rebecca." KatieAnn gave her a hug.

"It's church day tomorrow. We'd better join the family for prayers and get to bed early." Rebecca turned to leave the kitchen.

"Wait." KatieAnn grabbed Rebecca's arm. "I don't think I can attend church tomorrow. I don't know who else Clara told. I-I can't face everyone."

"If you don't go, people will think you have something to hide — that's *if* Clara told anyone else."

"Don't you think she did? You know her much better than I do. Be honest."

Rebecca stayed silent a moment. She sighed. "*Jah.* Unfortunately, I believe Clara probably couldn't keep from telling this juicy tidbit."

KatieAnn felt like she'd been kicked in the belly. She pictured herself as a kite flying high one minute and then crashing to the ground as the wind fizzled out. Her nose and eyes burned with unshed tears.

"You just hold your head high. You have no reason to be ashamed. The Lord Gott knows you are honest and *gut*. So do I. And so do other people."

"I-I don't know a-about t-the other people." KatieAnn's lips trembled.

"Well, you just stay strong and keep believing. The Bible says the truth will set you free, ain't so?"

"*Jah.*"

"Let's get in the living room before Samuel sends one of the little ones in search of us."

KatieAnn thought about Mamm's letter as she trudged upstairs behind Rebecca and the *kinner*. Her lamplight cast eerie, elongated shadows of large and small monsters creeping silently up the wall. She gave herself a little shake to dispel gloomy images and thought again of Mamm. She missed her parents and family. Mamm was probably very lonely. She would be by herself in the big house all day, cooking and cleaning with only her thoughts and memories for company. Daed, Elias, and Thomas rarely came into the house for anything.

How could she go home, though? As soon as she did,

Bishop John would expect her to kneel before the church to confess her sin of stealing — and now, her sin of disobedience. Surely running off to avoid confession would be deemed an act of disobedience. Would the Lord Gott want her to confess to something she didn't do? That would be a lie. Lying was wrong, too.

KatieAnn still had no idea how Deborah's money and that fancy watch got into her bag. But for sure and for certain, she did not put them there herself. She had not even touched them. She'd gone to work like always. Put her personal items away like always. Washed her hands and started baking like always. The whole thing was still a complete mystery to her.

"Huh?"

"The *kinner* are trying to tell you *gut nacht*," Rebecca explained. "Where are you?"

"I'm sorry. My mind wandered away."

"Was it visiting Persimmon Creek?"

"*Jah*, for a minute." KatieAnn bent to hug Jonas, Eli, Emma, and Elizabeth. Benjamin and Grace had already been tucked into bed.

"*Gut nacht, aenti*." The little voices echoed one another.

"Pleasant dreams," KatieAnn responded.

Rebecca sent the *kinner* to their rooms, promising to tuck them in shortly. She placed a hand on KatieAnn's arm. "Try not to worry. Remember to give Gott your cares."

"I'll try."

Rebecca gave KatieAnn a brief hug. "I'll expect you to be ready for church." She used an exaggerated stern voice.

KatieAnn nodded, even though she dreaded the very thought of attending church and enduring the stares and whispers that were bound to follow her.

Just as she reached her room, a knock on the front door

echoed throughout the silent house. She stopped in her tracks and listened.

Who in the world would be visiting at this hour? Granted, they were heading up to bed a little early, but still…it was late for visiting, especially since tomorrow was a church Sunday. Samuel pulled open the front door. KatieAnn strained to hear. Rebecca's head popped out of the girls' room to listen, as well.

"I'm sorry to call so late, Samuel. I had a late customer at the shop and then had my chores to do. Could I, uh…would it be possible for me to speak to KatieAnn for a few minutes? I promise I won't be long."

KatieAnn recognized the voice. It belonged to Luke Troyer.

CHAPTER THIRTEEN

From upstairs, KatieAnn noted Samuel's lengthy pause, like he had to ponder the request. "I'll see if she's gone to bed."

"I'm *kumming*, Samuel," KatieAnn called softly. What could Luke possibly have to say that couldn't wait until after church tomorrow? Her heart thumped so hard her whole body pulsated with the rhythm. Samuel and Luke must surely hear it in the otherwise quiet house.

"There's a lamp in the living room. I'll take yours to light my way upstairs, KatieAnn."

She nodded and passed her lamp to Samuel, and then turned wide eyes to search Luke's face. He swiped his black felt hat off his head and reached a hand to smooth down the static-filled golden strands of hair that tried to follow the hat.

"*Kumm* in." KatieAnn led the way into the living room with Luke following so closely she could smell his soap and some subtle spicy aftershave. Pleasant smells to be sure. "Please have a seat."

Luke perched on the edge of the sofa while KatieAnn settled awkwardly in the nearby wooden rocking chair.

"*Was ist letz?*" She feared the answer, but had to ask the question.

"I'm sorry to show up so late." Luke fidgeted. He twisted his hat, practically scrunching it into a ball.

What made him so nervous? Surely he didn't think this was a courting call. Courtships didn't usually begin this way. Didn't the fellow usually wait until the family had gone to bed and then toss pebbles at or shine a light into the girl's window? Luke looked so uncomfortable, but she didn't know how to alleviate his stress. She would have to wait for him to reveal his reason for the visit.

"I really didn't want to disturb the whole household," he began, "but I didn't want to just appear at your window either, you know?" When KatieAnn nodded, he continued. "I mean, it's not that I wouldn't want to *kumm* to your window to see you, but..." He stopped to take a breath. His cheeks turned cranberry red.

KatieAnn reached forward to gently touch his arm in reassurance. "Just tell me why you're here, Luke. Okay?"

"Okay."

She pulled her hand back and waited, about ready to start fidgeting herself. She searched his face and found compassion, concern, and caring written there. At least she hoped that was what she saw, and not pity or mistrust. She didn't think she was mistaken, but why was Luke having such difficulty expressing himself? It must be something bad. Tears congregated in her eyes. He must be afraid to tell her he and the other young folks didn't want to associate with her. Maybe she should spare Luke this agony, send him on his way, and then pack her bags to flee somewhere.

Luke cleared his throat and tried to speak. When not a single sound came out, he cleared his throat again. "KatieAnn, I heard through the grapevine something I can't quite believe."

She swallowed hard, hoping to dislodge the huge lump that had formed in her throat and threatened to completely cut off her air. She gulped back a sob and lowered her eyes to stare at her clasping and unclasping hands.

Luke grasped her cold hands in his big, rough, warm ones. "What I'm trying to say KatieAnn, is that I don't believe for a minute that you took anything that didn't belong to you."

She expelled a shaky breath. "Truly?"

"*Jah.*" Luke's smile melted the ice around her heart. "Anyone who knows you even a little bit wouldn't consider that a possibility."

"It's kind of funny that people I've known most, if not all my life, want me to confess before the church."

"They must all be *narrisch!*"

KatieAnn smiled. "They would probably think you're crazy for defending me when you hardly know me."

"I feel like I've known you a long time." Luke gave her hands a gentle squeeze.

"I'm not sure the exact tale you heard, but may I tell you what happened?" KatieAnn surprised herself. Here she'd been trying to hide in Maryland and not mention anything about the trouble in Persimmon Creek. Yet now she was eager to explain the circumstances to this kind young man who held her hands.

"You don't have to tell me anything."

"I know, but I-I'd like you to know the truth. May I tell you?"

"Tell away." Luke shifted slightly to assume a more comfortable position, but he did not let go of her hands.

Conflicting emotions tug-of-warred inside KatieAnn. If she explained what happened at the Old Time Bake Shop and Luke believed the evidence overwhelmingly pointed to her guilt, she would be devastated. If she explained and he still believed in her, then she'd made a true *freind*.

She should probably pull her hands away from his, but she didn't. She needed his strength and support. She blew out a slow breath and began to recount the events of that fateful day. Luke could choose what to believe. A single tear trailed down her cheek unnoticed.

"Whew!" Luke squeezed KatieAnn's hands again after she finished her tale. He reached to brush away more tears that trickled from her eyes. "That's quite a story. Someone wanted to make you look guilty. The so-called evidence doesn't make any difference to me." Luke lightly grasped her chin to tilt her head up. She had no choice but to look at him. "I believe you, KatieAnn. I know you would not steal anything. You are a *gut*, honest, Gott-fearing woman."

"*Danki* for believing me."

"I will support you and help you however I can. Do you have any clue who would want to make you look guilty?"

"*Nee*. I've worked with those ladies for quite some time. Of course, we were very busy, so customers could have slipped into the back room unnoticed, but why? Why would they hide those things in my bag? It seems to me they would just stuff the bag and watch into their own bags or pockets and be on their way."

"It doesn't make sense, that's for sure, but you did the right thing. You can't confess to something you didn't do."

"*Jah*, but nobody believes me." Tears threatened again.

"*I* believe you."

"I'm sure if you've gotten wind of this whole mess already then everyone else here has, too. What if they all believe as Clara does? I'm sure she thinks I'm guilty from the way she spoke to Miriam."

"Clara likes to gossip, but she can't make people believe her tales. Anyone who knows you..."

"But people here don't know me very well. They might think I ran away from home because I'm guilty."

"I think folks here are pretty fair."

"I hate the thought of everyone watching me to see if I will steal something."

"I really don't think they will. The fact that Miriam didn't say anything to you is a *gut* sign, KatieAnn. If she had believed Clara, she would have told you not to work at the store."

"Maybe. I know Grossmammi Sallie believes me."

"There you go!"

"*Jah*, but she's an old woman who doesn't always think too clearly."

"Grossmammi Sallie is highly respected, even if she is forgetful at times."

KatieAnn merely nodded. She still couldn't believe Luke had rushed here to talk to her and offer his support.

"You won't let this stop you from attending singings and other functions, will you?"

"I don't know, Luke. Maybe I should lie low."

"Hide, you mean."

"I don't want people to whisper about me and point to me, and.. ."

"If you stay away, you will look guilty."

"That's what Rebecca said when I told her I might not go to church tomorrow."

"She's right. Listen to your *schweschder,* if not to me."

"I-I'm scared."

"I'll be there to support you. So will your family and *freinden.*"

"*Freinden*?"

"Sure. You don't think Rosanna, Micah, Nancy, or Thomas will believe anything bad about you, do you?"

KatieAnn shrugged her shoulders.

"I know them well. You can count on them to believe in you. Okay?"

"If you say so."

"And Grossmammi Sallie will set everyone else straight or she'll whack them on the head."

KatieAnn laughed. She could picture that very thing happening.

"I'd better go before Samuel throws me out."

"*Danki*, Luke—for everything."

Luke headed for the door with KatieAnn following. He turned abruptly to face her, then jammed his black hat on his head, shadowing his face. "If I should tap at or shine a light in your window, would you let me in? That is, if you aren't courting someone back home."

KatieAnn thought briefly of Micah Kinsinger. He believed she was guilty. She knew by his attitude and the expression on his face. If she returned home tomorrow and he asked to court her, she would refuse him. She couldn't give her heart to someone who didn't trust her. Besides, his image had all but faded from her mind. And dear Timothy Yoder was a *gut freind*, nothing more. "There isn't anyone back home."

"Then, w-would you let me in?"

KatieAnn pressed her hands to her suddenly warm cheeks. "*Jah.*"

Saturday's heavy, gray clouds hung onto their precipitation all night, but threatened to release it in the form of snow or ice on Sunday morning. KatieAnn shivered as she quickly pulled on her *gut* church dress. She would have to either ask Mamm to send her more clothes or do some serious sewing, since it didn't look like she'd be returning to Persimmon Creek any time soon.

She took extra care smoothing her hair under her freshly ironed *kapp*, knowing she'd be the recipient of much unwanted, covert attention. Even if no one actually confronted her, she would be the object of scrutiny and the subject of whispered conversations. She ventured a peek into the little hand mirror. A pale, porcelain-like face with red-rimmed eyes and caramel-colored freckles across the nose stared back at her.

She dropped the mirror back inside the top dresser drawer and sighed. Nothing could be done about her pallor or the red-streaked eyes. It took all of her faith and courage not to dive back beneath the quilt and stay there for the foreseeable future. "Lord, help me get through this day."

The drive to church at John and Naomi Beilers' house was relatively quiet. Even the *kinner* sensed the tension and kept their chattering to a minimum. Full of nervous energy, KatieAnn jiggled her knee, making Grace bounce up and down on her lap. They arrived with barely enough time to file into the Beilers' house...thank Gott! There wouldn't be time to socialize. Large, downy snowflakes broke free from the clouds and fluttered to the earth as they entered the house.

From the moment they arrived, little pinpricks skated up and down KatieAnn's body. Various pairs of eyes studied her every movement. She followed Rebecca's advice and held her head high with her eyes focused in front of her, even though she wanted to dash back to the safety of the buggy — better to freeze outside than burn with embarrassment as people questioned her with their eyes.

Looking only at the house in front of her, KatieAnn did not see who approached as she waited with the other unmarried women to enter. Her gaze shifted slightly to the left for an instant at a subtle touch on her elbow. Rosanna smiled and mouthed, "It's all right." She jumped in line in front of KatieAnn while Nancy Swarey wormed her way in behind her. She relaxed a tiny bit, assured that she had the support of at least two other people.

The sudden warmth of the house did little to thaw her chill. Based on the frowns of a few older women, it did little to thaw their hearts, either. A few of the menacing scowls froze the blood in her veins. Rosanna patted her arm as they filed in to take their places on hard, wooden benches. The service stretched out before her like one of those mile-long trains that seemed to never end.

Determined to be optimistic, KatieAnn forced her gaze up out of her lap. A fleeting glance at the men's side of the room lightened her heart. Luke met her gaze and ever so briefly winked one sapphire eye. She allowed a sliver of a smile to lift her lips just enough to acknowledge him. He nodded slightly in response to her smile and graced her with a smile of his own. Released from its ice dam, her blood flowed again. She'd better not look at Luke anymore, lest she lend fuel to the fire of gossip threatening to engulf her.

Out of the corner of her eye, KatieAnn caught Gross-mammi Sallie's not-so-subtle wave and broad smile. At her age, Sallie was beyond caring what anyone thought or said about her. Certain behaviors were overlooked when a person became one of the oldest in the community. KatieAnn smiled and nodded at the old woman she had already grown fond of. Sallie had become KatieAnn's *freind* and surrogate *grossmammi*. With advanced age came respect, so KatieAnn gained some measure of comfort knowing Sallie championed her cause.

Not wanting to draw any more attention to herself — as if that was even possible — she settled herself between Rosanna and Nancy and prepared to sing the first hymn from the Ausband. Hopefully the ministers had not yet gotten wind of Clara's big news and would not deliver sermons on honesty or confession.

She tried hard to concentrate on the sermons, but her mind raced. Which of her new *freinden* believed the rumor? Which of them weren't sure what to believe? Who among them already believed her guilty?

Thankfully the snatches of sermons she caught were not directed at her. Not this Sunday anyway.

Her eyes wanted to stray away from the speaker and roam the room. She knew people secretly watched her. Their gazes pricked her like hungry mosquitos biting and sucking her blood. She willed herself to sit still on the hard bench. Forced her eyes to stay glued on the ministers. Would this service never end?

Yet when the service ended and people began to file out of the room, KatieAnn wasn't sure that was such a *gut* thing. Now she'd have to face the women in the kitchen and serve the men at the tables. Again she had the urge to dash out into the snow and scramble inside the cold buggy. Rosanna sent her a reassuring smile, but KatieAnn's effort to return the gesture fell short.

She scurried to and from the kitchen carrying platters and bowls to the makeshift tables. Several times conversations abruptly ceased when she entered the kitchen. Pretending to be brave, she bit the trembling lip that threatened to blow her cover.

"Hang in there." Esther cornered her in the kitchen and gave her a little hug.

"Y-You heard?"

"I heard some sort of nonsense, but I don't believe a single word of it. Keep your chin up."

"I'll try."

"*Gut*. Now *kumm* and get a plate."

"I'm not really hungry. Maybe I'll just…"

"You will *kumm* get a plate and eat something. Even if it's just cheese and crackers or pickles. You have no reason to hide. Besides, we can't have you wasting away."

"Bossy, isn't she?" Hannah laughed.

"She sure is."

"She is with me, too, so join the crowd." Hannah linked her arm with KatieAnn's.

"Well, look at you two little creatures." Esther shook her head at them. "I've seen bigger ants than the two of you."

"You aren't so huge yourself, you know," Hannah retorted.

"Then we'd better all go eat." Esther looped her arm through KatieAnn's free one and towed them all to the buffet table.

Bishop Sol's gaze fixed on KatieAnn as she approached with Hannah and Esther. Had he heard? Would he be paying a visit? Clara stared at her unabashedly. Technically, KatieAnn should be eating with the other unmarried women, but she had allowed herself to be swept along with Esther and Hannah. Maybe this breach of unspoken protocol heaped coals onto the rumor fire.

Stomach churning with unsettled nerves, she had no desire to eat. Nevertheless, in order to avoid dropping it, KatieAnn grabbed the plate thrust into her hands.

"Eat!" Esther commanded half under her breath. "And take a deep breath. You're the color of those bread-and-butter pickles."

She nodded and placed a few of the green pickles on her plate along with a spoonful of coleslaw. Esther plopped a dollop of macaroni salad onto the center of the plate, and KatieAnn thought for sure she would have to excuse herself and run for the bathroom.

Flanked by Hannah and Esther, she sat at the table and stirred the food around on her plate. She couldn't quite bring herself to raise a forkful to her mouth. Her stomach churned at the prickle traveling her spine from constant eyes on her back.

"Psst!" Esther hissed. "You have to *eat* the food, not play with it."

KatieAnn picked up a pickle and nibbled at it. If that went down and stayed down, she'd try a little of the coleslaw next.

∽

"At least you ate a little," Esther remarked when KatieAnn rose from the bench with her plate still half full.

"That's the best I can do."

Esther smiled and patted her arm. "I'll take this for you." She tugged the plate from KatieAnn's hands. "It will save you another trip to the kitchen. It's my turn to clean up along with Hannah, Sarah, and a few others. Why don't you grab some cookies or a piece of pie and relax a bit?"

"Relax? Is there some place I could just melt into the woodwork, or fade into the scenery?"

Esther and Hannah laughed. KatieAnn even managed a small smile.

"With that gorgeous auburn hair, I doubt you could disappear," Hannah said. "Besides, I have a feeling someone may be looking for you."

KatieAnn gasped. "Bishop Sol? Clara? Miriam, to tell me I'm fired?"

"You are jumpy." Hannah reached to hug KatieAnn. "I meant the young man behind you who can't keep his eyes off of you."

Hannah and Esther slipped away to the kitchen, giving Luke the opportunity to approach. "Hi, KatieAnn. Would you like some cookies?" He held out a napkin filled with an assortment of treats.

"I don't have much of an appetite...but I'll take one

cookie." She didn't want to hurt his feelings. "*Danki* for being so thoughtful." KatieAnn plucked a plump chocolate chip treat from the pile in the napkin. "Y-you aren't afraid to be seen talking to me?" She bit off a tiny crumb and forced it down her dry throat.

"Not in the least. I don't think everyone has heard."

"They will by the end of the day." KatieAnn nodded slightly toward Clara. The unpleasant woman stood in the distance, whispering behind her hand to another woman.

"Not everyone will believe Clara. Are you too cold to step out on the porch for a minute?"

"Probably not for just a minute or two, but you are already getting dirty looks. I wouldn't want to be the cause of any trouble for you."

"Don't worry about me. Dirty looks don't bother me at all."

"What about your parents?"

"My *daed* is out in the barn discussing the weather, the horses, or something similar with the other men. My *mamm* is probably talking to Naomi Beiler or Barbara Zook, but not Clara Schwartz."

"Have they already heard about me?"

Luke shrugged. "I don't know. I suppose so. They haven't said anything. That's just the way they are. They mind their own business. *Kumm,* let's just look at the snow for a minute." He pulled open the door and waited for her to exit in front of him.

"So pretty, but it doesn't seem to be sticking very much yet." KatieAnn admired the huge flakes. Only a few patches of greenish-brown grass boasted frosty crystals, though.

"I don't think it'll last long. The sky already looks a little lighter."

"The weather is sure different here. At home, clouds

like these would unload snow all day."

"Some years we get a fair amount of cold and snow. Last year set a record, I think. Other years we only get a dusting of snow — or none at all."

"I guess there isn't much sledding for the *kinner*, then."

"Hopefully they got their fill of that last winter. You're shivering. We should have grabbed your coat. We can go inside."

"In a minute." She couldn't tell Luke her trembling was mainly due to his nearness.

"Will you attend the singing tonight?"

"I-I don't know. I don't want to have to endure more whispers and stares. Anyway, if it keeps snowing, I probably won't ask Samuel to take me back out."

"I really don't think the snow will amount to much. And I'd really like you to attend."

"Maybe you shouldn't spend so much time with me or even be seen with me."

"Pshaw! I'm not the least bit concerned. I understand your feelings, but please don't lock yourself away. Okay?"

"Okay. But I'm still not sure about tonight."

Luke gave her arm a little squeeze. "I won't pressure you, KatieAnn. I just like talking to you and would like for you to *kumm* tonight. I'll understand, though, if you don't. Just don't shut me out. Please?"

CHAPTER FOURTEEN

The fickle weather warmed up again to nearly fifty degrees. Wednesday morning's cloudless blue sky promised another fair day. After being cooped up inside for two days helping care for a coughing, sneezing, miserable little girl, KatieAnn welcomed the brisk walk to Esh's store. She even hummed a little made-up tune as she swung her basket in time with the rhythm of her song. As soon as she got inside, she hung her bonnet, bag, and coat on a hook in the rear of the store and deposited her basket of treats on the counter.

"*Gude mariye*, Grossmammi." She greeted the old woman in the rocking chair first thing and planted a light kiss on the withered cheek. Sallie merely mumbled a greeting. She kept rocking and staring out across the store. KatieAnn patted the gnarly hand and turned to look at Miriam.

Miriam lifted her shoulders in an exaggerated shrug. "Not one of her *gut* days," she mouthed.

KatieAnn nodded in understanding. "I brought oatmeal raisin muffins, Grossmammi. Would you like one?"

"*Jah*." Sallie murmured a response, but her gaze

remained fixed on something across the room, real or imaginary.

KatieAnn tore a decorative paper towel off the role and placed it and a muffin chocked full of fat, juicy raisins in front of Sallie. Toasted oats atop the muffin provided a little decoration and crunch.

Sallie absently pinched off a chunk of the muffin and crumbled it between her thumb and forefinger. She then tried to get the crumbs to her mouth but mainly scattered them all over herself.

"Here, I'll cut it in pieces for you to make it easier." KatieAnn located a plastic knife and cut the muffin into manageable, bite-sized pieces.

"*Danki*." Sallie reached for a bite and popped it into her mouth. "Mmmm. *Gut*." She smacked her lips.

KatieAnn smiled before turning to face Miriam with a questioning look.

"*Danki* for the muffins, KatieAnn," Miriam said. "Grossmammi didn't eat much breakfast this morning, so she probably is hungry. I couldn't get her to eat more than two bites of oatmeal. She wouldn't touch the eggs or sausage at all."

"Is she sick?"

"I don't think so. It's just that some days she's too agitated and restless to even eat. We'll have to keep an eye on her. She's been wandering a bit today. I don't want her to get out the door in this state."

"I'll help look out for her."

"I'm thankful these days are few and far between." Miriam sighed. "It makes me sad, but there isn't anything to be done about it. We just have to keep her safe and make sure she eats and drinks."

"I'll help," KatieAnn promised.

"I appreciate that. She likes you and trusts you."

The store was busier than usual for a Wednesday, but

KatieAnn did try to keep track of Sallie. Several times she followed her around the store and then led her back to her rocking chair by the stove. KatieAnn handed Sallie her yarn and needles and encouraged her to knit. The old woman would set the needles clacking for a few minutes but soon lose interest in her project.

"KatieAnn, did you sell all the lavender sachets?" Miriam called just before lunch time.

"*Nee*. I don't believe I sold a single one."

"That's funny. I don't see any here, and I'm positive I had some. How about the cinnamon votives?"

"*Nee*. I didn't sell any of those either, that I recall."

"Very strange."

"Maybe they've just gotten out of place."

"I don't know." Miriam started to say more but was interrupted by the tinkling of the bell over the door.

Does she think I took them? KatieAnn's fears returned. Would she be accused of stealing the missing items? She began searching shelves to see if they had simply been misplaced.

"*Ach!*" Miriam cried when the customer had exited. "My last doll is gone. I know for certain I didn't sell that today, and I'm sure it was here this morning." The faceless Amish doll in authentic blue dress, black cape, apron, and bonnet always sat in a prominent spot on the end of a row. Her absence was obvious.

"I did see some *Englisch kinner* playing with her earlier, but their *mamm* put her back on the shelf. Maybe they moved her when everyone was distracted." KatieAnn searched in earnest now. Miriam's bewildered expression didn't escape her. Was there accusation in that look as well? Would she always be the first suspect when something went missing? KatieAnn pawed through everything on the shelves and then set things aright before moving to methodically search the next section.

"I don't see any sign of any of the missing items." Miriam rubbed her eyes as if that would help her see more clearly.

KatieAnn's heart sank. Now she be asked to leave, of course.

"Miriam, I'm getting hungry!" Sallie practically shouted from her corner near the stove.

"If you watch the store, I'll take Sallie . . . wait. If you'll run to the house and pick up the sandwiches I made earlier, I'll stay here."

Miriam didn't trust her alone in the store with only Sallie to watch her movements. KatieAnn could clearly see that. Miriam's sudden mistrust wrapped its evil tentacles around her heart and threatened to squeeze the life out of her. She wanted to cry but blinked hard to hold the tears at bay. Then she turned away, not wanting Miriam to see her pain, her tears. She slipped out the back door without even grabbing her coat off the hook, and ran to the house.

KatieAnn pretty much had her emotions under control by the time she returned to the store laden with sandwiches and cookies. She had wiped her eyes, blown her nose, and composed herself the best she could. As long as nothing else set off the waterworks, she should be all right.

"Here you go, Grossmammi Sallie." KatieAnn unwrapped a chicken salad sandwich and placed it on the little table beside the elderly woman. She spread a paper towel across Sallie's lap and handed her half of the sandwich.

Sallie took a bite and wrinkled up her nose. "Ugh!" She struggled to swallow.

KatieAnn fetched a bottle of water from the cooler, unscrewed the cap, and held it out to Sallie. "You don't like chicken salad?"

"She likes it," Miriam said around the bite of sandwich in her mouth. "She's being contrary today."

Sallie made a face when Miriam leaned over to take another bite of her sandwich. KatieAnn had to smile at the juvenile expression. Sallie pushed the sandwich away.

"Would you like another muffin?"

"*Jah.*"

KatieAnn removed a muffin from the basket on the counter and cut it into pieces for Sallie.

"You eat." Sallie held out a bite of muffin for KatieAnn.

"That's yours. I'll get something." She didn't feel much like eating, but wanted to encourage Sallie. She yanked her bag off the hook and reached for the ham and cheese sandwich inside. It had all the appeal of rat poison. Nevertheless, KatieAnn opened the baggie and took a tentative bite. Ugh. Sawdust. She chewed and chewed before gulping to swallow the lump, and then returned the sandwich to her bag. Maybe later she would have a better appetite.

"Cookies?" Sallie asked while still chewing a bite of muffin.

"After you finish your muffin." KatieAnn felt like a *mudder* with a little girl.

"You didn't eat." Sallie shook a crooked index finger at KatieAnn.

"I'll eat more later."

But what did 'later' have in store for her?

∽

The day dragged on. All afternoon, KatieAnn felt like a deer tick under a magnifying glass. Her every move was scrutinized, not by Sallie who snored softly by the stove, but by Miriam—who hurriedly glanced away whenever

KatieAnn looked in her direction. To say it made her uncomfortable would be an understatement. She considered
telling Miriam she needed to go home, but that would
scream, "Guilty!" At least the store stayed busy, which
offered some distraction from her tormented thoughts.

The pleasant temperature took a nosedive by late afternoon. KatieAnn had noticed a definite chill when she
ran to Miriam's house for sandwiches. At the time, she
attributed the chill to nerves combined with fleeing from
the store coatless. Now, as she began her walk home, she
realized the weather truly had changed again. Fall and
winter seemed set to play tug-of-war for control. Was this
normal for Southern Maryland? At home, when cold
weather arrived, it usually stayed.

Since customers had dwindled by late afternoon, Miriam had told KatieAnn she could leave a little before clos-
ing time. Levi had *kumm* in from his farm chores and
helped Sallie to the house after telling Miriam he would
return to help close the store if needed. KatieAnn felt sure
Miriam wanted her out of the way so she could discuss
the missing store items with Levi. She would not be at all
surprised if Miriam didn't count the money two or three
times to make sure none was missing. At least she hadn't
told her not to bother returning to work on Saturday.

Was she simply being paranoid? KatieAnn didn't
think so, but it certainly appeared she was doomed to be
labeled a thief. Maybe she should wear a sign and call out,
"Don't trust me!" like the lepers in the Bible cried out
"unclean" to warn others of their disease. *Lord Gott, please
help me. Please let this matter be resolved so people will trust
me.*

When she got home, KatieAnn hung her black coat
and bonnet on the hook inside the door. She stopped to
hug the four youngest *kinner* before shuffling into the
warm kitchen where the smell of bubbling beef stew and

baking cornbread permeated the air. Esther sipped tea at the table with Rebecca.

"*Ach*! Is it that late?" Rebecca jumped up from the chair.

"*Nee*. I'm a little early. Business died down, so Miriam let me go." KatieAnn spoke so softly that Esther cupped her hand to her ear, pretending she couldn't hear.

"Is something wrong?" Rebecca sank back onto the sturdy oak chair and studied her *schweschder*'s troubled expression. "KatieAnn?"

"Sit down." Esther patted the chair beside her. "You look like you've lost your best *freind*."

"I've lost my mind, I think."

"What happened?"

KatieAnn explained about the missing items at the store. "I know Miriam thinks I took those things, but I didn't. Unless I have multiple personalities. I read about that once. You don't think I could have another personality that steals, do you?"

"Of course not," Rebecca was quick to say.

"You are just fine." Esther gave KatieAnn's arm a reassuring squeeze.

"Then why do things keep disappearing when I'm around? Miriam kept a hawk eye on me all afternoon even though I'm sure she thought I didn't notice. If she tells anyone things went missing from her store, I'll be labeled a thief, for sure and for certain. Especially if she tells..." KatieAnn covered her face with her hands and tried to hold back the tears that threatened to flow.

"Clara Schwartz." Esther finished the statement for her. "I don't think Miriam will say anything she can't prove. She isn't a gossip."

"I-I hope y-you're right." Despite KatieAnn's best effort, tears trickled from her eyes.

"I'm going to get you a nice, calming cup of tea. I

brought just the right stuff." Esther slid from her chair and poured hot water over the herbs. "I've learned a lot about lavender since I've been growing it. Lavender tea is very soothing, very relaxing."

"It was your lavender sachets that were taken, ain't so? I'm so sorry. I should have been watching more closely. We were crowded from time to time, and Sallie was pretty agitated today, so I tried to keep an eye on her, too."

"It certainly isn't your fault. Besides, I can easily make more, so don't give it another thought. Here. Try this." Esther smiled as she set the hot cup of fragrant tea in front of KatieAnn.

"*Danki*, Esther. And *danki* for believing me, too."

"Of course I believe you. I may not know you extremely well yet, but I know you would not steal anything. Just let me get as many facts as I can, and we'll try to sort out all this confusion."

Rebecca put her hand in front of her face, winked at KatieAnn, and whispered behind her hand. "In case you didn't know, Esther is not only our herb expert, she's also our resident sleuth."

"Ha! Ha! I heard that, Rebecca Hertzler."

Rebecca smiled at her *freind*. "Actually, she is very *gut* at solving puzzling issues. If anyone can figure out what is going on, it will be Esther."

"Well, solve away. I need all the help I can get." KatieAnn risked a sip of the steaming tea.

The three women brainstormed as they drank their tea. They considered and rejected various possibilities but found no solution.

"*Ach*, I forgot. You got a letter today." Rebecca pushed her chair back and stood. She crossed the room to retrieve the missive from the kitchen counter.

"I hope it's not from Deborah again." KatieAnn's

hands shook as she set her cup on the table.

"I don't think so."

"That's a relief." KatieAnn took the envelope from Rebecca's hand, turned it over slowly, and scanned the return address. "It's from Grace Hershberger."

"You can go ahead and read it," Rebecca said. "I know you're anxious to find out what she has to say."

KatieAnn slid her finger under the flap to open the envelope. She extracted the single sheet of paper and skimmed the short letter. When she raised her gaze, she found Rebecca and Esther staring at her, obviously waiting to be enlightened.

"What does she say?" Rebecca clapped her hand over her mouth. "Oops, I'm sorry. It's your letter. You don't have to share the contents."

"That's okay. It's nothing personal. Grace says that Deborah's missing recipe book turned up."

"Really? Where was it?"

"Deborah found the book under some papers on her desk even though she had looked there before."

"How odd," Esther mused.

"Well, at least that clears you," Rebecca said. "You couldn't possibly have taken that book and slipped it back on her desk."

"That's true. Grace also says that Lizzie quit working for Deborah."

"Why would she do that?" Rebecca frowned in thought.

"She's going to work for Busy B's Bakery. You know Bea passed away and her sons have been running the business. Apparently they've been losing business and wanted a new baker."

"Lizzie is going to bake for them? I thought you said…"

"I know, Rebecca. It doesn't make much sense. Lizzie

doesn't know much about baking. Not unless she has learned a lot since I've been gone."

"I doubt she's learned a whole lot in only a few weeks." Rebecca's skepticism stretched across her face.

"Grace thinks Lizzie told Bea's sons that she baked for Deborah and that the specials were her creations."

"*Your* specials? Those *wunderbaar* treats you invented? Lizzie claimed them as her own? That took a lot of nerve!" Rebecca's voice rose.

"It took a lot of stupidity," Esther blurted out. "What will happen when they find out Lizzie can't bake any of those things? Then where will she be?"

"*Gut* question," KatieAnn agreed.

"Jobless!" Rebecca spat out.

"Grace said she'd keep me updated."

"The plot thickens." Esther rubbed her hands together vigorously. "But, alas, I must be off to cook my dear husband's dinner. I will ponder all these facts and see if I can solve the mystery." She wiggled her eyebrows.

Rebecca and KatieAnn laughed.

"You do that." Rebecca rose to follow Esther to the door and to check on her little ones.

"*Jah*, you do that," KatieAnn echoed.

CHAPTER FIFTEEN

"*Gude mariye!*" The bell tinkled above KatieAnn's head upon entering Esh's store Saturday morning. She pasted on a cheerful smile, hoping to hide the fair amount of trepidation that bubbled inside her. Had Miriam found the missing items? Had more things disappeared? Would she be told to go away and stay away? She forced those thoughts aside and crossed the room to greet Sallie.

Her eyes strayed to the shelf where the faceless Amish doll had reigned. Still empty. She did a double take when she glanced in the direction of the sachets and candles. A neat stack of sachets filled the space that had been empty on Wednesday afternoon. Either Miriam located the missing sachets or Esther spent Thursday and Friday making new ones. KatieAnn felt Miriam's eyes on her.

"Esther stopped by yesterday." Miriam responded to her unasked questions.

"*Kumm* here, girl," Sallie called from her perch.

KatieAnn raised her eyebrows and nodded in Sallie's direction in silent query.

"Better today," Miriam mouthed. "She slept better the last two nights. I think that helps."

KatieAnn hurried over to kiss the cheek Sallie offered. *"Wie bist* du *heit?"*

"I'm fine. My belly is a little empty, though."

KatieAnn chuckled at Sallie's sly smile. "Let's see if I can find anything in this bag to remedy that situation." She set her bag on the counter and pulled out a container filled with slices of marble pound cake. "Did you eat your breakfast?"

"I sure did. I ate oatmeal and applesauce."

"Then I guess you can have a sliver of cake," KatieAnn teased.

"Hmph! I'll take more than a sliver. I need to see it with these old eyes and taste it. I can't taste a sliver."

KatieAnn laughed and tore a paper towel off the roll stashed behind the counter. "Is this big enough?" She set a medium-sized piece of cake on the little table beside the elderly woman.

"It will do for a start."

KatieAnn grinned and left Sallie to eat. She brushed off her hands and prepared to greet the first customer. If Miriam didn't mention Wednesday, then she wouldn't either.

The day was busy but relatively uneventful. Many *Englischers* wanted something unusual or handmade to give as Christmas gifts. KatieAnn had a few moments of panic when Clara Schwartz walked in under the dinging bell. She held her breath, waiting for Miriam to confide in Clara about Wednesday's missing objects, but Miriam must have decided to keep mum about the whole business. Clara exhibited her usual scowl whenever KatieAnn happened to catch her eye, but KatieAnn did her best to remain pleasant. She forced her facial muscles to relax and even coaxed them into a weak smile. Nevertheless, she heaved a sigh of relief when Clara left with her small bag of purchases. She had the distinct feeling Clara only came into the store to check on her.

"That woman always looks like she's eaten sour grapes," Grossmammi Sallie called out. She puckered up her face in imitation.

"Now, Grossmammi, be nice." Miriam tried to be stern but smiled through the admonition.

"I'm being truthful, Miriam. At my age, I'm allowed to say what I think."

"Who made up that rule?" Miriam faced the old woman with fists on her hips.

"It's a given. I've lived long enough and seen enough to speak my mind."

"If you say so." Miriam rolled her eyes.

"How about another piece of that cake, dearie, if there's anything left but crumbs. And if there are only crumbs, I'll take those."

"Feisty today," Miriam muttered.

"What's that, Miriam? My hearing is still pretty *gut*, you know."

Miriam rolled her eyes again. KatieAnn had to turn aside to keep from laughing. She fetched a slice of cake to appease Sallie.

∞

"KatieAnn, will you *kumm* here, please?" Miriam stood at the counter, shortly after five o'clock, figuring out the day's sales.

KatieAnn finished straightening the row she'd been working on, flipped the sign on the door to "closed," and approached the counter. "What can I do for you?"

"Here, you count this money and see if you get the same thing I did."

KatieAnn's heart hiccupped. There must be some problem. When Miriam stepped aside, she slipped into her place and began counting the money. Only the ticking of the wall clock broke the tense silence in the room. KatieAnn finished counting and looked at the register receipt. Her stomach churned. She turned wide eyes to Miriam. "It seems to be twenty dollars short."

"That's what I got, too."

"Let me count again." KatieAnn's hands shook as she tried to separate dollar bills. She knew she counted correctly the first time, but a recount couldn't hurt. If the count truly was off, would she be accused of stealing money — again?

"Same thing?" Miriam asked.

"*Jah*." KatieAnn's voice was barely above a whisper. *Here it kumms. Now she'll accuse me of stealing.* KatieAnn braced herself for the accusation and lifted her gaze to Miriam's face.

They were all momentarily distracted when the back door flew open.

"Still working?" Levi called out. "It's nearly half past five."

"I've got a little money problem to figure out," Miriam answered.

"Are you short?"

"A little."

"Did Grossmammi tell you I had to borrow twenty dollars when Jeremiah delivered some tools?"

"*Nee*, she didn't. That's it, then. I'm exactly twenty dollars short."

KatieAnn grew weak with relief. Her legs shook so much she feared she'd collapse. *Thank you, Gott.*

"Why didn't you say something to me or leave a note, Levi? It would have saved time and aggravation." Miriam fussed at her husband.

Levi held up a hand. "Whoa! You were busy when I came in. Jeremiah was waiting so I just told Grossmammi Sallie."

"Next time, Levi—"

"*Jah, jah.* Next time. Let's close up now. I'll help Gross-mammi inside if you lock up."

"Okay. *Danki* for staying, KatieAnn, and for all your help today. You go ahead and get home. I'll finish up here. Rebecca will be wondering what happened to you."

"Okay. See you next week, Miriam."

KatieAnn didn't notice the cold on her drive home. She probably wouldn't have noticed howling winds and driving snow. She was so happy the money wasn't actually missing that she even sang a little song along the way. The horse stepped lively, almost in time to her tune. He threw his head back and snorted, obviously glad the day was over and he could get home to warmth and food.

"You aren't half as glad as I am," she told him. She let him trot a little faster.

～

Everyone else had retired a couple hours ago, and the house was totally silent when KatieAnn finished reading and placed her Bible on her nightstand. Tomorrow was not a church day, so she didn't mind staying up a bit later tonight, but she was a bit tired. She reached for her *kapp,* but before she could remove it and pull the pins from her hair, something thudded softly against her bedroom window. Was it sleeting or raining? Had the wind picked up?

She padded to the window, though she doubted she would be able to see anything in the dark. A sudden flash of light startled her. What was that? Then the light briefly illuminated a face. Luke Troyer. Luke was tapping and shining a light at her window!

Surely he wasn't here to court her. She'd only known him a few weeks. Of course, what she knew of him she liked. Very much. And he was quite handsome—so tall she barely reached his shoulder, hair like spun gold, and those dazzling sapphire eyes. But she shouldn't think of those things. As much as she'd like to, she couldn't in *gut* conscience let him court her. Somehow she would have to discourage him. She smoothed her hair, straightened her *kapp*, and slipped from the room.

Skipping the squeaky step, KatieAnn silently crept downstairs and made her way to the front door. It opened noiselessly. She stepped out onto the porch and wrapped her arms around herself to ward off the cold. "Luke?" She whispered into the darkness.

The beam from his flashlight bobbed closer, and then Luke appeared from around the corner of the house. "*Ach*, KatieAnn, you'll freeze without a coat."

"W-what...?"

"I'm sorry to disturb you," Luke interrupted, "but I had to see you. I haven't had a chance to talk to you since after church last Sunday. You didn't attend the singing. I missed you."

"I didn't think I could handle any more whispering or dirty looks. I had enough at church and in the kitchen."

"I don't think any of the young people would have made you feel uncomfortable."

"I was afraid to take that risk." She rubbed her arms briskly and struggled to keep her teeth from chattering. "*Nee*." She put a hand out to keep Luke from shedding his coat and offering it to her. "Let's go inside for a few minutes. Everyone else went to bed ages ago."

Luke switched off his flashlight and followed her inside. Putting an index finger to her lips, she tiptoed past the stairway and into the living room, where she perched on the edge of the cushion at one end of the sofa.

Luke dropped down at the other end. Either nervous or embarrassed or both, he began twisting his black felt hat. KatieAnn reached to still his hands before the poor thing became misshapen beyond recognition.

He cleared his throat. "KatieAnn, I'd really like the chance to get to know you better. I..."

KatieAnn considered her words. How could she tell him she'd also like that chance, but she would probably have to leave or might even be asked to leave? "Let me tell you what happened this week before you say anything else."

"Okay. I'm listening."

KatieAnn took a deep breath and recounted the happenings at the store on Wednesday. She finished with the money episode from earlier that day.

"But Levi explained about the money," Luke reasoned.

"He did, but before he came in, I could see the doubt in Miriam's eyes. She thinks I'm responsible for the missing merchandise. She was ready to believe the worst about me today."

"But she didn't say anything or accuse you."

"Not yet. I don't know what she would have said or done if Levi hadn't entered the store when he did."

"I can't believe Miriam would think poorly of you."

"I never in my wildest imagination would have believed Deborah, my boss at the bakery, or even my own family, would doubt my integrity. They've always known me to be honest. Yet when the money and watch were found in my bag, I was declared guilty, even though I still don't have a single clue how they got there."

"Those people were wrong. KatieAnn, I may not have known you long, but I feel drawn to you. I feel a closeness to you. Maybe it's the Lord Gott tugging me in your direction. I don't know. But I do know that I trust you. I believe in you. I, uh...care for you."

"I appreciate your support, Luke. Truly, I do...and I wouldn't want to see you hurt. What if I have to leave here? What if your bishop wants me to confess or leave like Bishop John back home? Sometimes I think I *should* leave before I bring shame on Rebecca, Samuel and the little ones. Before I hurt you."

"You can't run away, KatieAnn. You have to stand strong. The truth will win out. With Gott's help, we'll find a solution to all this. Please don't shut me out. Please don't leave." Luke reached a large, calloused hand to KatieAnn's face. He tilted her chin so she would have to look at him.

A tear trickled down her cheek and dropped onto Luke's fingers. "I don't want to leave. I am not guilty of any wrongdoing. I just don't want you to be hurt or declared guilty by association."

"I'm tough. I'm willing to face whatever may happen. I'll be your most loyal defender."

KatieAnn almost giggled. "You make yourself sound like a faithful hound dog."

"I can be that too." Luke smiled. "Can you accept me as your loyal dog and *freind*? Can we spend some time together and get to know one another better?"

KatieAnn stayed silent so long Luke began picking at his hat again. "I-if you're willing to take the risk, then I-I'd like to get to know you better, too."

Luke's smile split his face. He squeezed KatieAnn's hand and then apologized, afraid he'd hurt her.

"If the pressure gets too great or you feel the situation is too embarrassing, I want you to tell me. I will understand if you change your mind."

"I won't, so don't even think about that. I have faith in you, and I have faith in Gott. He doesn't give us more than we can handle. He'll provide a way out of this dilemma."

KatieAnn certainly hoped that would be soon. She wasn't at all sure she could handle much more of this stress and worry. "*Danki*, Luke." She squeezed his hand.

Reluctantly, Luke got to his feet. "Will you go for a ride with me tomorrow afternoon, say around two o'clock?"

"*Jah*, unless you *kumm* to your senses overnight and decide to steer clear of me."

"That won't happen. I guarantee it."

We'll see. KatieAnn kept that thought to herself.

CHAPTER SIXTEEN

Sunday turned out to be a slow, relaxing day. A bright sun dominated the cloudless blue sky, yet the air held a nip that produced rosy cheeks and runny noses — but not bone-chilling, teeth-chattering cold. KatieAnn spent time outside playing with Eli, Jonas, and Emma for a while, and then herded the *kinner* inside for indoor games and coloring projects.

Little Elizabeth still had sniffles, so she had to stay inside with Grace and Benjamin, who were just showing signs of catching her cold. Rebecca plied them all with warm tea and honey to soothe irritated little throats. Elizabeth whined her displeasure at being left out of playtime with her *aenti*.

Sensitive to the little girl's feelings, KatieAnn involved the older three in a board game so she could color with and read to Elizabeth. The little girl instantly perked up at having her *aenti* all to herself. Benjamin and Grace became cranky and miserable, so Rebecca put them down for early naps.

Looking up from the picture she was coloring, KatieAnn caught sight of a buggy proceeding up the dirt driveway. "Company, Rebecca," she called into the living room. Obviously exhausted from caring for sick *kinner*, Rebecca had finally dropped onto the sofa beside Samuel.

"*Ach*! It's Bishop Sol and Lena!" Rebecca cried. "I wonder what they want."

"Perhaps just to visit, Fraa." Samuel patted her arm.

KatieAnn's heart flip-flopped, then plummeted to her feet. Her throat went dry, and her hands turned icy. Maybe if she and Elizabeth kept coloring and stayed quiet as mice, the bishop wouldn't even know she was around. She prayed he wasn't there to talk about her. From her chair at the kitchen table, she listened as Samuel open the front door to greet their guests. Maybe she should run out the back door. No...that would be totally unacceptable. She would have to face and deal with whatever lay ahead, like an adult.

"I know one of your little ones wasn't feeling well last Sunday, Rebecca." Lena King's voice drifted through the house. "When you didn't make it to the quilting bee at Barbara's yesterday, I got a little worried."

"*Jah*, Elizabeth was sick with a nasty cold all week, and now Grace and Benjamin are getting it. I didn't want to bring them around other people and cause an epidemic."

"You've had your hands full, then."

"For sure. I'm thankful KatieAnn has been around to help."

Why did Rebecca have to mention her? KatieAnn wanted to be out of sight and out of mind.

"That truly is a blessing," Lena agreed.

"Where is KatieAnn?" Bishop Sol's voice echoed through the house.

"She's been entertaining the older *kinner* while I've tended to the twins. Can I get you both some pie and *kaffi*?"

"*Danki*, dear, but we won't stay long. I told Sol I was

concerned, so he decided we should check on you all."

Please, Gott, let them leave soon! KatieAnn didn't want them to be here when Luke arrived.

"That was thoughtful of you both." Rebecca's voice broke into her thoughts. "Elizabeth is much better, and I'm hoping the twins don't get as sick."

"We'll certainly keep you in our prayers."

The bishop spoke to Samuel in a low, rumbling voice. KatieAnn couldn't make out his words or Samuel's replies. They must have been a little farther from the kitchen door or else they deliberately kept their voices low. Were they discussing her? If only she could hear them! But all she heard was the conversation between Lena and Rebecca about the quilting bee.

Lena and the bishop left after only a few minutes and didn't even poke their heads into the kitchen. Intent on coloring, Elizabeth hadn't made a sound to give away their presence. KatieAnn released her held breath and relaxed her hunched shoulders. "*Gut* job," she whispered to Elizabeth.

Promptly at two o'clock, KatieAnn saw Luke coming up the Hertzlers' driveway. He'd brought his open courting buggy since it would be inappropriate for the two of them to ride unchaperoned in an enclosed vehicle. Now that he was here, KatieAnn had serious misgivings about riding with Luke even in his open buggy. What if Bishop Sol saw them? Would being with her damage Luke's reputation? Worse yet, what if Clara Schwartz saw them? The grapevine would sizzle.

Could she change her mind with any grace now that he had made the trip here? Maybe she could tell him it was too cold...but he'd never believe that. Although it was a brisk day, it was not brutally cold. Besides she'd lived in Pennsylvania all her life. She was used to a colder climate than this.

Think, KatieAnn. What can you say?

"*Kumm* in," KatieAnn heard Samuel say. For some reason she understood those words clear as spring water on a summer day, but she hadn't been able to decipher a word of Samuel and Bishop Sol's conversation. She'd try to pump Rebecca for information later.

"KatieAnn, you have a visitor," Rebecca called. "She's in the kitchen, Luke. Go ahead in."

Luke swiped his hat off his head as he awkwardly clomped into the kitchen.

"Hi." KatieAnn smiled. Luke looked a mite nervous. How could she put him at ease? He put her in mind of a cat in a room full of rocking chairs. Biting back an unexpected giggle, she looked into his dazzling blue eyes and then dropped her gaze to Elizabeth's picture.

"Hi." More like a croak than his usual deep rumble. Strange. He hadn't been the least bit tongue-tied during their previous conversations. Maybe knowing Samuel and Rebecca could most likely hear his every word made him skittish.

He cleared his throat and spoke again. "*Wie bist du heit?*"

"I'm fine, Luke. Elizabeth and I have been coloring."

"That's a nice picture." He looked over Elizabeth's shoulder and peered at her scribbling. The little girl beamed her pleasure.

Luke turned his bluer-than-blue eyes back to KatieAnn and smiled. "Are you ready? Uh, do you want to go for a ride?"

"Luke, I've been thinking..." She wasn't sure how to continue. Already, Luke's shoulders slumped and his smile disappeared. KatieAnn took a deep breath and lowered her voice to just above a whisper. "I would like to go for a ride with you, truly I would. But I, uh...I think it's better if—well, if you aren't seen with me. I don't want people to get the wrong idea."

"You don't want people to think we want to see each other? Are you embarrassed to be seen with me?"

"*Ach! Nee*, Luke! It's not that at all." KatieAnn jumped up from her chair and moved to stand right in front of him. The top of her head barely reached his shoulder. She had hurt his feelings, something she never wanted to do. *Help me, Lord Gott. Give me the right words.* "It's not you at all. I don't want you to be criticized for being seen with me. I don't want you shamed."

"That could never happen."

"People talk, and it isn't always kind or true. I wouldn't want people to treat you badly because you're with me."

"You are a *gut* person."

"I fear there are some people who may disagree with that."

"Most people don't pay a lot of attention to Clara Schwartz, if that's who you mean."

"If people in my own hometown, who have known me all my life, can think I would steal, then people Clara has talked to might believe I am guilty of stealing from my employer, too. They might look on you unfavorably because you are with me. Guilty by association, you understand?"

"I'm willing to take that chance."

"I appreciate that, Luke. Really, I do. I just don't want to be the cause of any problems for you."

"So, you'll never..."

"Hey! I've got an idea. How about if we go for a walk around here? There are plenty of fields and woods we can walk through. That way we can spend some time together and not set tongues wagging."

Luke's face instantly brightened. His sapphire eyes sparkled, and a slow grin spread across his face. "Great idea! Let's walk!"

"Let me get my coat and bonnet." KatieAnn leaned down to hug Elizabeth, who had been coloring furiously, oblivious to the dilemma of the adults around her. "*Gut* job, Elizabeth. You finish while Luke and I walk. Okay?"

Elizabeth's little blonde head nodded up and down. Her fingers never paused in their scribbling.

KatieAnn poked her head into the living room to let Rebecca know her plans. She tied the black bonnet strings beneath her chin and pulled gloves from her pockets.

"You don't think you'll be too cold?" Luke opened the back door and waited for her to exit first.

"*Nee.* I was out earlier with the older *kinner*. It's brisk, but as long as we're moving, I should be warm enough."

"You're so small, you probably get cold easily." A worried frown creased Luke's forehead.

"I'm tougher than I look. Don't worry about me."

He smiled. "Okay, if you say so. Which way?"

Conversation flowed easier once they walked a ways from the house. They set out at a brisk pace to keep warm in the chilly air.

"I think the temperature has dropped a few degrees since I was out a little while ago."

"Are you too cold?"

"Not at all. I'm fine for now."

Luke gently squeezed her arm. "Let me know any time you want to go back inside."

She giggled. "I will, but I promise I'm not as delicate as I look."

They entered the woods and shuffled through dried leaves and pine needles. Loblolly pine and cedar trees mingled with leafless maples and oaks, providing a touch of green to the otherwise barren landscape. The scent of evergreens floated on the air.

"Look!" KatieAnn pointed to a spot a few feet into the woods. "That's running cedar, and over there is some crow's foot. I'll have to make wreaths for the doors. Rebecca probably won't have time to do that, especially if Grace and Benjamin end up with Elizabeth's cold."

"There are a few holly trees, too."

"The berries would add color to the wreaths. I'll have to remember where I saw all these plants."

They ambled along, talking of their childhoods, their families, their work, whatever came to mind. Totally at ease with each other now, even the silences were companionable rather than awkward.

"Shhh!" Luke pulled KatieAnn close to him and pointed. "Look over there."

KatieAnn's gaze followed his finger. She smiled when a doe with two spotted fawns came into view. "They're beautiful," she whispered.

They watched in silence for a few moments as the deer munched low vines. Then, as though they sensed they were being watched, the animals stopped in mid-munch. Leaves dangled from their mouths as they stared at the humans, who stared back at them. At some silent cue, all three turned and leapt away into the woods.

"I love the deer." KatieAnn spoke softly in case they were still nearby. "They're so graceful. I could watch them for hours."

She also liked being close to Luke but didn't mention that. When he reached for her hand before they continued their walk, she allowed him to take it.

Wind blasted them as they left the woods and started across the open field. KatieAnn ducked her head against the blustery cold. "Where did this arctic air *kumm* from?"

"The wind must have picked up strength while we were in the woods. The trees sheltered us there."

"I suppose you're right."

"Are you okay?"

"*Jah*, but I think I'm ready to head for the house." The wind snatched the words from her mouth and threw them aloft. Luke nodded his understanding. They concentrated on walking faster and focused on breathing instead of talking.

"Would you like some hot cocoa or *kaffi* with a slice of peach pie?" KatieAnn paused with her hand on the door knob to look up at Luke.

"Did you make the pie?"

"I did."

"Then I know it will be *wunderbaar* — like the person who made it. *Jah*, I would love a slice of *your* peach pie."

KatieAnn smiled. Her cheeks grew hot, but they were probably already reddened by the wind. She washed her hands and poured milk into a pan to heat for cocoa. After uncovering the pie, she sliced a large, triangular piece for Luke. "Have a seat and I'll bring your pie and cocoa."

"I can help. Where's your pie?"

"I think I'll have a cookie instead. You can have both, if you'd like."

"Sure."

KatieAnn nestled two cookies alongside the chunk of pie. She handed Luke the plate and a mug of cocoa and carried her own mug and cookie to the table. "Mmm. The cocoa hits the spot."

Luke forked a big bite of pie into his mouth. "This is even better than I expected."

At his wink, KatieAnn felt her cheeks flush again. She quickly looked down and nibbled at her cookie.

They talked until their mugs and plates were empty. Luke leaned close to wipe a bit of chocolate from her mouth. He stared into her eyes and didn't move away after he lowered the napkin. Her heart flipped several times. She feared Luke would kiss her if she didn't do something quick. Not that she didn't want him to kiss her. *Ach,* she didn't know what she wanted!

"Did you get some pie?" Rebecca's voice sounded close.

Luke jumped back just before Rebecca entered the kitchen.

"We did. Actually, Luke just finished a piece." KatieAnn hoped her voice didn't betray her flustered emotions.

"*Gut.* The babies are up, so I'm just going to get them a little snack." Rebecca bustled about, obviously trying to ignore the young couple at the table.

"I really need to be leaving." Luke pushed his chair back from the table.

KatieAnn followed him to the door. "I'm sorry about the change in plans, but I enjoyed our walk."

"So did I. I'm glad I came over. I think the walk was an even better idea than the drive." He dropped his voice so only KatieAnn could hear. "I could concentrate fully on you and not worry about keeping the horse in line."

Heat traveled up KatieAnn's cheeks, across her forehead, and up her scalp.

"Could we do it again? Soon?" Luke took KatieAnn's hand in one of his big, calloused ones.

"I-I think that would be all right."

"Will you be at the singing next Sunday?"

"I don't know about that."

"Rosanna and the others would like you to attend, too."

"I'll have to wait and see."

"Then I'll check with you again later." Luke squeezed her hand. "See you soon?"

"*Jah.*"

He plopped his hat on his head, gave her a final

lopsided grin, and winked one sapphire eye. Then he bounded down the steps whistling a happy tune.

KatieAnn sighed as she closed the door. What on earth was she thinking? She was a horrible person! She'd let Luke think everything was fine and normal, like they could possibly have a relationship. Even if she wanted to pursue one with him—and she felt pretty sure she'd like to do that—how could she? She didn't even know how long she would stay in Maryland, or even if she'd be allowed to stay if anything else went wrong. She sighed again, this time deeper and louder.

"What's that heavy sigh for?" Rebecca looked up as KatieAnn entered the kitchen. Benjamin and Grace sat in high chairs eating small pieces of bread spread with apple butter.

"Life, I suppose."

"Rebecca, what did Bishop Sol talk to Samuel about?" KatieAnn hadn't intended to blurt out the question, but somehow the words tumbled out before she could stop them.

"Well, um..."

"I hate to put you on the spot, but was it about me?"

Rebecca lowered her voice. "The bishop asked Samuel how you were doing, and if there were any problems."

"In other words, have I stolen anything from you or anyone else that you know of?"

"*Ach*, KatieAnn. I don't think the bishop meant it that way. He's actually a fair man for all his stern demeanor."

She sighed. "I'm sorry to be so jumpy. I'm just tired of having people judge me and finding me guilty. Was I such a horrible little girl, Schweschder? Is that why people back home are so quick to believe the worst about me?"

"Of course you weren't." Rebecca hugged her. "You were not bad at all. A little mischievous, maybe, but not more than most *kinner*. So what else about life caused that great big sigh?"

"Isn't that enough?"

"I'm thinking there was more to it."

"Uh, I'm just a terrible person, I guess. Seems like a black cloud follows me around everywhere. I feel like I'm being punished for something."

"KatieAnn, I don't believe the Lord Gott punishes us by allowing bad things to happen. He loves you. Sometimes bad things happen because of something someone else did. We can grow stronger and grow closer to the Lord or we can grow bitter. Please don't grow bitter."

KatieAnn sniffed. "I'm trying not to."

"Remember, Gott promises that things will work out for *gut*. One of my favorite Bible verses is from the book of Jeremiah. Gott knows the plans He has for us—plans to prosper us and not harm us, plans to give us hope."

KatieAnn nodded against Rebecca's shoulder.

"Luke doesn't seem to be bothered by any rumors he may have heard."

"That's another problem," KatieAnn wailed.

"How is that a problem? It seems more like a blessing. Luke is a very sensible, kind young man."

"I agree. I should not have encouraged him in any way, that's all. I'm just a visitor here and may even have to run from this place, too."

"You can't run away from your problems, you know, and I don't think anyone will force you to leave here."

"My life is back in Persimmon Creek."

"One great thing about life is that it always changes, just like the weather. There are cloudy days and sunny days. We need to be open to change. It may just be what the Lord has in mind for us. Maybe you'll want to stay here permanently."

"I don't want Luke to be criticized because of me. I-I

like him too much to cause him any pain."

"He didn't seem concerned about that to me."

"He says he isn't."

"Believe him. I'm not saying you should marry Luke Troyer, but there's not any harm in getting to know him, ain't so? Things have a way of working out for the best."

"I guess you're right. I hope you are."

"Just see where the Lord Gott leads you."

KatieAnn nodded. She wiped her eyes with the back of her hand, gave a final sniff, and pasted a shaky smile on her mouth. "We'll see."

CHAPTER SEVENTEEN

Grossmammi Sallie seemed a little agitated and out of sorts when KatieAnn arrived at Esh's store on Wednesday. She improved somewhat while eating the sweet treat KatieAnn brought but then went back to drumming her fingers on the wooden arms as she rocked the old chair furiously. Occasionally she would wander around the store for a few moments.

Whenever KatieAnn had a break, she'd sit beside Sallie and knit rows on the last of the Christmas presents she was making for the *kinner*. As long as KatieAnn sat beside her, Sallie remained calm and crocheted blue or white squares she planned to assemble into a bed covering.

"I don't know how you work with that cotton thread and those tiny needles." KatieAnn nodded at Sallie's hands. "I can barely see the stitches myself."

"These old fingers know what to do without my even looking." Sallie's gnarled fingers flew, proving her words true. She behaved in a perfectly calm, normal manner while crocheting and talking with KatieAnn.

"You're *wunderbaar* with her, and she has really taken to you," Miriam said later, after Sallie had dozed off. "I may have to hire you just to take care of her!"

"I love spending time with her," KatieAnn replied. "She's very special, like my own *grossmammi*."

"I appreciate your help with her."

Business remained steady but not quite as hectic as Saturdays usually were. Shortly before lunch time, Rosanna entered and set the little bell above the door tinkling. A blast of cold air ushered her inside. "Whew! I think winter may have arrived for *gut*." The door slammed closed behind her.

"*Kumm* get warm here by Grossmammi Sallie. She'll share the stove with you," KatieAnn called out.

Rosanna hurried across the store. "It's *gut* to see you, KatieAnn. I missed you at the last singing. And you didn't stay long after the meal on Sunday, so I didn't get to talk to you."

"Rebecca had a sick little one and wanted to get her home."

"You could have returned for the singing, though, ain't so?" Rosanna set her bag down and rubbed her hands together to warm them.

"I-I suppose I could have. I, well, I was uncomfortable during the service and meal. Too many eyes followed me around. Too many whispered conversations stopped abruptly when I entered a room."

"I understand." Rosanna patted her arm. "But I think you should attend the next singing. Everyone missed you."

"Everyone?"

"Everyone I know of. KatieAnn, people will always talk about the latest 'news,' but after a bit, something newer happens along and they forget all about the previous tidbit."

"Do you think talk about me has died down?"

"Probably. I know the Bontragers just got back from

visiting family in Ohio. I'm sure any news they have is clogging up the grapevine by now."

"They most likely don't have any news as juicy as a thief among the community."

"You're not a thief. Anyone who even slightly knows you would never think that of you."

"Tell that to the folks back home." KatieAnn mumbled the words mainly to herself.

"It will all be okay. Trust the Lord Gott."

"I'm trying to do that. Rebecca says the Lord always has a plan for *gut* for us. I'm hanging onto that."

"She's right. Anyway, I know Nancy, Micah, Thomas, and Luke all want you to *kumm* to the next singing. Especially Luke." Rosanna nudged her *freind*.

"*Ach*, Rosanna. What have you brought me?" Miriam hurried from the storage room.

Rosanna lifted her bag and carried it to the counter. As curious as Miriam, KatieAnn followed.

Miriam peered over Rosanna's shoulder as she opened her bag. "Something smells *gut* in there."

"I made more candles. I wrapped them separately so the scents wouldn't intermingle." Rosanna unwrapped pale yellow candles. "These are lemon vanilla."

Miriam took a deep breath. "Mmm! They smell tasty."

"These..." Rosanna unwrapped red candles. "...are cinnamon spice."

Miriam and KatieAnn sniffed in appreciation, but Rosanna wasn't quite finished. "Chocolate!" she cried, pulling out brown candles.

"These really do smell *gut* enough to eat." Miriam held a candle to her nose to give it another sniff. "These should sell well. You've been busy."

"Indeed I have."

"I'm sorry I haven't gotten back to watch you make candles again. I had wanted to do that," KatieAnn said.

"That's okay. This is a very busy time of year, and I know you've been helping Rebecca with the *kinner* and the housework in addition to working here. Maybe after the holidays you can visit again."

"I'd like that."

"Well, I really need to get home to help my *mamm*. Church is at our house this Sunday, and Mamm cleans for days beforehand."

"*Danki* for bringing the candles, Rosanna," Miriam called out as she placed the candles on the appropriate shelf.

"Please *kumm* to the singing, KatieAnn." Rosanna dropped her voice to a whisper. "Miriam doesn't seem to be bothered by any rumors."

"She hasn't said anything to me. Yet."

"Think positive thoughts!"

"I'll try."

"And please attend on Sunday evening."

"I'll see." That was the best KatieAnn could offer. She wouldn't make a promise she might have to break.

Rosanna gave her *freind* a quick hug before making her way to the front door.

"How about another treat?" a sleepy voice called from the corner near the stove.

"I'll be right there, Grossmammi." KatieAnn smiled as she walked toward the tiny old woman who had just awakened from her nap. "I don't know where you put all those treats!"

"I always have room for sweets." Sallie threw back her head and cackled. She licked her lips and patted her stomach. Then she reached for KatieAnn's hand. "You go to that young people's singing." She winked. "You see, sometimes I really am just resting my eyes and I know everything that's going on."

"So I see." KatieAnn laughed and doled out another

cookie.

∽

"Oh no! My ring!" The distraught wail came from around the corner where an older *Englisch* woman and her daughter had been browsing.

KatieAnn had almost forgotten the women were still in the store. She hurried down the aisle and stopped beside them with her heart pounding like a drum. "What happened?"

Miriam dropped the box she was getting ready to unload and rushed over. "Are you all right?" She panted to catch her breath.

"Nooo!" the younger woman wailed again. "My ring is gone."

KatieAnn's heart thudded even harder. "Did you drop it?" She began searching the area.

"Did you have it on when we came inside?" the older woman snapped. "You're always playing with it. I've told you and told you to get it made smaller."

"I—I don't remember, but I must have had it on. Oh, I don't know. When I'm cold the ring slides on and off so easily."

"Perhaps it's in the car," Miriam suggested.

"It could be anywhere!" The mother did not seem at all sympathetic.

Her daughter threw her a dirty look. "The ring is important to me, Mom. Danny gave it to me for my birthday." Her voice quivered as a tear slid down her cheek.

"What does it look like? I'll look all through the store." KatieAnn felt sorry for the distraught young woman.

She sniffed. "It's got a white gold band. The stone is a large sapphire surrounded by diamonds. You know what a sapphire looks like, don't you?"

Sometimes *Englischers* amazed KatieAnn. They

seemed to think the Amish were clueless about things. Just because they chose to avoid worldly things didn't mean they weren't aware of their existence. "Sapphires are my favorite stones." She almost said they reminded her of Luke's eyes so of course she knew what they looked like. "I'll start looking."

"It's kind of a gaudy thing, if you ask me," the older woman muttered. "The stone is too big."

"Mom! The ring is beautiful!"

"I'm sure it is." KatieAnn tried to smooth the girl's ruffled feathers. She rummaged through each shelf and checked the floor. Miriam did the same.

The young woman pulled a wadded-up tissue from the pocket of her leather jacket and swiped at her eyes and nose. She stood completely still, as if in shock.

"I'll go look in the car," her mother finally offered.

Thirty minutes later, all searchers came up empty-handed. The ring was nowhere to be found.

"Leave us your name and number. We'll call you if the ring turns up," Miriam offered. "When my husband gets home, I'll get him to move some of the shelves so we can look behind them."

The young woman nodded and continued to wipe her nose.

"Here, dear." Sallie appeared as if by magic, holding out a pen and a piece of paper. KatieAnn hadn't even known Sallie was paying attention.

The young woman printed her name and phone number and handed the pen and paper back to Sallie. "You'll be able to call me?"

"Of course we will," Miriam assured her.

"It's probably at home anyway," the mother mumbled. "Or else it's gone for good. Come on, Julie, let's go."

"Thank you for your help." The young woman trailed out of the store behind her mother. The bell tinkled as the door closed behind them. Their arguing voices still reached the women inside the store who all stared at one another.

KatieAnn's knees nearly buckled. Would she be accused of another jewelry theft?

Sallie wagged her head and broke the silence. "*Englischers* have way too many baubles."

∞

KatieAnn crawled out of bed and began working in the kitchen earlier than usual on Friday morning. She wanted to bake today since she would be helping out in the store tomorrow. By the time the family assembled for breakfast, she already had a pan of walnut fudge brownies cooling on the kitchen counter and had stirred together the dry ingredients for two carrot cakes.

She set her mixing bowls aside to ladle steaming oatmeal into seven bowls while Rebecca slid fried eggs and crisp bacon onto plates. Emma carefully carried cups of milk to the table for the *kinner* while Elizabeth placed napkins at each place. The *buwe* and Samuel, freshly scrubbed after completing outside chores, plopped down at the table to wait.

"This ought to warm me up." Samuel nodded at the bowl of oatmeal and cup of *kaffi* KatieAnn set in front of him. "The wind has a real bite to it today."

When plates, cups, and bowls had been distributed around the table, everyone bowed their heads for silent prayer. At Samuel's cue, heads lifted and forks scraped against plates. The *buwe* slurped their milk.

"Use your napkin." Rebecca frowned when she caught Eli about to wipe his mouth on his sleeve.

"*Jah*, Mamm. Hurry up, Jonas. We don't want to be late."

"Why are you in such a hurry to get to school?" Jonas

spoke around the bite of bacon he'd shoved into his mouth.

"I don't want to be late and have to make up the time at recess."

"Have you had to do that?" Rebecca laid down her fork and studied her son.

"*Nee*, but Will Brubaker and Joseph Stoltzfus have."

"If you leave in ten minutes, you should have plenty of time."

"Okay, Mamm, if you say so." Eli looked skeptical but didn't argue with his *mamm*.

Rebecca smiled at her son who was growing up so fast. She turned to look at Samuel. "You'll be at the cheese factory today, ain't so?"

"I will. I'll drop the *buwe* off at school first. It's pretty cold this morning."

KatieAnne willed everyone to eat fast and get out of the kitchen so she could clean up and continue with her baking.

The combined sweet scents of carrots, cinnamon, and raisins permeated the kitchen even before KatieAnn pulled the two fat carrot cakes from the oven. She set them on the counter to cool. Later she would drizzle a cream cheese frosting over them. She glanced out the kitchen window as she washed dishes. "Someone is here."

Rebecca dragged her dust mop across the room and hurried to peer out of the curtainless window. A car had stopped in front of the house. "I wonder who that could be."

A tall, lanky young woman with mousy brown hair peeking out from her black bonnet climbed out of the car. She pulled a traveling bag out behind her and handed the driver what appeared to be a wad of money.

"Are you expecting someone, KatieAnn?"

"Not me. But she does look familiar." When the girl turned around, KatieAnn knew who had arrived. "*Ach!* It's Lizzie Krieder from back home. What is she doing here?"

"The Lizzie you worked with at the bake shop? The girl that lied and said she was the baker and made up *your* recipes?"

"That would be the one."

"What *is* she doing here?"

"I guess we're about to find out."

The two women watched as the dark green van drove off. Lizzie gazed at the house as if unsure what to do. After a moment, she took hesitant steps toward the front porch.

Rebecca stowed her mop away as KatieAnn dried her hands on the striped dish towel. Both headed in the direction of the front door just as the first rap of knuckles hit the wood. Rebecca pulled it open before another knock sounded through the house. KatieAnn stood behind her *schweschder* but out of the visitor's view. She stared at Lizzie, who gazed at Rebecca, a confused expression on her face.

"I-is K-KatieAnn Mast here? I'm Lizzie Krieder." She paused for a moment. "From Persimmon Creek."

"I'm Rebecca Hertzler, KatieAnn's *schweschder*. *Kumm* in." Rebecca held the door open and stepped back enough to allow Lizzie to enter. While she behaved in a welcoming manner KatieAnn could tell that her protective older *schweschder* wasn't altogether thrilled at the girl's sudden appearance.

"Lizzie, whatever are you doing here?" she blurted out.

"H-hi, KatieAnn." Lizzie twisted her hands round and round on the handles of her bag, obviously at a loss now that she had gained entrance into the house.

"How did you find me?"

"I, um…Clara and Noah Schwartz stopped in to see Mamm when they were in Pennsylvania. They, um, mentioned that you were here."

"Now I know how Clara happened to return with a rumor," KatieAnn mumbled more to herself than to Lizzie.

"Clara told me I could visit her so, um, so here I am."

"Let's go sit in the kitchen. I'll get us some hot tea." Rebecca hurried to the kitchen.

They all sat at the big oak table with their hands wrapped around mugs of tea, each waiting for someone else to speak.

Rebecca broke the tense silence. "Are you staying with Clara?"

"*Jah*, for a few days."

"But you came here first?" KatieAnn couldn't help but voice her questions. "Why? I heard from Grace that you were starting a new job."

Lizzie fidgeted with her paper napkin until it began to disintegrate.

"Um, I am, but—well, KatieAnn, I need your help." Lizzie's voice trailed off.

"Her help?" Rebecca exploded and then calmed herself with obvious effort.

KatieAnn blinked. Rebecca must be quite upset to get so riled up. Her older *schweschder* had always been her protector and did not seem to want to relinquish that role now.

"How can I help you?" KatieAnn's curiosity got the best of her.

"Can you teach me how to bake like you and give me your recipes?"

"Didn't you get a job as baker at Busy B's? That's what

Grace wrote."

"I did. Deborah wouldn't let me bake even after you left."

"How did you get the job at Busy B's if you don't know how to bake?" Rebecca asked

KatieAnn watched Lizzie closely. Would the girl confirm what Grace had written, or would she try to worm her way out of the falsehood she'd supposedly told?

"I..." Lizzie swirled her mug of tea until it sloshed over the rim. "I sort of told them I baked all the specials at The Bake Shop."

KatieAnn gasped. The revelation should not have been a surprise since Grace had alluded to this very thing in her letter, but hearing the admission aloud from Lizzie's own lips felt like a punch in the belly.

"You what?" Rebecca's voice rose. "Why would you do such a thing?"

"Deborah wouldn't let me bake. She wouldn't even give me a chance. She just said, 'Wait on the customers, Lizzie. Clean the counters and tables, Lizzie.'"

Lizzie did such a *gut* imitation of Deborah that KatieAnn almost smiled. "We all did those things when we were finished with our other work."

"Other work!" Lizzie cried. "That's just it. Those were my only jobs."

"Is that what you were hired to do?" Rebecca had gotten control of her voice.

"Well, *jah*, but..."

"And you lied to get a better job. You deceived your new employer."

"If KatieAnn helps me and gives me her recipes, then it won't really be lying. You can start with those yummy-looking cakes over there." Lizzie pointed to the counter where the carrot cakes cooled.

"That's a rather twisted way of looking at things, don't

you think?" Rebecca used her best stern parent voice. "You want KatieAnn to partner with you in your deception, ain't so?"

Lizzie remained silent, her finger trailing through the puddle of tea on the table.

KatieAnn couldn't believe her ears. "Do you really think it would be fair to your new employer or to me if I did what you're asking?"

"Well, I don't see what's wrong with your helping me."

"Lizzie, I don't mind helping anyone, but you want me to be your partner in crime."

Lizzie rolled her eyes. "Don't be so dramatic."

KatieAnn was sure she knew her *schweschder*'s thoughts. Rebecca most likely wanted to shake some sense into the seventeen-year-old girl sitting at her table.

"It certainly wouldn't be fair to pass KatieAnn's creations off as your own. I don't know how you can think otherwise."

"KatieAnn is in Maryland. I'll be in Pennsylvania. I think we're far enough apart that it won't matter."

"It won't matter to whom?" KatieAnn snapped. "What if I want to return to Persimmon Creek and start my own business? I wouldn't be able to use my own recipes — the recipes I spent time and energy and money creating — because you are already claiming them as your own."

"Are you planning to *kumm* back and make your confession?"

"I don't have anything to confess."

"You think it would be stealing if you gave me your precious recipes, but what about you stealing from Deborah?"

"Lizzie, you know in your heart I would not have stolen Deborah's money or that watch."

"Do I? Those things were found in your bag. Deborah caught you red-handed."

Tears clouded KatieAnn's vision. "Lizzie, how could you believe such a thing?"

"And yet you traipse to Maryland and want KatieAnn's help to save your own hide?" Rebecca sputtered. "That really takes a lot of nerve."

"I would gladly have helped you improve your baking skills, but I would never just hand my recipes over to you so you could pretend they were yours. I won't help you try to fool whoever is in charge at Busy B's since Bea passed away."

"It's her sons. And they need an experienced baker."

"They think that's what you are, ain't so?" Rebecca softened her tone. "They didn't even ask for references or for you to provide some baked items for them?"

Lizzie hung her head. A dark strand of hair had worked itself loose from her bun. She swiped at it with one long, bony hand to get it out of her face. "You won't help me?"

"Not right now," KatieAnn replied. "If you go back to Bea's sons and tell them the truth, then I would be willing to help you be the best baker *you* can be. I'll not give you my recipes to use as your own."

"They'll fire me. Then I won't have any job. Mamm needs me to work to help her out since Daed died."

"Bishop John is your uncle. He'll help. Even if he wasn't your uncle, as bishop he'd see to it that your family is cared for." KatieAnn hoped to reason with the girl.

"Mamm doesn't want charity."

"We all help each other, ain't so?"

"But you won't help me!"

"I won't be untruthful or deceitful for you."

Lizzie stood abruptly. "I guess this trip was a waste of what little money I have. Tell me how to get to Clara's house, please." She picked up her bag and started for the door.

"It's cold out, Lizzie. If you wait a few minutes for one of us to hitch up Brownie, we'll drive you," Rebecca said.

"Don't trouble yourself." Sarcasm dripped from Lizzie's voice. "It's colder than this at home. I can walk. Just point me in the right direction."

Rebecca walked to the door with Lizzie and described the shortest route to take to the Schwartzes' house. Before the door closed, she touched Lizzie's arm. "Had you thought that maybe baking is not your talent? The Lord Gott gives us all special abilities. Maybe your gift is something entirely different."

Lizzie shook off Rebecca's hand and shrugged her shoulders without answering. She trotted down the steps and plodded off in the direction Rebecca indicated.

Rebecca closed the door and hurried back to the kitchen. "Who'd have ever thought such a thing? She has a lot of nerve! Are you all right?"

"I would never have expected such a thing in a million years." KatieAnn paused in stirring together the confectioner's sugar, vanilla, and cream cheese for her frosting. "That girl needs to grow up. I do feel a little sorry for her, though."

"You did the right thing, KatieAnn. Stand by your beliefs. The truth is always best, and the whole truth will be discovered. You just keep believing that."

CHAPTER EIGHTEEN

Bearing one of her carrot cakes, KatieAnn arrived at Esh's store early on Saturday morning. Grossmammi Sallie already smacked her lips, savoring her first piece of cake, by the time Miriam unlocked the front door to officially open the store for business. KatieAnn cut most of the cake into small chunks into which she inserted wooden toothpicks so customers could munch on a treat. She squirreled away extra pieces for Miriam, Levi, and Sallie to enjoy later.

"This is one *gut* cake, dearie." Sallie licked cream cheese frosting from her fingers.

"Here, Grossmammi, I'll get you a paper towel," Miriam offered.

"Don't bother, Miriam. This cake is too *appeditlich* to waste a single speck. I declare, KatieAnn, every treat you bring in here tastes better than the one before. I think this is the best carrot cake I've ever eaten."

"You like anything sweet," KatieAnn teased.

"I do, but I especially like your treats. Can I have another sliver?"

"Later, if you're *gut*." Miriam shook her finger at

Sallie, and all three women laughed.

The front door banged open to admit a cold blast of air and Esther Fisher, loaded down with handmade holiday wreaths and door swags.

"Let me help you!" KatieAnn rushed to the door to lend a hand.

"I'm glad you're here. I thought that was the Hertzlers' buggy up near the barn." Esther passed the box of wreaths and swags to KatieAnn. "I have a few more in the buggy." She turned toward the door.

"Do you need some help?"

"*Nee*. I only have a few more."

KatieAnn stuck her nose in a wreath and inhaled. "I love the smell of pine and cedar. It makes me feel all warm inside, the same way the scents of cinnamon and apples do."

"What have you brought me?" Miriam walked closer to investigate.

"I got carried away making wreaths and such," Esther said. I have plenty to sell, so I thought I'd see if you wanted some."

"For sure. They're lovely."

"I'll be right back. I've got to run out to the buggy for just a minute."

∽

While KatieAnn helped Miriam find the best location to display the wreaths and swags, Esther returned to the buggy she'd left near the door. She gently patted her horse's head. "No need to unhitch. I'll be right back."

She reached inside the buggy to grab a bag of bows to tie on the wreaths. Not wanting them to get smashed in transit, she'd packed them separately, with plans to affix the bows to the wreaths after she got the greenery safely inside the store.

As she backed out of the buggy clutching her bag to her, a movement grabbed her attention. From the opposite direction, she spied a lone figure approaching. It looked like a rather tall, thin woman hurrying up the driveway toward the store. Esther was unable to identify the woman. It certainly wasn't someone easily recognizable, and she hadn't heard of any visitors to the area. She shrugged her shoulders and hurried back inside. "I guess I'll find out if she *kumms* inside."

~~~

Lizzie thrust her hands deeper into her pockets. The weather was almost Pennsylvania-cold. She should have taken Clara up on the offer to use her buggy. She shuffled along, kicking larger rocks as she came to them. She felt like she had been kicked.

Why couldn't things ever work out for her? Why couldn't she be pretty and happy and successful? She hoped to catch a minute with KatieAnn without her nosey big *schweschder* around. Clara said she would find KatieAnn at the store on Saturdays, so Lizzie set out for the Eshes' place. She would try one more time to persuade KatieAnn to see things her way. *Kumm* Monday, she'd have to head back to Persimmon Creek. She wanted to get started on those recipes and make the owners at Busy B's glad they hired her. She was running out of time and money. KatieAnn had better help her!

Lizzie kicked a few more rocks in the gravel parking area just because it made her feel better to kick something. Several larger rocks and numerous pebbles skittered away with her last effort. A shiny, blue object sparkled in the space the rocks had vacated. "That can't be a rock," Lizzie said aloud.

She pulled a black-gloved hand from her pocket and bent to pick up the glittering object. A ring. A beautiful blue ring surrounded by diamonds. "This must be worth a lot of money." She deposited the ring in her pocket before giving the door a yank.

"I tell you, Esther, Levi and I looked everywhere," the older woman said as she arranged the wreaths and swags. "We even moved as many shelves as we could. We still didn't find that ring."

"That poor young woman must feel so sad." KatieAnn fluffed a wreath. "It seemed like it was something special to her."

"Maybe she found it at home," Esther offered.

Lizzie paused to process the snatch of conversation she'd just overheard. Her brain hatched a plan that just might get her out of the mess she was in.

A gust of air brought a pause to the conversation. Along with Miriam and Esther, KatieAnn swung around to see the thin young woman who'd entered the store. She groaned inside as the wind closed behind Lizzie with a loud slam.

"What happened to the bell?" Miriam looked above the door where the little bell usually hung.

"I'm afraid I knocked it off when the wind pushed me and my load inside," Esther replied. "I meant to pick it up but forgot."

Lizzie snatched up the bell and crossed the room to where the women stood. She held out the item.

"*Danki.*" Miriam took it from the newcomer's hand. "I'll have to put that back up."

"I'll do it for you." KatieAnn held her hand out for the bell. "By the way, this is Lizzie Krieder from Persimmon Creek. She's, uh, visiting Clara." KatieAnn finished the introductions and pointed out Grossmammi Sallie sitting in her customary spot by the stove. She seemed to be taking in the action like a spectator at a ball game. She nodded as she was introduced but never slowed the rocker.

"Did you need something, Lizzie, or did Clara send you on a mission?" Miriam asked.

"*Nee*. I actually came to talk to KatieAnn."

Halfway to the door with the bell, KatieAnn stopped in her tracks. She looked over her shoulder at Lizzie. "We talked already." She snatched up the stepstool and carried it to the door.

Esther and Miriam resumed arranging the display. KatieAnn could hear them talking softly but couldn't decipher their words.

"KatieAnn, please listen. Won't you help me?"

"We've been through this, Lizzie."

"I thought you might have changed your mind."

"I haven't."

"KatieAnn..."

"Lizzie, what about the other bakers at Busy B's? I know Bea was the main baker, but she had other bakers as well. They certainly won't want you taking over their jobs."

"They quit."

"All of them?" KatieAnn had a hard time believing her ears. "Why would they all quit?"

"They, uh, couldn't stand working for the sons after Bea died. Don't you see, KatieAnn? Now is my chance. They need me to bake. Please at least give me your recipes. It shouldn't be that hard to follow directions."

KatieAnn almost rolled her eyes. Lizzie's few attempts to bake at Deborah's shop had been disastrous. The poor girl had followed the recipes—simple ones—from Deborah's recipe book, yet none of the final results had looked appetizing or even recognizable. The taste had been nothing to write home about either.

Still, she didn't want to hurt Lizzie's feelings by reminding her of those culinary disasters. "Lizzie, we've discussed this. It's not right to take my recipes and claim them as your own. Besides a lot of my recipes are in my head." KatieAnn climbed onto the stool to hang the bell.

"You could write them down for me."

"You aren't listening at all. It's wrong to deceive your employers. Don't you want to succeed honestly, on your own merit?"

"I don't have time for that! Besides, you're a fine one to talk about deception and honesty." Lizzie turned her back on KatieAnn and stomped across the store. She turned slightly to mumble over her shoulder. "I gave you a chance. Now I have no choice."

"What?" KatieAnn climbed off the ladder, shaking her head. What on earth was Lizzie talking about? Why was she heading back through the store instead of leaving? Whatever was the girl up to now?

KatieAnn put the stool away, and then walked around Lizzie to look at the display. "These are perfect. They look so festive." Out of the corner of her eye, she saw Lizzie smirk and reach into her pocket.

"*Ach*! I almost forgot." Lizzie pulled her hand out of her pocket and thrust it into KatieAnn's face. "You must have knocked this out of your buggy or dropped it when you got out." The girl replaced the smirk with a wide-eyed, innocent expression.

KatieAnn looked down. The missing sapphire and diamond ring nestled in Lizzie's hand. She gasped and tried to make her voice work, but couldn't.

"You always did like jewelry." Lizzie shook her hand in KatieAnn's face. "Here. Take it."

"I-it's not mine, and it wasn't in my buggy." KatieAnn's voice was a mere whisper. "It's that *Englisch* lady's lost ring."

"It's not yours? It sure looked like it fell from your buggy. Unless — did the *Englischers* park up there where you do?"

KatieAnn plucked the ring from Lizzie's hand and turned to hand it to Miriam, who stared at her, obviously horrified. A scowl shadowed Esther's face, as well. Did both women think she had taken the ring?

"Clara's here." Lizzie pulled her gaze from the window and spoke in a syrupy voice. The little smirk returned to her face. "She's showing me around today. I don't want to keep her waiting. Have a *gut* day, KatieAnn." She sped across the room and pushed open the door. The little bell KatieAnn had just rehung jangled wildly.

"Wait!" Esther cried. She dropped a wreath and ran for the door. KatieAnn stared after her. Lizzie had already reached Clara's buggy by the time Esther got outside, leaving the door wide open behind her. "Lizzie!"

The girl never acknowledged hearing Esther's voice. Esther shook her head as she re-entered the store. She closed the door firmly, setting the little bell crazy again.

"I-I have no idea how that ring got near my buggy. I-I never saw it when I got out. How could it suddenly appear there?"

Miriam's face still registered shock. "Let me find that woman's number." She spun around and headed for the counter.

"Miriam..." KatieAnn didn't know what to say. Should she proclaim her innocence, or would attempting to defend herself make her look more guilty?

"I'm not at all sure it did suddenly appear by your buggy." Esther laid a hand on KatieAnn's arm.

"Huh?"

"I don't think Lizzie was near your buggy."

"But she said she found the ring outside where I

parked. The other day a young *Englisch* woman was in the store and became upset when she realized she didn't have her ring—a sapphire and diamond ring."

"I saw Lizzie as she walked up the driveway. She wasn't walking by your buggy, at least not while I was outside."

"*Ach*, Esther. I didn't take that ring. Now Lizzie will tell Clara and the grapevine will vibrate with the news. I might as well pack my belongings." KatieAnn struggled not to cry.

"Don't you do any such thing. It doesn't matter where Lizzie found the ring. Nobody will accuse you of taking it."

"Didn't you see Miriam's expression? She looked horrified."

"She was probably shocked to see the ring, for sure, but that doesn't mean she thinks you took it."

"Lizzie had to go and say how I liked jewelry. I did like jewelry during my *rumspringa*. I even bought cheap costume jewelry, but I gave all that up when I joined the church. That stuff doesn't even appeal to me now. Some of it is pretty, but I don't want it. Really, I don't."

"Calm down. I believe you." Esther patted KatieAnn's arm. "Don't worry. We'll sort this out," she whispered as Miriam approached.

"The lady was overjoyed we found her ring. She'll *kumm* by for it later. I'll hold onto it for safekeeping." Miriam shuffled off in the direction of the storage room.

Because you don't trust me. KatieAnn almost said the words aloud. Instead she nodded at Miriam. She bent to help Esther clean up pine needles scattered on the floor around the greenery display.

"Don't you do anything foolish like leaving here, KatieAnn Mast. You have people here who believe in you."

"They won't after Clara spreads the latest news."

"Most of us don't pay a lot of attention to Clara's ram-blings. Luke and Rosanna wanted me to persuade you to attend the singing tomorrow night."

"How could I possibly think of going now?"

"How can you not go? Don't go burying your head in the sand. That screams, 'guilty.'" Esther lightly grasped KatieAnn's chin and forced her to look up into her warm, chocolate eyes. "And we both know you are not guilty of any wrongdoing. You hold your head up and go have fun with the young people who care about you."

"You tell her Esther!" Sallie called from her rocking chair. Smile lines crinkled around her mouth and eyes.

"That old woman doesn't miss a thing," Esther whis-pered, causing KatieAnn to smile despite her troubles. "Grossmammi Sallie might come in useful."

"For what?"

"My investigation."

CHAPTER NINETEEN

The morning proved to be another tense one for KatieAnn. She tiptoed all around the subject of the recovered sapphire ring and avoided talking with Miriam whenever possible. She couldn't decide whether to broach the subject before Miriam did, or simply wait to be dismissed. At least the store had a steady stream of customers to keep them busy.

KatieAnn spent her lunch time with Sallie. As promised, the tiny, old woman received a second generous slice of carrot cake after eating nearly two-thirds of her ham and cheese sandwich.

"It looks like I did better than you." Sallie pointed to KatieAnn's chicken salad sandwich—still perfectly intact except for a tiny bite out of one corner.

"I guess I'm not very hungry today."

"You've got to keep up your strength, girlie. You're too little as it is."

"I've always been small."

"Well, if you don't eat that sandwich, you're going to disappear entirely."

KatieAnn smiled. "I don't think it's quite that bad."

"Pretty close. Don't you let that girl upset you. You are a *gut* person. I know that—here and here." Sallie pointed first to her head and then to her heart.

KatieAnn hugged the woman's bony shoulders. "You are a *gut* person, too. I feel like you are my *grossmammi*."

"I'd be delighted to be your honorary *grossmammi*."

"*Danki*." KatieAnn leaned over to kiss the withered cheek.

"Now eat!"

"I'll try." KatieAnn nibbled a few more bites. But when Sallie looked down to spear a bite of cake with a plastic fork, she stuffed her mostly uneaten sandwich back into her bag.

"I saw that!"

"Is there anything you don't see?"

"These old eyes are still pretty sharp. Besides, I've raised too many *kinner* not to know their tricks."

"I know. I don't like to be wasteful. It's just that my appetite took a hike and hasn't returned."

"More like a buggy ride, ain't so? But don't you fret. You can cast your cares on the Lord. He cares about you."

"I know, Grossmammi."

"Then buck up. And you go to that singing tomorrow night. Do you hear?"

"I hear. I'll think on it."

"Pray on it."

The door opened to admit two *Englisch* women, thereby ending the conversation. The ladies browsed around the store a bit before the younger one approached the counter. She was tall and thin but not boney. Long, curly dark hair fell well past her shoulders. Her baby blue eyes were fringed by dark lashes, and her smile was kind.

"May I help you with something?"

"Ooh. Are these carrot cake samples?"

KatieAnn smiled. "They are indeed. Help yourself."

The young woman selected a chunk of cake and popped it into her mouth. "Mmm!" She licked remnants of cream cheese frosting from her lips. "This is the best carrot cake I've ever tasted. I'm a baker, too, but my carrot cake isn't nearly this good." She plucked another sample off the tray by its wooden toothpick. "Gina!" she called to the other, slightly older woman. "You've got to taste this cake. It's the best." She turned back to KatieAnn. "Who made this?"

"That girl you're talking to made it." Sallie tapped her cane on the floor for emphasis "Everything she makes is *appeditlich* — delicious."

Heat crept up KatieAnn's face and traveled up the part in her hair the way mercury rose in a thermometer on a hot July afternoon.

"Really? My compliments to the baker." The woman offered a friendly smile and gave a little bow. "My name is Abby Spencer."

"KatieAnn Mast." She clasped the woman's outstretched hand and gave it a brief shake.

"Well, KatieAnn, would you be willing to bake me a couple of these ap- ap-"

"*Appeditlich*," KatieAnn supplied.

"Right. Would you bake me a couple of these *appeditlich* cakes? I'd pay whatever you ask. I'm having a gathering of friends and coworkers, and they simply have to try this carrot cake."

"I-I guess we could work something out."

Out of the corner of her eye KatieAnn spotted Grossmammi Sallie's broad smile.

"I own a bake shop. I may have work for you if you're interested."

Before KatieAnn could answer, the other woman joined them. She took the offered cake sample and slid it off the toothpick with her teeth. Her brown eyes grew wide. "This is absolutely wonderful! I could eat the rest of the samples on the tray!"

"My feelings exactly," Abby agreed. "Can we arrange for two cakes?"

The women discussed dates and prices. KatieAnn couldn't believe Abby was willing to pay her so handsomely for the cakes, and tried to negotiate the price.

"No way," Abby said. "Don't sell yourself short. These cakes will be worth every penny. Trust me." They finalized the agreement, and Abby left a business card for KatieAnn. "Please think about baking for me."

Well, there's one ray of sunshine to counter that black cloud that keeps following me around.

∞

KatieAnn could scarcely believe her eyes when Lizzie entered the store an hour after Abby Spencer left. The familiar black cloud instantly swallowed the one little glimmer of sunshine she'd glimpsed for a moment. She sighed. *Please, Gott! I do not want to rehash everything with Lizzie yet again.* Her heart jumped in her chest and her breath caught midway between her lungs and nose when Clara Schwartz pranced through the door behind Lizzie. KatieAnn panicked. Was this the way people felt when they were about to pass out? She grabbed the edge of the shelf she had been straightening to steady herself. Why would Clara *kumm* here now? The desire to flee almost overtook all rational thought. But *nee*. She would hold her head high, just like Esther said. She had done nothing wrong.

"Hello, Lizzie, Clara." KatieAnn spoke as cheerfully as she could manage.

"Where's Miriam?" Clara demanded without exchanging pleasantries.

Thankfully, the only two customers scooted by Clara

and Lizzie and left the store.

"*Was ist letz?*" Miriam called as she hurried from the back of the store.

"Do you have to ask me what's wrong?" Clara bellowed. She sat her bag on the counter and crossed the room. She grabbed Miriam's arm, ushered her to a far corner, and lowered her voice a few decibels before speaking again.

Hoping to avoid any further conversation with Lizzie, KatieAnn crept past the counter to reach the corner where Sallie snored softly by the wood stove. With her back to Lizzie, she reached out to gently pull the afghan up over Sallie's frail form. She couldn't see what Lizzie was up to. Hopefully the girl would just stand in the doorway and wait for Clara.

"I really think you should be smart about this." Clara's voice carried all the way back to where KatieAnn stood. "Think of your business. Think of your reputation."

KatieAnn cringed, well aware that Clara spoke of her and her presumed untrustworthiness. When she glanced at Lizzie, the girl mocked her with a self-satisfied smirk. She quickly turned back to Sallie.

"I could probably help you clear this up." Lizzie had crept closer and kept her voice low. "You know, if…"

KatieAnn held up a hand to ward off Lizzie's stream of words. "I'll not be a part of your deception."

"Suit yourself." The girl flounced away.

Clara retrieved her bag from the counter. "Here, Miriam. I want to purchase a few of these sachets Esther made so Lizzie can take them home with her."

"How nice. *Danki*, Clara." Lizzie feigned the innocence of a newborn *boppli.*

"*Ach*! Where is my money?" Clara pulled only a few dollars from her purse. "I had more than one hundred dollars in here from selling some of my things at the market." She rummaged through her bag. "I had the money when I came in here!" She glared at KatieAnn. "See? Do you see now, Miriam?" Her voice had risen to a near shout. She tossed the sachets on the counter and grabbed Lizzie's skinny arm. "*Kumm.*" She stormed out of the store with the girl on her heels.

Sallie cranked one eye open. "Did she get a bee in her bonnet? Or maybe a whole swarm of them?"

KatieAnn couldn't help but smile at Sallie even though her lips quivered as she fought back tears.

Miriam finally pulled her gaze from the door and faced Sallie and KatieAnn. Her face was chalky white and her mouth still hung open in shock. KatieAnn's heart thumped so hard she feared it would rip right through her purple dress. She couldn't force a squeak out of her throat even if she had a clue what to say.

"Close your mouth, Miriam," Sallie said. "You know better than to pay attention to Clara Schwartz."

"Do I?" Miriam whispered. Then she snapped her mouth shut, whirled to face the counter and pressed a hand to her forehead as though suddenly experiencing a headache. As if in a daze, she shuffled behind the counter, opened the cash drawer and began counting the money inside.

"What in the world are you doing?" Sallie stopped rocking.

"Shh!" Miriam started counting over again.

"Your money is all there."

"How do you know? Things have been mysteriously disappearing around here lately — dolls, sachets, candles, rings, money. It seems mighty strange. We've never had such problems before."

"Coincidence." Sallie commenced her rocking.

"Hmmph!" Miriam kept counting.

KatieAnn watched the interchange in silence. She felt

like she sat on the rafters looking down on the surreal scene. She jumped when Miriam slammed the cash drawer closed.

"All there, ain't so?" Sallie queried.

"As best I can tell."

"See!"

KatieAnn looked from one woman to the other, her nerves wreaking havoc with her stomach. She placed one hand across her abdomen and willed her couple bites of lunch to stay down.

"KatieAnn, I think business has tapered off for today, so you can go ahead home."

"A-are you sure?"

"I'm sure. And Wednesday, Sarah will be here so you won't have to *kumm* in. I don't know yet about next Saturday."

"Miriam, are you trying to tell me you don't want me to work for you anymore?"

"Maybe not right now. Sarah can probably help out now and then. I'm sure Rebecca could use your help..."

"I understand. I-I'll get my things." She sniffed and bent to hug Sallie. "I'll still bring you treats if you like, Grossmammi."

"I'm counting on that." Sallie hugged KatieAnn with a strength that surprised the younger woman. "You just remember that all things work for *gut* to them that love the Lord. Stay strong, dearie. The Lord is on your side. So am I. And so are lots of other folks."

KatieAnn choked back a sob, kissed the old woman, and jerked her coat and bonnet off the hook. "See you soon," she whispered to Sallie. Then she grabbed her bag and fled.

Should she prepare for another visit from the bishop tonight?

CHAPTER TWENTY

KatieAnn fumbled to hitch Brownie to the buggy, her vision blurred by unshed tears. Her fingers trembled, making the ordinary task troublesome.

"Hey, do you need some help?" Levi called from the barn.

"I've got it, but *danki*."

"You're leaving early today, ain't so?"

KatieAnn nodded, afraid to trust her voice not to betray the fact she was on the verge of out-and-out sobbing. It was a *gut* thing Brownie was a docile creature as far as horses go. He accepted the bridle and bit with no fuss and was raring to go by the time she situated herself inside the buggy. She gave a little shake of the reins, and the horse set off at a moderate trot.

Brownie could find his way home blindfolded, which was a *gut* thing since KatieAnn's eyes were clouded by tears. Because the winding road was still a little unfamiliar to her and the Saturday afternoon traffic a bit heavier than usual, KatieAnn looked for a place to pull off the road and calm herself. She'd prefer not to be sobbing when she walked into her *schweschder's* house. Better to get any crying over with now.

The next gravel drive led to the school house. That should be a nice, quiet spot since school was not in session today. She steered Brownie toward the school.

A quick, brisk walk might improve her outlook. She hopped out of the buggy, looped the reins around the hitching rail, and shuffled through the crackly, dried leaves. Gazing up at the bare tree branches scraping the sky, she imagined she felt exactly the way those trees must feel—stripped of dignity, bending with the blows life dealt, and reaching for the Almighty's help. The sobs she'd held at bay burst forth against her will, leaving her gulping and gasping for air.

"KatieAnn?" a soft voice called.

She jumped, hastily swiped her hands across her tear-soaked face, and turned to identify the person who had discovered her. So much for a deserted school yard.

"I didn't mean to startle you," Hannah said. "I came to drop off some things for the teacher who replaced me. Since she lives in another district, I knew I wouldn't see her at church tomorrow." Hannah paused momentarily. "What's wrong?"

KatieAnn didn't want to burden anyone else with her problems, but she couldn't keep the words from tumbling out. "*Ach*, Hannah! My whole life is such a mess!"

"Do you want to tell me about it? I'm a *gut* listener."

"I-I don't want to trouble you." Another tear slid from the corner of KatieAnn's eye and rolled down her cheek. She thought she'd run out of tears, but apparently she had more stored away. How many tears could a human produce anyway?

"You won't trouble me at all. Let's sit on the school steps if you aren't too cold."

KatieAnn allowed Hannah to link arms with her and lead her across the yard to the little white school building.

They settled themselves side by side on the top concrete step. Hannah turned to KatieAnn with an expectant expression on her face, but she didn't press for an explanation.

After exhaling a long, quivering breath, KatieAnn spoke softly. "Why do people want to believe the worst about others?"

Hannah reached to clasp one of KatieAnn's hands. "It's human nature, I suppose. I think some people feel their own sins don't seem so terrible if they believe bad things about others. Are you still worried about the rumor Clara brought back from Pennsylvania?"

"There's more fuel she can add to that fire now."

"How so?"

Haltingly, KatieAnn related the condemning events of the day, ending with Miriam's roundabout way of dismissing her from her duties at the store.

'I'm so sorry." Hannah loosened her grip on KatieAnn's hand and threw her arm around the younger girl's shoulder, drawing her close in a hug. "Somehow everything will work out, KatieAnn. Keep trusting Gott. If He could straighten out all the trouble I was in when I came here, then He will surely help you, too."

KatieAnn nodded against Hannah's shoulder. She had heard how Hannah arrived in Southern Maryland as a crime witness in need of protection. She had pretended to be Amish and even taught in one of the schools. Now she really was Amish and had recently married Jacob Beiler. Things had turned out well for Hannah. Might things turn out well for her, too?

"*Ach!* Who could that be?"

KatieAnn lifted her head and blinked the moisture from her eyes. A horse and buggy clip-clopped up the school driveway. This place was busier than she'd have ever guessed.

When the buggy drew nigh, KatieAnn recognized the driver. Luke. Her face must be red and tear-streaked, but there was nothing she could do to change that. She straightened her bonnet and wiped her face with her gloved hand.

As soon as his buggy stopped rolling, Luke jumped out. "Is everything okay? Is someone hurt or sick?" The creases in his forehead and between his eyes revealed his worried mind. Some other brief emotion that KatieAnn couldn't identify crossed his handsome face.

"We're fine," Hannah assured him.

Luke suddenly appeared ill-at-ease, as if unsure whether he should stay or go. "Can I do anything to help?"

Hannah jumped to her feet. "I need to be getting home and seeing to supper. I'm sure KatieAnn wouldn't mind visiting with you, Luke." Hannah looked down at KatieAnn, winked and whispered, "I believe you will be in capable hands here, if you want to stay a while."

"*Danki* for listening, Hannah. Why don't you let me drop you off at home so you don't have to walk?"

"The walk is *gut* for me. I'm a fast walker, anyway. I was a runner in my old life, you know." Hannah laughed. "You keep your chin up. If you want to talk again, please drop by and visit."

"I will."

"Bye, Luke." Hannah gave a little wave and set out at a brisk pace.

KatieAnn scooted over a little, giving Luke room to sit on the step without actually touching her. She tucked the edge of her cloak beneath her leg to get it out of the way.

On second thought, she put her hands on the step, prepared to push to a standing position. "You probably should not to be seen with me." She hitched a breath. "That might—I mean, that would be best."

Luke thrust out a hand to indicate she should remain seated. "Best for whom?"

"You, of course."

"And why wouldn't I want to be seen with such a pretty young lady?"

"You know the rumors."

"*Rumors.* I don't put stock in rumors or fabrications." He lowered his tall, muscular frame and wiggled to fit into the space vacated by Hannah. "Now, do you want to tell me what has you so upset?"

"Not really."

Luke's face fell. "I thought we were *freinden.*"

"We are. It's, uh, just..." She sighed. "Well, it's news that doesn't cast me in a favorable light."

"Nothing could make you fall out of favor with me. Tell me why you've been crying."

Luke's gentle tone and his expression — so caring and sincere — touched KatieAnn deeply, and she nearly burst out sobbing again. She took a deep, shaky breath and once again launched into the story of her miserable day.

"So you see, even Miriam believes the worst about me. I'm sure she has doubts about my trustworthiness since she pretty much asked me not to return to work at her store. She probably thinks I stole the money, the ring, the doll, the sachets, and anything else that might be missing."

"I can't believe Miriam would be judgmental. That isn't like her."

"I don't know if it's like her or not, but I'm sure she believes all the evidence points to me. Think about it. Things only go missing at the store when I'm working. Pretty big coincidence in her mind, I'm thinking."

Luke remained silent, obviously deep in thought.

"I really didn't steal anything from Miriam or anyone else!" KatieAnn's outburst brought on a flood of new tears.

"It's okay." Luke patted her hand. "I believe you. Honest."

"Why? How can you believe me when others are clearly ready to believe the worst?"

"I know you. I may have only met you a few weeks ago, but I know you inside. I'm absolutely convinced you are a *gut* person."

"I appreciate the trust you have in me. Truly, I do. But still, for your sake, we shouldn't be seen together. I wouldn't want to tarnish your reputation. You are held in high regard, and I don't want to spoil that."

"What kind of person would I be if I turned my back on a *freind*?" Luke's voice dropped to barely above whisper level. "I feel more than *freindship*, to be completely honest."

KatieAnn hung her head and stared at her gloved hands in her lap. "You shouldn't say that."

"Look at me."

She tried not to, but the plaintive note in his voice compelled her to look into his clear, bright, sapphire eyes.

"Now tell me you don't feel something special between us. Tell me you want me to go away and leave you be."

"I-I want you to l-leave..." She dropped her eyes to her lap.

"*Nee*. Look at me."

"I-I can't," she whispered.

"Why not?"

"If I look at you, I can't say what I need to say."

"What do you *want* to say?"

"I-I..."

"KatieAnn, please look at me." He gently grasped her chin to tilt her head up. "Now tell me."

"I feel a connection between us, too." The words

sneaked out whether she wanted them to or not. "But I still think we should keep our distance, at least until my problems are resolved. If they are ever resolved."

Luke wanted to turn cartwheels across the yard. KatieAnn had feelings for him. The spark between them wasn't merely his own imagination. Relief and happiness rendered him almost giddy. He smiled down into her up-turned face with the adorable little brown freckles dotting her nose and nearly lost himself in the huge, dark-fringed hazel eyes. What would it be like to kiss her pink bow-shaped lips? *Better not go there.*

He forced his thoughts back to the issue. "The problems will be resolved. I am sure of that. But you need to know that I could *nee* more keep my distance from you than a newborn calf could keep its distance from its *mudder.* I will only avoid you if you ask me to. Are you asking that?"

KatieAnn remained silent for so long Luke feared she'd had a change of heart already. "I-I am n-not asking you to." He strained to hear her whisper. "Even though I think that is best, I can't."

"*Gut.*" He squeezed her hand.

"But maybe we should not be, um, obvious about our, um, relationship. At least for now?" Her voice took on a questioning, pleading tone.

"I understand." He sighed. "I don't like it, but I do understand."

KatieAnn let out the breath she must have been holding. "*Danki.*"

"You'll be at the singing tomorrow, right? Rosanna, Nancy, and the others all want you there."

"They haven't heard the latest news yet."

"Pshaw! They won't pay any mind to that."

She raised an eyebrow. "It depends what their parents say, I'm thinking."

"Trust, KatieAnn. Trust Gott and your *freinden*. We all care about you, you know."

"I-I'll think about the singing."

Luke dared not ask for more.

CHAPTER TWENTY-ONE

Fat, fluffy snowflakes twirled through the air and silently floated to the ground on Sunday morning. Daylight merely hinted at the sky when KatieAnn gave up all hope of sleep and crept from her warm bed. Awe and wonder and praise for the Creator washed over her as she stared out the bedroom window at nature's crystal wonderland. Despite the cold, she couldn't resist throwing open the window for a moment. Somehow, the silent snowfall always instilled peace. KatieAnn craved peace.

Shivering, she lowered the window and hopped over to a throw rug to get her bare feet off the cold wood floor. She prayed for strength to get through, not so much the church service, but the common meal afterwards, with the possibility of whisperings and accusing looks directed her way. Briskly rubbing her hands up and down her arms to generate warmth, she jumped to another rug to dress and wind her long auburn hair on top of her head. *Lord, give me strength.*

KatieAnn tiptoed down the stairs to the kitchen. The cold house remained dark and quiet. She lit a lamp in the kitchen, stoked the fire, and started the *kaffi* pot perking.

A chill snaked its way up her body and set her teeth a-chatter. She filled a kettle with water and set it on the stove. It was definitely a *gut* morning for steaming, rib-sticking oatmeal. The mere thought of warm cinnamon oatmeal sliding down her throat calmed her shivering.

She'd stay close to the stove until the room heated up a bit. A little time remained in which she could be alone with her thoughts and fears, before the family clamored around the table for breakfast or until Rebecca entered the kitchen to help with breakfast preparations. The scent of brewing *kaffi* filled the air. KatieAnn's stomach rumbled, though the growl was due more to nerves than hunger.

"You're up early." Rebecca rushed into the kitchen, nearly breathless.

KatieAnn jumped. So lost in thought, she hadn't even heard Rebecca's approach. "*Jah*, I had trouble sleeping so figured I might as well get up. I thought you were still asleep."

"*Nee*. I got caught up in my Bible reading when Samuel and the *buwe* went out to tend the animals. Now I guess I'm running behind."

"The *kaffi* is almost ready. I was getting ready to make oatmeal, if that's not too much work for the Lord's day. I thought it would be better for this snowy morning instead of cold cereal."

"Snowy?"

"Haven't you looked outside?"

Rebecca hurried to peer out the window.

KatieAnn shuffled close to look around her *schweschder* at the snow glossing over the grass and coating tree branches like vanilla frosting on chocolate cake. "Beautiful, ain't so?"

"It is. I wonder how long it will keep up?"

"It looks pretty steady right now." The heavy, gray

clouds seemed intent on hanging around until their contents had been completely discharged.

"The *kinner* will be so excited. Are you okay here? I'll go hurry them along. Samuel and the *buwe* will be inside soon."

"I'm fine. I'll slice some banana bread to have with the oatmeal."

"Okay." Rebecca flew from the room to collect the younger children.

∞

Huge snowflakes continued to float to earth as the church service concluded and the women headed to the house. The Zooks' barn had been comfortable enough, with several kerosene heaters and the heat of many bodies providing warmth. Still, KatieAnn had kept her heavy black cloak pulled tightly around her.

The initial blast of cold air when she exited the barn momentarily shocked her system. She hustled inside the cozy house, where she shed her outerwear and bonnet and added them to the collection in the living room. She stuffed a black glove inside each pocket. Even though all the coats and bonnets looked alike, the women never had a problem picking out their own belongings when the time came to leave.

KatieAnn kept to the fringes of the hustle and bustle as much as possible. If she could have slithered beneath the big kitchen table and remained hidden there, she surely would have done so. Rosanna and Nancy attempted to enlist her help in carrying platters and bowls to the barn, but she preferred to blend into the woodwork. Her presence in the kitchen probably spoiled the chance for gossip, though. Surely the grapevine had been quivering with news, and more than a few women would be about to burst from holding their comments inside.

"*Wie bist du heit*?" Esther sidled up to KatieAnn and spoke in a whisper.

"I've been better."

"You just hang in there. Things will work out. Have faith."

"I don't see how things are going to get better, but I suppose they can't get much worse, ain't so?" KatieAnn tried to smile, but the corners of her mouth pulled down instead of up. To her horror, her lips began trembling as much as her hands. She caught her bottom lip between her teeth to stop its involuntary movement. *I will not cry here. These people will not see how upset I am. I will not give them more to talk about.* She straightened her shoulders and blinked hard.

Esther patted KatieAnn's arm. "Let's move over to the counter and cut the pies."

KatieAnn nodded and followed the older woman, grateful she understood the desire to stay out of the way today. She picked up a wood-handled knife and quickly sliced a peach pie into six uniform triangles. Esther did the same with an apple pie. "These look delicious. Which scrumptious dessert did you make?" Esther glanced around at the array of treats on the counter.

KatieAnn saw right through the older woman's attempt to distract her from all the whispering in the corner of the room where Clara uncovered bowls of macaroni salad and coleslaw.

"The carrot cake."

"I'll be sure to save room for that."

When KatieAnn could no longer endure hiding in a corner of the now-stuffy kitchen, she stepped out onto the front porch for a quick breath of air. The men would most likely still be gathered in the barn, and the *kinner* would be running around in the snow that had begun to accumulate in little, fluffy piles.

With her nerves stretched so taut, one more furtive glance in her direction would sever them completely. A little gulp of air to clear her mind would give her strength to withstand the remaining time until Samuel and Rebecca decided to head for home. She hoped.

Not bothering to extract her cloak and bonnet from the pile, she quietly inched the front door open. She shouldn't need her outerwear for such a short time outside.

"Maybe we can write to each other."

KatieAnn was pretty sure who uttered the words, but to whom were they addressed? She widened the crack in the door. Lizzie stood close to Luke, gazing into his face and batting her stubby dark lashes. KatieAnn couldn't hear Luke's mumbled reply, but she didn't have any problem hearing Lizzie.

"I'm so glad I came here and got to meet you." The girl seemed unable to stop the constant flutter of her eyelashes.

Luke nodded and said something else KatieAnn couldn't hear. She gasped when Lizzie stepped even closer and boldly laid a hand on his arm. Did Lizzie glance toward the door? KatieAnn couldn't be sure, but she had seen and heard enough. She pushed the door closed, barely resisting the almost overpowering urge to slam it.

"There you are…" Rosanna seemed to swallow whatever else she planned to say. She looked from KatieAnn to the front window that framed Luke and Lizzie like a photograph. "I-I'm sure that's nothing." She nodded in the direction of the cozy twosome.

"I'm not sure of anything anymore." KatieAnn hated the tremor in her voice. "Maybe he runs after every female visitor."

"KatieAnn! You know Luke better than that!"

"Do I?"

"He's been your most staunch defender, along with me and Nancy and Thomas and Micah."

"Maybe he wasn't sincere."

"I've known Luke Troyer all my life. He doesn't have a mean or dishonest bone in his body. He's probably only trying to be polite to her."

"Well, I certainly didn't see him move away from her or hear him discourage her in any way."

As if he knew he was the topic of conversation, Luke glanced toward the window. KatieAnn shrank back, hoping she'd moved out of view.

"Maybe you didn't hear him clearly."

KatieAnn didn't mention that she hadn't heard Luke's words at all. She shrugged and shuffled to the far corner of the living room, which was empty at the moment.

Rosanna followed. "I wanted to make sure you were planning to attend the singing this evening. If the snow keeps piling up, we'll sled behind the schoolhouse and maybe have a bonfire too."

"It's probably best not to count on me." KatieAnn stared at the floor.

"You need to get out. We'll have fun, and you can forget all about your problems for a while."

"I doubt that will be possible. They keep mounting up like the snow, only they aren't pretty and they won't melt away."

The girls' conversation ceased when the front door banged open. KatieAnn slunk back even farther into the shadows, but Rosanna remained in plain view. KatieAnn was tempted to grab her *freind's* arm and yank her into the shadows, too, to keep from giving her presence away to the newcomer.

"*Ach*, Rosanna! Have you seen KatieAnn?" Luke's gaze swept the room, but he quickly turned when Lizzie very obviously pretended to stumble as she entered. He reached out to steady her.

"*Danki,* Luke. I surely would have fallen if you hadn't caught me in your big, strong arms." Lizzie clung to Luke's arm and gave him a big, toothy smile.

KatieAnn rolled her eyes but used the distraction as an opportunity to escape. She slipped past Rosanna and sped toward the kitchen. *Please let Rebecca be ready to go home.*

"KatieAnn, wait!" Luke's voice rang out behind her.

She refused to turn her head or even acknowledge having heard him.

"Let her go, Luke." Lizzie's voice came loud and clear. "She's so moody."

KatieAnn ground her teeth and bit back a retort. She would be kind. Mamm taught her to be kind. *Remember that, KatieAnn. Remember.* She unclenched her teeth and half expected to spit out any that had loosened. *Be kind.* When had she curled her hands into fists? She unclenched them. *Keep moving.*

All conversation ceased when she stepped into the kitchen. What a surprise! Whatever could they have been discussing? *Be kind. Be kind.* The words became her mantra. Where on earth was Rebecca? She desperately wanted to leave.

"There you are!" Rebecca entered the room through the back door. "I was checking on the *kinner*. I sent Eli and Jonas out to see if Samuel was ready to head home. The snow doesn't seem to be letting up. If anything, I believe it's snowing harder."

KatieAnn's sigh was audible. "I'm more than ready to go."

Rebecca gave her a quick, sad smile and patted her arm. "Let's get our things and get the little ones ready to go outside."

KatieAnn plucked their cloaks and bonnets from the

collection on a living room chair and returned to the kitchen. Acutely aware of the other women gathered around the periphery, she tried hard not to make eye contact with any of them. She didn't want to see the doubt and suspicion etched on some faces or the pity in the eyes of her supporters.

After handing Rebecca's things to her, she thrust her arms into the sleeves of her own heavy, black coat, and then plunged her hands into the pockets to retrieve her knit gloves. As she pulled her right hand from the pocket, a wad of money flew out with the glove. She sensed every eye in the room on her and heard several gasps.

KatieAnn bent to pick up the dollar bills. "I-I don't know where this came from." Her hand shook as she held the money away from her as if it was a king cobra. Rebecca closed her hand around KatieAnn's and took the money from her.

"How much is it?" A voice KatieAnn recognized as Clara Schwartz's called out loud and clear.

Rebecca carefully straightened out the bills and counted. KatieAnn counted silently along with her. "One hundred fifty-five dollars."

"The exact amount I'm missing from yesterday." Anger and accusation tinged Clara's voice.

"It's just like at the bake shop in Persimmon Creek," Lizzie piped up.

All eyes turned to Lizzie and then to KatieAnn, who felt as though her life had drained out through the soles of her feet. Her knees wobbled, threatening to give up their responsibility to keep her upright. Her head swam, and she couldn't seem to form a coherent thought. How could this happen again? She swayed. Was she going to faint right here in front of everyone? Rebecca tossed the money onto the table and wrapped an arm around KatieAnn to steady her.

She looked at her *schweschder* through watery eyes. "Honest, Rebecca, I didn't take that money." A single tear dribbled down her cheek.

Rebecca hugged her tighter. "I know you didn't."

"Did the money just jump from my bag to your pocket yesterday?" Clara's voice rose loud enough to be heard in neighboring Charles County, shattering the stunned silence in the room.

The screech echoed in a pounding rhythm in KatieAnn's head. She absently rubbed little circles across her forehead and summoned up the tiny bit of courage that had gone into hiding the minute she pulled her hand from her coat pocket. She surveyed the faces in the room. Some registered shock, some disbelief, and some anger. She saw concern only on Hannah's and Rosanna's faces. Something akin to determination crossed Esther's face, and KatieAnn had a feeling the other woman's sleuthing instincts had kicked into high gear.

Finally, KatieAnn looked at Lizzie, whose long, thin face mocked her. The girl's small brown eyes showed a total lack of concern. Though careless about her duties, Lizzie had always been pleasant at the bakery when they worked together. KatieAnn had even stuck up for the flighty girl on several occasions when Deborah had been frustrated to the point of firing her.

Not a speck of loyalty or kindness crossed Lizzie's face now.

The room closed in and oxygen grew scarce. She gasped to catch her breath. "I didn't do it!" She spun and raced for the door. Air. She needed air.

The cold wind slapped her in the face as she stepped onto the porch. She gulped in huge breaths, desperate to calm the erratic heartbeat that made her head and ears pound. Groups of men were making their way from the barn to the house to gather their families. KatieAnn drew in one final gulp of air before running down the steps. She had to escape. Now.

"KatieAnn, I—" Luke began.

But she sprinted past him and Micah without slowing her pace.

"Is Rebecca ready to leave?" Samuel called.

She ignored him as well. KatieAnn ran to the buggy and threw herself into a back corner. She would have run all the way home, but snow still fell from the heavy, gray sky with a vengeance. *Gray. Always gray. Where is the sun?* She wanted to scream.

CHAPTER TWENTY-TWO

"What was wrong with everyone, Fraa?" Samuel asked.

They were all settled in the buggy and finally headed for home. The horse wanted to hurry and get out of the cold and snow, but Samuel reined him in. The anxious animal's breath hung in the air as if frozen. He tossed his big head and whinnied, but he obeyed the command. "All the women looked like they'd been told we were going to be buried under ten feet of snow."

"We'll discuss it later." Rebecca spoke softly. "Too many little ears."

KatieAnn figured they'd hear the tale soon enough. Other scholars at school might tease Eli and Jonas about their thieving *aenti*. How would they handle that? Rebecca and Samuel would have to discuss this embarrassing issue with the *buwe* before sending them to school tomorrow. They needed some sort of warning of what they might expect.

Ach! The trouble and shame I've brought to Rebecca's family. KatieAnn wished she could slide right out of the buggy and stay buried in a snow drift. The *kinner's* chatter about the snow was the only conversation during the rest of the ride.

KatieAnn helped hustle the little ones inside and get them out of coats and hats, and then she made a beeline for her room. Maybe she could hide in there for the remainder of the day—or the rest of her life. She shuffled across the room to stare out the window at the mounting snow.

What would Samuel say when Rebecca told him what happened? Would he think she was a bad influence on his *kinner*? Would he want her to leave? She'd heard he had asked Hannah to leave because he feared for his family's safety. They weren't in any danger from her unless Samuel thought she might steal from them, but he wouldn't be happy. That was for sure and for certain. Maybe she should just pull out her bag and start packing. But where would she go? She couldn't go home to Persimmon Creek. Kneeling beside the bed, she reached under it for her travel bag.

"Dear Gott, why is this happening to me? I don't understand. Help me know what to do. Please make things right." Unbidden tears coursed down her cheeks. She jumped practically to the ceiling when a knock sounded at her door. *Please don't let it be one of the kinner.* They shouldn't see her like this. Hastily, she rubbed at her eyes and sniffed. Tears kept flowing, and she didn't even have time to reach for a tissue before the door creaked open.

"KatieAnn?" Rebecca peeked into the room. Her eyes grew to saucer size when she took in the travel bag on the bed. She flung the door wide open. "*Ach*, KatieAnn, what are you doing?" She rushed across the room and picked up the still-empty bag. "What on earth are you planning?" She fixed her younger *schweschder* with a motherly stare.

"I can't bring trouble into your life or Samuel's life or the *kinner*'s lives."

"Don't be ridiculous."

"Does Samuel want me to leave?"

"Of course not. Why would you think that?"

"He wouldn't want to harbor a criminal."

"It sounds like you read the same books as Esther." Rebecca attempted a smile, but the tremor in her lips gave away her emotion.

"He put Hannah out."

"That was a bit different. There were some bad people after Hannah. Samuel only wanted to keep us safe. You aren't a threat to anyone."

"He isn't afraid I'll steal something?"

"Definitely not! We love you and believe in you. We want you to think of this as your home."

"The bishop will probably visit."

Rebecca paused a moment. "That's a possibility, but we have nothing to hide. You haven't done anything wrong."

"But don't you see?" KatieAnn's voice trembled as it rose in volume. "It's Persimmon Creek all over again. More valuables were found in my possession, and I don't have a clue how they got there."

"We'll work this out. Everything works for *gut* for those—"

"I know. I know. But when? I've been waiting and waiting for the truth to be made known. Instead, things keep getting worse. I-I c-can't take any more." KatieAnn threw herself into Rebecca's arms as great sobs wracked her body.

Rebecca patted her younger *schewschder's* back. "Have faith, dear one. Trust Gott. He knows everything. He will help."

"B-but w-when?"

"In His own time. We aren't to question Him. We are to trust Him."

"I'm trying. It's so hard." KatieAnn sniffed again.

"I know. Keep believing, *jah*? And let's put this bag away. You won't be needing it."

"Y-you don't think the bishop will ask me to leave? H-he looks so stern."

"He does look stern. I guess he has to. He takes his calling seriously, but Bishop Sol is a fair man. I don't believe he'll ask you to leave. Truly I don't."

"I hope you're right."

"*Kumm* down by the stove. The *kinner* would be happy to have you read to them or play with them."

KatieAnn allowed Rebecca to lead her downstairs where the family lounged in the living room. Wood popped and sizzled in the stove, making the room warm and inviting. A slight smoky smell permeated the air, a scent KatieAnn usually found comforting and homey. She forced a smile as she stepped into the room. Samuel looked up from reading The Budget and nodded but did not utter a sound. At least he didn't scowl, ask questions, or reprimand. She tried to relax her stiff shoulders.

"Play, *aenti*?" Elizabeth looked up with a hopeful expression.

"Sure. I'll play with you." KatieAnn situated herself on the floor beside her young niece.

"Can Jonas and me play, too?" Eli asked.

"I," Rebecca corrected. "Jonas and I."

"Do you want to play, too, Mamm?"

"*Nee*, son. I was correcting your grammar."

"Why don't we get out a board game we can all play?" KatieAnn stretched to reach the games on a low shelf.

"I don't know how." Elizabeth's lower lip poked out in a pout.

"I'll help you. We'll be partners." KatieAnn tickled the little girl under her chin.

"The snow has almost stopped." Rebecca nodded

toward the window. "It's turned to small, fine flakes now."

"Aw, then we'll have school tomorrow," Jonas whined.

"I'm sure you will." Rebecca laughed at her son's downtrodden expression.

"Can we go out to play in the snow again?"

"In a little while. Wait until right before chore time so you only have to get cold and wet once."

An hour later, KatieAnn stretched her cramped legs out in front of her and bounced them up and down to dispel the tingling. She looked toward the window. Sure enough, even the flurries of snow had ceased. The sky remained heavy and gray, though, like her heart. Oh, for the sun to shine in the sky and in her soul!

"Play again?" Elizabeth tugged on her sleeve.

"Your *aenti* needs a little break." KatieAnn tweaked her niece's nose.

"Can we go outside now?" Jonas asked.

Rebecca gave the answer he'd obviously been waiting to hear. "Get your things. They should be dry now. *Ach*! Who's heading up the driveway?"

All eyes turned toward the window. A lone gray buggy slowly plodded through the snow toward the house.

"It looks like Rosanna Yoder. She must be here to see you, Schweschder. It looks like she has someone with her."

KatieAnn stood and peered out the window. "Nancy Swarey."

The two young women jumped from the buggy and headed for the house. Rebecca had the door open before they could stomp the snow from their boots. "*Kumm* in and get warm."

"We can't stay," Rosanna answered. "We just came to

fetch KatieAnn to the bonfire and sledding."

"Are you sure there's enough snow for sledding?" Rebecca cast a wary glance outside. "It doesn't look very deep."

"We can at least go down Zooks' hill a couple times before we hit grass," Nancy replied. "Where is KatieAnn?"

Rebecca nodded toward the living room.

"KatieAnn..." Rosanna began.

KatieAnn didn't even let the other girl finish her statement. "I can't go."

"Why not? We'll have fun."

"I-I just can't. You...you know why."

"Nobody believes you took Clara's money." Nancy fisted her hands on her hips. "*We* sure don't believe that."

"A certain someone asked if you were attending. A certain tall someone with blond hair and blue eyes." Rosanna winked.

KatieAnn's cheeks burned. "That someone will be fine without me there."

"Your *freind* Lizzie will be there," Nancy added.

Some *freind!* Nancy was obviously unaware of the damage Lizzie had caused. "Well, maybe Lizzie can keep that certain someone you mentioned occupied for the evening." KatieAnn didn't want to appear jealous but feared that was exactly how she sounded.

"I thought Lizzie would be getting ready to go home tomorrow," Rebecca called from the doorway.

"She can't," Nancy explained. "Pennsylvania is getting hit much harder with the snow. Her travel plans had to be postponed."

"Too bad." KatieAnn knew her comment sounded sarcastic and silently chided herself.

Nancy continued her explanation. "Lizzie was a little worried about her job, but she reached her *mudder* who said she'd let Lizzie's boss know about the delay."

"My, you seem well informed." Rebecca stated the thought that had raced through KatieAnn's brain.

"*Jah*. My *mamm* visited with Clara a bit this afternoon."

That certainly explained Nancy's wealth of knowledge, however erroneous it might be. *Be kind, KatieAnn.*

"Pleeease *kumm* with us." Rosanna dragged out the word and fixed KatieAnn with a pleading look.

"I really don't feel up to it." KatieAnn didn't want to hurt the girls' feelings. They had shown such loyalty. "Maybe next time."

"Okay, but if you change your mind—"

"If she changes her mind, Samuel or I will bring her over to the Zooks' place," Rebecca interrupted.

"All right. We'll miss you, KatieAnn." Rosanna grabbed Nancy's arm and tugged her toward the door. "By the way, I'm making candles tomorrow—those chocolate ones that smell so heavenly—and I'm decorating some holiday candles. Do you want to *kumm* over?"

KatieAnn glanced at Rebecca who nodded encouragingly. "Well, okay. I'd like to watch or help or whatever."

"Great. I'll probably start around nine, but you can *kumm* whenever you'd like."

"*Danki*." KatieAnn smiled at Rosanna. Her *freind* tried so hard to include her in the community. "Have fun sledding." She wished she could go along. She loved the snow, but didn't enjoy being the center of attention at all, particularly if the attention was so negative.

The wind howled around the corner of the house the rest of the afternoon, rattling the glass in the living room windows. KatieAnn shivered, despite sitting as close to the woodstove as she dared. The temperature had steadily dropped all afternoon. Now she was glad she didn't go sledding with the others.

While the *kinner* ate a snack in the kitchen, she pulled out her needlework bag to knit a few more rows on the lap robe she'd begun for Grossmammi Sallie. The weight of the yarn on her lap should help warm her up.

Rebecca, Samuel, and the little ones had gone out of their way to cheer KatieAnn up since she'd been relieved of her store duties. Relieved of? Fired, was more like it. Again. Soon, not a living soul would take a chance on hiring her for fear their merchandise would be stolen.

She sighed as she drew the knitting needle through a loop and wrapped the strand of sunshine yellow yarn around it. But Rebecca had urged her to leave everything to the Lord Gott, and that's what she planned to do. She'd simply concentrate on this project and let Gott work things out in His way.

Giggles floated in from the kitchen, and KatieAnn found herself still able to smile. Rebecca's *kinner* brought her such joy. Regardless of the circumstances surrounding her visit to Maryland, she cherished the time with her family.

An unexpected, furious pounding on the front door sent her needles to the floor in a loud clatter. Who would be out visiting on such a raw day, and who would bang at the front door instead of entering at the back as most *freinden* would do? Samuel reached the door before KatieAnn could persuade her legs to move.

"Miriam! Is something wrong?"

KatieAnn held her breath so her ragged inhalations wouldn't muffle the voices. Was something else missing from the store and Miriam braved the cold to accuse her? Surely not. Today was Sunday. Miriam wouldn't be in her store on the Lord's day.

"She isn't here, is she?"

"Who?" Samuel stood back to allow the distraught woman to enter.

"Sallie."

KatieAnn jumped to her feet, allowing her knitting to tumble to the floor. "Is Grossmammi missing?" She hurried to the door where Miriam stood as if in a daze.

"I haven't been able to find her. She wanders a bit now and then, you know. Anyway, I've searched the whole house, high and low. Levi has scoured the barn and out-buildings. He and close neighbors are combing the woods."

KatieAnn ran to jerk her heavy cloak and bonnet from the peg on the wall. She thrust her arms into the sleeves and fished her gloves from the pockets.

"What do you think you're doing?" Samuel asked.

"I'm going to find Grossmammi."

"It's too cold. You'll freeze out there." Rebecca hurried in from the kitchen and looked from Miriam to Samuel to KatieAnn.

"So will Grossmammi if we don't find her soon." KatieAnn secured her bonnet and wiggled her fingers into the woolen gloves.

"The men will search. You stay here with Miriam and Rebecca." Samuel grabbed his own jacket and hat.

"I have to help." Without waiting to hear any additional comments from the other three, KatieAnn ran out into the blustery wind. She didn't take time to hitch the horse. She'd leave that to Samuel. Her pounding heart should keep her plenty warm. She ducked her head against a wind gust and started in the direction of the Esh farm. *Please, Lord Gott, let me find her along the way.*

"Sallie! Sallie!" The wind snatched KatieAnn's voice and tossed it through the trees. She prayed the sound would reach Grossmammi. Where would the woman go? *Think, KatieAnn!* Sallie had shared so many stories of her younger years. KatieAnn had been enthralled by each of them. Now she had to remember some place that might have been special to Sallie.

Story after story came to mind as she hiked and shouted. The school house. Sallie loved school. She had taught before marrying her childhood sweetheart. Would she have gone there for some reason? The quickest route would be through the woods.

Brambles snagged her clothes and tried to drag her down, but she plodded on. If this hunch didn't pan out, she didn't know what she would do next. Daylight faded quickly this time of year and would take with it that tiny speck of warmth the muted sun provided. Once she cleared the briars and thorns, she ran.

The front of the school looked completely normal—and completely empty. Fear snaked up KatieAnn's spine. She raced around back and stopped so abruptly she nearly lost her balance. Grossmammi Sallie sat on the top step with her arms wrapped around her knees. She spoke, but KatieAnn couldn't hear the words. Perhaps she was singing a song from her scholar days.

KatieAnn forced a calmness she didn't feel. She strode toward the steps. "Grossmammi?"

"*Ach*, KatieAnn."

Praise the Lord Gott! The elderly woman recognized her and was not locked somewhere in the past. "What are you doing out here, Grossmammi? Aren't you cold?" KatieAnn wiggled her way onto the step beside Sallie. She stripped off her cloak and wrapped it around the trembling little woman.

"It's our anniversary."

"Your wedding anniversary?"

Sallie nodded so hard she nearly shook off her *kapp*.

Poor lady hadn't put on a bonnet, either. KatieAnn removed hers and tied it under Sallie's chin. "Did you *kumm* here to remember better?"

"I did. We fell in love here at the school. He was ahead of me, of course, but he never looked at another girl. He waited for me." She cast a furtive glance in every direction and lowered her voice. "Don't tell anyone, but he carved our initials in an oak tree out back. It's getting too dark to see it now."

"That's very sweet. You must have loved him very much."

Sallie gave a gentle nod this time. "I have *wunderbaar* memories."

"I'm glad." KatieAnn tucked a hand under Sallie's elbow. "If I help you, can you stand? We need to walk around front so I can ring the bell. Folks have been looking for you."

"I'm not lost, am I?"

KatieAnn smiled. "Not at all."

Together they shuffled around to the front of the school so KatieAnn could sound an alert. She wrapped an arm around the frail woman to add extra warmth and tried to ignore her own chattering teeth.

What seemed like eons later, several gray buggies drove into the school yard. Miriam jumped from Samuel's buggy as soon as he shouted, "Whoa!" Apparently she hadn't heeded Samuel's advice to stay inside, either. She ran toward the building with tears streaming down her face. The occupants of the other buggies followed.

"Sallie! You gave us such a fright! Are you all right? You didn't even take your cloak and bonnet."

"As right as rain. And I'm plenty warm. My girl here took care of me." She squeezed KatieAnn's arm.

"Gracious, child. You don't have on a cloak. You must—you gave yours to Sallie."

KatieAnn nodded. "She needed it more than I did."

"*Danki*." Miriam sniffed and swiped at her eyes. She

turned back to Sallie. "Are you ready to go home?"

Sallie nodded. "I am now." Her gaze took in the small crowd gathered around. "I appreciate your concern. This girl is a *gut* girl. She braved the cold to help a foolish, old woman. Don't you all forget that."

CHAPTER TWENTY-THREE

Monday morning presented another heavy, gray sky, but at least the clouds didn't spit out any snow. When breakfast was over, Eli and Jonas trudged off to school and Samuel returned to the barn.

KatieAnn helped Rebecca with the laundry early. She would head to Rosanna's for the candle making afterward. Hard work kept her hands occupied, but her mind wandered again and again to the money that flew from her pocket the previous day. How would she ever refute that condemning evidence?

"KatieAnn!" Rebecca called down to the cellar where KatieAnn fought with the old wringer washing machine.

"Be right there." She hoisted the laundry basket to her hip and climbed the stairs. A few flaps in the cold air should dry the clothes quick or freeze them stiff as boards. *"Was ist letz?"*

"Bishop Sol just arrived. He's out talking to Samuel."

KatieAnn gasped. The basket on her hip suddenly felt like it contained boulders instead of wet shirts and pants. "W-what do you think he wants? Will he *k-kumm* inside?" She blinked back sudden tears. "Never mind. We know what he wants. He'll ask me to confess or to leave or both."

"Now, *Schweschder*, we don't know that."

KatieAnn raised an eyebrow as if to say, "Really?" But she said nothing aloud.

"Here, I'll hang out the clothes." Rebecca reached for the basket her younger *schweschder* held in a death grip.

"*Nee*. Stay with me."

"I can have the clothes on the line before he gets in here, if he even enters the house."

"I-I don't think so." KatieAnn nodded at the window. Bishop Sol and Samuel approached the house in long, determined strides. She gulped hard but couldn't quite swallow or even get air past the peach-sized lump in her throat. Maybe she'd die right here on the spot. That would get her out of this mess.

"Breathe!" Rebecca tugged the laundry basket out of KatieAnn's stiff hands. She dropped it to the floor and gave the younger girl a quick hug. "Everything will be all right."

"I wonder if Joan of Arc's family said the same thing to her."

KatieAnn's heart thudded when the door banged open and heavy footsteps drew near. She searched the solemn faces for a hint of a smile above the dark beards, but found none.

"KatieAnn, the bishop would like to have a word with you." Samuel's voice sounded as stern as when he reprimanded his sons.

She nodded, not trusting her voice to emerge if she attempted to speak. Samuel beckoned for Rebecca to join him. Great! Now she would be alone with the bishop. Her always-protective big *schweschder* couldn't help her at the moment. She was on her own. Rebecca patted her arm as she scurried across the kitchen to join her husband.

"Can we sit?" the bishop asked.

"Of course. C-can I get you something to drink?"

"*Nee*. I'm fine." He dragged out a chair at the big, oak table.

KatieAnn did likewise. She feared her poor heart would explode any moment.

The bishop cleared his throat. "I understand there was a little problem at the Eshes' store on Saturday that was resolved yesterday."

"I-I guess so."

"Do you want to tell me what happened?"

"I-I don't really know." KatieAnn couldn't keep the quiver out of her voice. She inhaled deeply, hoping to calm her racing heart. "Clara Schwartz came into the store Saturday afternoon with Lizzie Krieder from Persimmon Creek. When she reached into her bag for money to pay for some sachets, it was gone."

"What was gone?"

"Her money. She said she had more than one hundred dollars from her market sales, and it wasn't in her bag."

"Where was it?"

"I-I don't know. I never saw it. I was clear across the room covering up Grossmammi Sallie with an afghan."

"Did Clara find her money?"

"*N-nee*. She and Lizzie left the store."

"This Lizzie is a *freind* of yours from your home?"

"Lizzie and I worked together at a bake shop. She's a few years younger, so..."

"So you were not close *freinden*."

"W-we were always nice to each other but not close *freinden*."

"Hmmm. Then what happened?"

"Miriam asked me to leave." Those pesky tears threatened again. She couldn't speak above a whisper. "A-and she said she wouldn't need my help at the store anymore."

"Why?"

"She said Sarah would help her, but..."

"But what?"

"I don't think she trusts me. I've never given her a reason not to, though."

"What happened to Clara's money?"

"I don't know. When I pulled my gloves out of my pocket yesterday, the money just flew out."

"Was that your money?"

"*Nee*. I didn't put money in my pocket. I don't have any idea how it got there."

"Was it Clara's money?"

"It was the same amount that she was missing, so I assume it was hers. Honest, Bishop Sol, I did not take Clara's money." KatieAnn swiped at an escaped tear with the back of her hand.

"Was that money in your pocket when you got home from the store yesterday and put the gloves in your pocket?"

"I didn't put my gloves in my pockets when I got home, so I don't know if the money was there. And I put them in my pockets so quickly after church yesterday that I didn't notice if anything else was in there."

"I've heard other items were missing from the store."

"A few little things. But I didn't take them either."

"Were there problems in your home town?"

"There were a few missing items from the bakery where I worked."

"Were these things found in your possession?"

"Uh, *jah*, but I promise I didn't take them either." KatieAnn saw herself falling deeper and deeper into a chasm that she'd never be able to claw her way out of. All the evidence pointed to her as the thief, at home and here. If it looked that convincing to her, surely the bishop would be ready to condemn her.

"Did you *kumm* to Maryland to run away?"

"I wanted to see my *schweschder*." She stopped. That was only part of the reason. She had to be truthful. "And-I couldn't confess to a sin I did not commit." There. She'd said it all. Now her fate hung in Bishop Sol's hands. *Please, Gott, don't let him tell me to leave.*

The man rubbed his big hands across his face and drew dark, bushy eyebrows together, obviously trying to collect his thoughts. The ticking of the kitchen clock sounded like the ticking of a bomb. KatieAnn braced herself for the impending explosion.

The bishop cleared his throat. "Well, KatieAnn, it looks like you've been a big help to Rebecca."

Confused at this change of topic and wondering where the conversation was going, she simply nodded but then figured some sort of response should be given. "I've tried to be."

"It seems you've been a blessing to Grossmammi Sallie, too."

How did he know anything about her relationship with Sallie? "I've grown very fond of her."

"And she of you, I gather. Sallie talked to me a bit before her family left for home yesterday." He paused and tugged on his beard.

KatieAnn held her breath. She wished the man would issue his verdict and be done with it. Her family must have already left when the bishop had this conversation with Sallie. She struggled not to tap her foot, but she sure wished he would get to the point. Her nerves were about to shatter.

"Sallie told me not to believe everything I hear and that things aren't always as they seem."

KatieAnn nodded again.

"Wise woman, Grossmammi Sallie. I'm going to take

her advice—for now—and see what happens. I'm trusting you to search your heart and to *kumm* to me if you have anything you'd, uh, like to unload. I'm also trusting you to stay out of trouble."

She nodded again. Did he think she went around seeking out trouble? For some reason, it kept finding her all by itself. The bishop pushed back his chair. KatieAnn summoned the courage to ask a question. "Bishop Sol, do you think someone else could have put that money in my pocket, thinking it was her own coat?"

"I don't know, but anything is possible." The bishop hoisted himself to his feet and strode from the room without looking back.

That's it? The interrogation is over? I don't have to leave?

KatieAnn breathed a huge, shaky sigh of relief. Now how in the world did she keep away the trouble that lurked at her doorstep?"

The meeting with Bishop Sol ate up precious minutes, and KatieAnn got a later start than she had intended. She finally had Brownie hitched and settled herself inside the family's buggy for the trip to Rosanna's house. The temperature had warmed and the snow had been steadily disappearing, but gray clouds still hung in the sky the same as they hung over her life. Unbidden, the song the little red-haired girl sang in the one show she ever attended flitted through her mind. She hummed, unsure of the words. All she could remember was, "the sun will *kumm* out tomorrow." When exactly would her tomorrow be? When would bright sunshine dispel the gloom that hung over her?

She stopped humming abruptly. If Bishop Sol heard that she'd been humming a worldly song, she'd be in even more trouble, if that was possible. She should tell

Rosanna not to include her in any more activities. The more KatieAnn kept to herself, the less chance she had of anyone else being drawn beneath the black cloud hovering over her. But she didn't have a way to cancel on Rosanna today and didn't want to appear rude by not showing up.

She tried on a smile. She *would* be joyful. Time spent with Rosanna *would* be fun. If she kept telling herself these things, she might eventually believe them.

"There you are!" Rosanna skipped down the steps, letting the door slam behind her. "I thought you'd forgotten."

"*Nee*. We had a visitor, and that made me late leaving the house. I hope you haven't finished your candle making."

"Hardly. I'm about ready to stir in the fragrance, though."

"I'm glad I didn't miss that part."

KatieAnn unhitched Brownie and turned him loose in the enclosed pasture. She hurried into the kitchen and tied on the old work apron Rosanna had draped across the back of a kitchen chair, and then picked up a wooden spoon and stirred as her *freind* added fragrance.

"Mmm! This chocolate smells heavenly." Visions of chocolate cake with fudge frosting danced through KatieAnn's head. "It makes me want to take a bite."

"You'd better not unless you want your lips sealed shut."

"That might not be such a bad idea." Both young women laughed. It did feel *gut* to laugh.

As they poured wax into molds, KatieAnn tried to explain her decision to distance herself from people. "At least until the trouble blows over." As an afterthought she added, "If the trouble blows over."

"*Ach*, KatieAnn! I don't believe any of those nasty

rumors. I don't care what anyone else says, I know you didn't take anything that didn't belong to you." Tears filled Rosanna's big gray eyes.

"I appreciate your support. That surely means a lot to me."

"You're my *freind*, ain't so?"

"Of course. Please don't misunderstand, Rosanna. You are a great *freind*. I like visiting with you and doing things with you, but I don't want to cause a blight on your character."

"I'm not worried about that in the least. I know this whole mess will be cleared up soon." Unable to free up her hands, Rosanna twisted to wipe her tears on her sleeve.

"I hope you're right." KatieAnn felt like crying again herself. She had to think of something that would lighten the mood or they'd be blubbering too much to accomplish anything. "You know, it would be really cute to pour this wax into brownie or cupcake molds, but then I guess you might have to worry about someone eating them."

"That's an excellent idea." Rosanna clapped her hands. "I could decorate them like chocolate treats. That would be so much fun...but you're right. Someone might be tempted to take a bite."

"Can you imagine if someone bought pastries and candles and reached into the wrong bag for a snack?" Both laughed so hard that they didn't hear the peck at the door and were startled when footsteps approached.

"*Ach*, Lizzie. You nearly scared me to death." Rosanna panted to catch her breath.

"I knocked."

"I guess we didn't hear it."

KatieAnn's heart rate quickened. What was Lizzie doing here? She thought the girl would be well into her journey home by now since the weather had improved. She said just that.

"I had to postpone my trip home," Lizzie said. "They're practically having a blizzard there. Travel is not advised."

"Oh."

Lizzie turned toward Rosanna. "I heard you mention you were making candles, so I thought I'd stop in to watch."

Rosanna glanced at KatieAnn and lifted her shoulders and eyebrows slightly, indicating she hadn't been expecting Lizzie's visit. "We're about done with this batch. We're getting ready to pour the wax into the molds."

"And then I'll have to go." KatieAnn's voice came out whisper soft.

"So soon?" Rosanna's shoulders slumped and the edges of her mouth drooped.

"We missed you last night, KatieAnn." Lizzie threw a smirk over her shoulder.

"We?"'

"Luke and me and the others. We had a lot of fun. In fact, I stopped in to see Luke before I came here."

"You interrupted his work?" Rosanna's expression registered her shock that Lizzie would be so bold.

"He didn't seem to mind."

"He was too polite to tell you," Rosanna muttered. She reached out to help support the pan KatieAnn nearly dropped.

"*Danki*. That would have made a huge mess. I'll help you clean up and then I'll have to get home."

"Can't you stay a little longer?" Rosanna held the mold steady while KatieAnn poured.

"Don't leave on my account," Lizzie interjected.

KatieAnn rolled her eyes. She wanted to tell Lizzie she didn't want to be in the same room with her, but that would be unkind. She didn't say a word as she carried the empty pan to the sink and began to scrub.

"I can clean up if you really need to go." Rosanna followed KatieAnn to the sink and poked her with an elbow.

"Okay. Let me get my coat and bonnet, then."

Rosanna followed her *freind* to the door. She squeezed KatieAnn's arm. "I really didn't know she would show up."

"That's okay. I'll see you next church day. *Danki* for asking me over."

"Sure." Rosanna didn't get to say more since KatieAnn skipped down the cement steps so quickly.

Before KatieAnn could get Brownie hitched, Luke rushed from the machine shop and practically sprinted over to her buggy. "KatieAnn, wait!"

"Hello, Luke."

Without being asked, he helped her finish her task. "We, uh...I missed you last night."

"Really? I heard you had a great time."

"Everyone else seemed to, but I kept wishing you were there."

"Lizzie was there."

"So?"

"So I'm sure she kept you...occupied. She said she just visited you in the shop."

"She did." Luke looked at the ground and kicked at some pebbles. "I wish she hadn't done that."

"Really? She seemed to think you were overjoyed at the interruption."

"Not so."

"Actually, it's none of my business. I apologize, Luke. You can certainly see or be interested in whomever you like." KatieAnn turned to climb into the buggy.

Luke laid his hand on her arm to halt her progress. "It's not like that at all. Lizzie doesn't mean anything to me. She seems like a confused little girl."

"I thought you were going to be pen pals when she goes home." *If she ever goes home!*

"Why would you think that?"

"I overheard her asking you to write. Oops! There I go again not minding my own business." She shook off Luke's hand and climbed into the buggy. "It's probably better for you to be interested in Lizzie anyway. I'm trouble for everyone." Tears flooded her eyes. "I have to go."

Before Luke could reply, she clucked to the horse and set out at a brisk trot. A quick glance behind her showed Luke, open-mouthed, staring at the retreating buggy. Her tears multiplied and spilled onto her cheeks. She allowed them to flow unchecked and hoped the crying jag would be over by the time she reached home.

Somebody's buggy sat near the back door of the Hertz-ler house. KatieAnn didn't want to face any guests. Maybe she could sneak in and start baking her carrot cakes. That *Englisch* lady, Abby Spencer, planned to pick them up tomorrow early in the afternoon. If she baked them today, she wouldn't feel so rushed tomorrow. She hadn't dared to mention her plan to bake while she was at Rosanna's house. Perhaps it wasn't very kind of her, but she didn't want Lizzie to invite herself over to study her every move in the kitchen. She was having a difficult time trusting Lizzie now or even believing anything the girl said. To tell the truth, she'd be ever so glad to have Lizzie completely out of her life.

After putting the buggy away and caring for Brownie, KatieAnn slipped through the back door and into the mud room. Voices, women's and *kinners'*, reached her from the kitchen. She might not get to put her baking plan into action after all. She poked her head into the kitchen. She would politely greet whoever came to visit and then dart to the stairway.

"*Ach*, KatieAnn!" Rebecca called. "You're back early."

"*Jah*. Rosanna received another visitor so I thought I'd *kumm* home and get started on my cakes." She turned to Rebecca's guests. "Hello, Lydia, Esther. How are you both?"

"*Gut* to see you again." Lydia smiled. Apparently she and her little girl had accompanied Esther for a visit. Ella sat at the table with Rebecca's *kinner*. All the children nibbled on apple slices, a safe snack even for Ella, with her celiac disease.

"We'll be leaving soon, so feel free to do your baking." Lydia glanced at Esther, who nodded.

"Please don't rush off on my account." KatieAnn untied her black bonnet and shrugged out of her cloak.

"We've both got to think of preparing supper, so we'll need to head home soon."

"Are you all right?" Esther crossed the room to stand in front of KatieAnn.

"Sure. Why do you ask?"

"You look like you've been crying."

"Maybe it's the cold weather."

"Maybe it's not. What's wrong?"

"I'm just silly." KatieAnn gave a half-hearted laugh. She lowered her voice. "It's hard to keep my distance from people to protect them, and it's even harder to be in the same room with Lizzie."

"Ah. She was Rosanna's other visitor."

KatieAnn nodded.

"I don't think you need to cut yourself off from people."

"It's better not to get involved with anyone. Then they can't get into trouble because of me. And if I keep to myself, people don't have to struggle to be polite or pretend they don't believe the rumors."

"What makes you think people are pretending? I think they truly believe you." Esther squeezed the younger woman's arm. "We really do care, you know."

"Maybe some of you do."

"Give me a little time. I'm trying to investigate."

Lydia chuckled. "Well, Sherlock Holmes, are you ready to head home?"

Esther wrinkled her nose at her older *schweschder*. "Go ahead and make fun of me, but you know I'm pretty *gut* at putting clues together." She turned back to KatieAnn. "Don't fret. Things will work out."

KatieAnn offered a weak smile. Rebecca moved closer as their guests donned outerwear. "Esther's right, dear one. Gott has a plan."

As Rebecca followed the guests to the door, KatieAnn called out. "I'll start baking my carrot cakes now if you don't need the oven."

"It's all yours. I've got stew simmering on the stove. I can bake biscuits later."

KatieAnn pulled bowls and pans out of cabinets. She removed carrots from the gas-powered refrigerator and grated them into the big glass bowl. With all her heart she wanted to believe everything would work out for *gut*, as Esther and Rebecca said. For the life of her, though, she didn't see how that was going to happen.

CHAPTER TWENTY-FOUR

After the breakfast dishes had been washed and Samuel and the *buwe* had cleared the kitchen, KatieAnn set about baking pretzel knots for afternoon snacks. She handed Emma and Elizabeth and even Grace and Benjamin little clumps of dough to roll around and pat into shapes. The older girls had great fun, but the twins soon grew bored and toddled off to play, leaving a trail of flour behind them.

KatieAnn rolled the dough and molded it in crisscross braids. She showed Emma and Elizabeth how to form their own pretzels. Emma followed directions pretty well, while Elizabeth had fun rolling balls of dough through the mounds of flour.

Once the pretzels were formed, KatieAnn brushed the knots with egg white. She sprinkled some with coarse salt and some with a blend of cinnamon and sugar. She planned to spread leftover cream cheese frosting from the carrot cakes over the remaining knots.

KatieAnn kept out enough dough to make a few regular pretzels in case Samuel and the *buwe* preferred large ones. The girls wanted to bake their lumps of dough, so she guided their little hands to form some semblance of pretzels, and then cleaned up the floury mess while the treats baked. Emma and Elizabeth stayed as close to the oven as they dared, eager to see their finished products.

By the time KatieAnn finished frosting the cakes, the pretzels and knots were ready to extract from the oven. Elizabeth hopped up and down in anticipation, her eyes shining. KatieAnn barely caught her little hand before she touched the hot pan. "We have to let them cool. You'll burn your hand and your mouth if you try them now. I'll tell you when they're cool enough. Okay?"

Elizabeth nodded but was obviously disappointed.

"Why don't you and Emma color here at the table? That way you can watch me decorate the cakes." Abby Spencer hadn't said she wanted her cakes decorated, but KatieAnn thought a few green holly leaves with red berries would lend a nice holiday touch.

Shortly after she and Rebecca cleaned up after the noon meal and all four little ones had settled down for naps, someone rapped at the front door.

"It must be your *Englisch* lady." Rebecca hurried through the house to answer the door.

"I hope she likes what I've down with the cakes." A sudden nervousness overcame her, and KatieAnn wiped damp hands on a towel. She smoothed stray wisps of hair back under her *kapp* and ran her hands down her dress to smooth out wrinkles.

"I'm Rebecca Hertzler, KatieAnn's *schweschder*." KatieAnn listened to the introduction from where she stood in the kitchen.

"Nice to meet you. I'm Abby Spencer." The *Englisch* lady had a soft, musical voice.

"Follow me. My *schweschder* is in the kitchen."

Two sets of footsteps approached. She moved the cakes from the counter to the just-scrubbed table.

"Hi, KatieAnn. It's good to see you again."

"Hello, Miss Spencer."

"Abby...please." The woman pushed a long, dark braid back over her shoulder. A few strands of hair had escaped and curled around her face. She glanced at the table and smiled. "Are these my cakes?"

"*Jah*." KatieAnn bit her bottom lip.

"They're beautiful. The decorations are perfect. I'm glad you thought of that. I know everyone will agree with me on how good your cakes are. What are these?" Abby's gaze strayed to a plate of pretzel knots covered with plastic wrap. "They look like the twisted parts of pretzels."

"They are. I call them 'knots.' When I was little, I always pulled my pretzels apart to save the knots for last. It didn't matter if they were hard or soft pretzels. The knot was my favorite part to eat." At Abby's encouraging nod, KatieAnn continued. "When I started making up my own recipes, I thought I'd make just the twisted parts. Now I make them all kinds of ways and call them 'knots.'"

"This looks like cinnamon on some of them. Is this frosting on others?"

"*Jah*. I try to top them with different things. Today I used cream cheese frosting on some, cinnamon and sugar on some, and only salt on others."

"They look delicious."

"Would you like to try them?"

"Sure."

KatieAnn unwrapped the plate so Abby could make her selection. The young woman studied the plate before choosing a cinnamon knot.

What will she think of my strange idea? KatieAnn held her breath and watched Abby's face as she chewed.

"This is absolutely yummy." Abby licked the cinnamon from her lips. "What a great idea! You know, I always broke my pretzels apart as a kid, too." She lowered her voice as if divulging some deep, dark secret. "I still do, to be perfectly honest, but I thought I was the only one who did that."

"You're not alone." KatieAnn smiled and relaxed.

"I could easily sell these. You are a gifted baker, if your cakes and knots are any indication. Would you be interested in working with me in my shop?"

"Uh..." KatieAnn looked at Rebecca, who shook her head ever so slightly. "We, uh, don't work in *Englisch* establishments, even though I do miss working in a bakery."

"You worked in a bakery before?"

"At home in Pennsylvania. I'm only visiting here right now."

"Oh." A wave of disappointment rolled across Abby Spencer's face.

"We're hoping she'll stay a *gut* long while and maybe even make this her home," Rebecca interjected.

"Do you think you could do some baking for me while you're here? I could give you orders—plenty of orders—once folks find out how tasty your treats are. I could come pick up the items, and you wouldn't even have to come to the shop. Would that be possible?"

"I guess I could ask the bishop." KatieAnn glanced at her *schweschder* again. Rebecca lifted her shoulders as if to say she didn't know.

"I'll check with the health department to make sure I wouldn't be violating any codes or procedures." Now Abby's face lit with excitement.

KatieAnn caught the other woman's enthusiasm. "I'd really like to be a baker again. I'll talk to Bishop Sol." She tamped down the fear that the bishop would say she'd cause trouble or couldn't be trusted or some other negative response. Everyone said he was a fair man. She'd see how fair he actually was. What harm could there be in selling her baked items to this *Englisch* store owner? Other Amish women sold homemade products at the farmers' market. A spark of joy lit KatieAnn's heart.

Abby pulled out her wallet and counted out the bills. KatieAnn silently counted along with her. When Abby pressed the entire wad into her hands, KatieAnn protested. "*Ach!* This is more than we agreed upon." She tried to hand some of the money back.

Abby stepped back and refused to accept the bills. "You did extra. You decorated the cakes. And you let me sample your knots. Do you have other original recipes as well?"

"Sure. I experiment with different combinations of ingredients all the time."

"Great! I sure hope we can do business together."

"I think I would like that—if it's allowed."

"We'll both check on proper procedures, okay? We don't want to do anything wrong."

"For sure." She had been accused of quite enough wrongdoing.

"I can stop by again after I've checked with folks at the health department, if that's all right."

"Sure."

"Thanks, KatieAnn. I know these cakes will be a big hit. It was nice meeting you, Rebecca." Abby reached for the cakes.

KatieAnn pulled out a plastic grocery bag. "Here let me pack them for you. I'll put in some of the knots, too, if you like."

"Wonderful. I'll be back soon."

The woman practically danced from the house. KatieAnn felt like dancing herself. Could this little ray of sunshine indicate some kind of break in her prevailing gloom?

∽

"I'll go out with them," KatieAnn offered.

Rebecca had bundled up the *kinner* and shooed them outside for some fresh air and to allow for a few quiet moments before the older ones arrived home from school. A pot roast surrounded by potatoes and carrots already bubbled in the oven. They would heat up other vegetables and roll out dough for biscuits later.

"You must be as tired as I am. Why don't you rest a bit? They know to stay in the back yard where I can watch them out the kitchen window."

"I don't mind, Rebecca. I could use a little fresh air, too."

She pushed one child then another in the swing. Samuel had suspended it by thick ropes from a thick limb of the massive oak tree at the edge of the yard. The *kinner* giggled, demanding to go higher and higher. Their *aenti* laughed along with them, and some of the tension eased from her neck and shoulders. Laughter *was* great medicine.

Buggy wheels crunching on gravel captured her attention. She looked up from pushing Elizabeth. This must be the day for visitors. She shaded her eyes against the sun's glare but couldn't determine who had come to call. She couldn't identify the caller, but it didn't look like Clara Schwartz, so that was a definite blessing.

Instead of heading to the house, the person—a man— walked toward her. *Please don't be Bishop Sol.* She did want to ask the bishop about baking for Abby Spencer, but if he sought her out, it probably was not a *gut* thing. When the man drew closer and moved into the shade, she recognized him. Younger than the bishop, and clean-shaven.

Luke Troyer. Why was he here? Hadn't she squashed his interest in her?

"Push!" Elizabeth cried. KatieAnn's attention returned

to the little girl. She quickly set the swing in motion again.

"Hello, KatieAnn."

"Hi, Luke. What brings you here?"

"You."

"I thought we finished our, uh, discussion at Rosanna's house yesterday."

"You might have finished, but I didn't."

"Oh." KatieAnn wished the earth would swallow her. She did not want to be mean, but for his own *gut*, Luke needed to leave her alone.

"Push!" Elizabeth demanded again.

"*Kinner*, time to *kumm* in!" Rebecca called from the back door.

KatieAnn grabbed the ropes to stop the swing's motion. She was sorry Rebecca called the little ones in. They provided a great distraction. The four rosy-cheeked youngsters ran for the house, leaving KatieAnn to face Luke alone. She was tempted to trot to the house, right behind the twins. Instead, she stayed rooted to the spot, her hands still grasping the ropes.

"Are you too cold to stay outside?"

She wanted to say she was, so she could escape, but she couldn't be untruthful. "I'm okay."

Luke stared at the ground for a few moments before raising his sapphire gaze to hers. "I appreciate that you want to protect me, but you don't need to do that. I can take care of myself. And I really don't much care what other people think. I do care about you, though. And you are not trouble to me—nor to anyone else."

"But people think I'm trouble. They think I steal things. I see the way they look at me, Luke—the way they guard their belongings when I'm around, like they're afraid I'm going to go through their pockets. I wouldn't want to expose anyone else to that kind of treatment."

"I can't change the way people act or react, but I'm not

really worried about them. I know what I believe, and I believe you are innocent."

"Things got taken by someone. I'm the newcomer who had similar problems at home. I can see where people would jump to conclusions. They just jumped to the wrong conclusion."

"Then we need to prove them wrong."

"Not *we*. I need to prove them wrong. You're better off with Liz-"

"Stop! I don't have any intention of getting involved with Lizzie. She needs to grow up. And she needs to go home!"

"Luke!"

"I'm sorry, but I think she will cause more problems by staying longer. She fans the fire Clara started, I'm thinking."

"I-I need to go inside and help Rebecca." KatieAnn inched toward the house.

"Don't run away again, KatieAnn. Please." Luke reached out to grasp her arm.

"Please try to understand." Tears sprang into her eyes. "I-I can't get involved with you right now—even if I wanted to."

"Do you want to? At least tell me that."

KatieAnn pulled away and ran for the house. She clapped a hand over her mouth to muffle her sob.

Luke's raised voice floated across the cold air quite clearly, even over her sniffling.

"I'll take that as a *'jah.'*"

CHAPTER TWENTY-FIVE

On Friday evening, the scholars would present their Christmas program. Everyone attended the community event whether they had scholars or not. Jonas and Eli both had recitations that they had practiced so much even KatieAnn had them memorized. School work would be on display, and everyone would sing. Of course, there would be cookies, brownies, and other sweet treats to enjoy while socializing afterward.

The *kinners'* excitement was contagious. Eli and Jonas chattered nonstop until they finally pulled on their black jackets, knit gloves, and black felt hats before traipsing off to school that morning.

"I don't know how poor Teacher Mary is going to make it through the day." KatieAnn jumped when the *buwe* slammed the door shut behind them.

"I'm sure it will be hard, her being so young and all." Rebecca shook her head. "Hannah volunteered to help her out all day, though, so that's a plus."

"I guess I should get busy baking." KatieAnn pulled out mixing bowls, brownie pans, and cookie sheets. She'd moped around the past few days, and counted on baking to put her in better spirits now. And she did look forward to watching all the excited scholars in the evening, even if she planned to observe the program from the shadows where she hoped she wouldn't be noticed.

∞

Despite the frosty evening outside, the little school house fairly crackled with heat—from the wood stove and from the throng of bodies crowded into the cramped space. All the cajoling in the world from Rosanna and Rebecca couldn't entice KatieAnn to abandon her post in the back corner of the room. She could see the scholars perfectly fine and wouldn't have to be the subject of any twittering or frowns. Attention should be on the *kinner* who had worked so hard, not on her.

KatieAnn mouthed the recitations along with Jonas and Eli and willed them to remember the words. Both spoke in little, shaky voices at first, but finished clear and strong, without a hitch. KatieAnn knew Rebecca breathed a sigh of relief along with her. The whole program progressed as planned. Teacher Mary had done a *gut* job. Parents and guests smiled their approval at the conclusion.

"KatieAnn, *kumm* help me serve refreshments." Rosanna tugged on her arm.

KatieAnn hesitated. She liked her spot in the shadows, but she didn't want to seem uncooperative.

"Please?" Rosanna's voice took on a pleading tone.

KatieAnn didn't want to refuse her *freind*. She allowed herself to be dragged from her hiding place. Maybe everyone would be anxious to get a snack and would ignore her altogether. She could only hope so. She relaxed a bit as she handed out cups of juice and cider.

"Say, did you by chance see what I did with my little candle-making book the other day?" KatieAnn instantly stiffened at Rosanna's whispered question. "It's a small spiral notebook where I wrote down mixtures for dyes and fragrances."

"*Nee.* I don't think you had it out when I was there." *Does she think I took the book? Will she accuse me of stealing, too?*

"Never mind, then. I probably forgot where I put it. I'm so scatter-brained." Rosanna giggled.

Not true. Rosanna was far from scatter-brained. In fact, she was meticulous with every aspect of her candle making. "Did you show it to Lizzie? Maybe you put it some place different."

Rosanna snapped her fingers. "That's it! I kept trying to get her to stop asking questions about Luke. I pulled out the book to distract her."

"Lizzie!" The voice carried from across the room.

All conversation stopped. All eyes fastened on Esther and Lizzie, who faced one another near the rows of coats suspended on pegs on the far wall. Esther's frown was visible even from the refreshment table. "Why are you back here in the coats?"

"Just getting something." Lizzie tucked her right hand behind her back.

"Getting something or putting something in a pocket?"

Lizzie didn't reply. Her expression held defiance.

"What's in your hand?"

"That's my business."

Esther held out her hand. Her foot tapped hard on the wooden floor.

"I don't have to give anything to you."

Esther continued to stare at the younger woman. Suddenly Lizzie seemed to wilt. Her cheeks flushed a bright red. She dropped her gaze to the floor and slapped a little notebook into Esther's outstretched hand. Esther flipped through the book. "This is Rosanna's candle book. Where were you going to put this?"

Lizzie kept her eyes on the floor.

Mudders sent older girls to entertain the young *kinner* and get them out of earshot. Rosanna crossed the room, pulling KatieAnn with her. Bishop Sol and the other ministers strode toward the back of the room. Other adults closed in to listen.

"You took my book?" Rosanna's voice shook a little. "Why?"

"I j-just b-borrowed it."

"Whose coat were you planning to put it in?" Esther seemed determined to ferret out the truth.

"Hers," Lizzie whispered. She pointed at KatieAnn.

KatieAnn gasped. "Why, Lizzie?"

"P-people already believe you t-take things."

"But I don't take things, Lizzie, and you know it."

"Who took Clara's money?" Esther grasped Lizzie's arm.

Lizzie stared at her black shoes.

"Lizzie?" Bishop Sol joined in the interrogation.

"I-I did. But I wasn't going to keep it. I put it, uh, in–"

"In my pocket!" KatieAnn finished the statement for her.

"What about that *Englisch* lady's ring?" Esther was on a roll.

"I found it outside the store, like I said."

"But it wasn't anywhere near KatieAnn's buggy, was it?"

"How would you know that?" Lizzie's head snapped up. Her eyes blazed at Esther.

"I happened to be at the store unloading my wreaths. I saw you *kumm* from the opposite direction."

"So? Maybe I walked around before going inside."

"But you didn't." A different voice drew everyone's

attention. Grossmammi Sallie pushed through the sea of green, blue, and purple dresses. "I wasn't sleeping. It just so happens that I glanced out the window about the time you came kicking rocks up the driveway. I saw you pick up something in the parking area."

"Why didn't you say anything at the store?" Lizzie's harsh tone bordered on disrespectful.

"I guess I did drift off while Esther brought things in and you women got to talking. Your voices must have lulled me to sleep."

"There! So you don't know anything for sure."

"Lizzie!" Bishop Sol's voice had a sharp edge. "You need to show respect for your elders."

"Sorry." But Lizzie didn't look sorry at all.

"I was alert enough when Clara's money went missing, young lady." Sallie's voice grew stronger. "I know KatieAnn was fussing with the afghan covering me. She wasn't anywhere near Clara's purse."

"You didn't say anything about that at the time, either, so you really don't have any facts." Lizzie's dark eyebrows drew together in a fierce scowl.

"You're right that I didn't see *you* take it, but I know for sure and for certain that KatieAnn didn't take it."

"Why did you want to make me look like a thief?" KatieAnn wanted desperately to make some sense of this whole ordeal. Did Lizzie hate her that much? Why?

"Everybody already thought you were a thief anyway. Besides, I gave you a chance, remember? But you wouldn't help me."

"I would have gladly helped you with your baking, but you wanted me to lie for you, to deceive your new employer. *That* is what I wouldn't do."

"Is that the truth, Lizzie?" Bishop Sol turned his sternest look on the gangly girl in front of him.

Lizzie glared at KatieAnn, then at Esther, and then at

the bishop. She sighed. Her shoulders slumped, and she again looked at the floor.

KatieAnn patted Sallie's arm and smiled into the sweet, wrinkled face before shuffling over to stand next to Lizzie. Gently, she grasped the other girl's arm. "Did you take the money and watch at Deborah's shop and put them in my coat pocket, Lizzie? Then, did you deliberately knock down the coat tree so everyone would see them fall out of my pocket?"

Lizzie burst into tears. "Y-you're beautiful. You're the b-best baker around. D-Deborah wouldn't even give me a ch-chance. You had T-Timothy. Y-you had everything I-I wanted."

Though she was shorter and slighter, KatieAnn pulled Lizzie into her arms and patted her back. "In the first place, Timothy Yoder and I have been *freinden* since we started school together. *Freinden*, Lizzie, nothing more. Understand?" Lizzie nodded against KatieAnn's shoulder. "I would have helped you learn to bake if you had asked. You never asked. In fact, you didn't even seem serious about working at the bakery—you came in late almost every day and complained a lot. That's probably why Deborah didn't let you bake."

Lizzie sniffed and raised her head. "I h-had a hard time remembering orders and d-dropped things. I would have b-been better back in the k-kitchen."

"Why did you take Rosanna's candle book?" Esther was obviously still in investigation mode.

Lizzie pulled back from KatieAnn's embrace and swiped a hand across her eyes. "When KatieAnn wouldn't give me her recipes or help me, uh—"

"Trick your bosses?" Esther inserted.

"*Jah*. Well, then I thought of something Rebecca said."

"Something *I* said?" Rebecca stepped forward and wrapped an arm around her *schweschder*.

"You said maybe baking wasn't my calling or gift, that maybe I had some other talent. I watched Rosanna make candles, and that looked like fun. I only wanted to copy her mixtures in case I decided to try candle making. I was going to give the book back."

"By way of KatieAnn's pocket." Esther shook a finger. "Why?"

"I don't know. I-I guess I figured Rosanna might think someone took her book if she noticed it was missing."

"So you figured you might as well let KatieAnn take the blame for that, too."

Lizzie hung her head as tears flowed again. Rebecca pressed a tissue into her hand. She gulped and raised her eyes to meet KatieAnn's. "I'm sorry. Because of my jealousy, you lost your job and had to leave your home. I know I don't deserve it, but can you ever forgive me?"

"I've been very hurt, but *jah*, I will forgive you." KatieAnn sniffed back tears of her own. "I'm sure there are things you are *gut* at, Lizzie, things you can do better than other people. You need to ask Gott to show you."

Lizzie nodded.

"Well, we've solved everything except for the missing sachets and doll from Miriam's store." Esther tapped her chin in thought.

"Actually, that's not a mystery any more either." Miriam stepped forward.

"How so?"

"Levi and I decided to turn Grossmammi Sallie's mattress to see if that would help her sleep better. When we pulled the mattress out, we found those missing items underneath."

"What?" KatieAnn couldn't believe her ears.

"I suppose during one of Grossmammi's restless days she plucked the things off the shelf and squirreled them away."

"I'm so sorry, dear," Sallie said. "I'd completely forgotten. I found those things in my bag but didn't remember putting them in there. I stuffed them under the mattress and planned to take them back to the store. But I was under the weather for a few days and completely forgot about them."

"That's okay." KatieAnn hurried to the old woman's side and wrapped her in a hug. "*Nee* harm was done."

"Harm was done to you, and I'm so sorry." Sallie raised her voice. "Listen up, everyone. This girl is the sweetest thing ever. She is innocent of any wrongdoing. And that's the truth of it."

KatieAnn smiled through her tears. "*Danki*, Grossmammi. I love you."

"And I love you as one of my own." Her fierce hug brought a gasp of surprise from KatieAnn. "Pretty strong for an old woman, ain't so?"

KatieAnn laughed. Rebecca, Esther, Hannah, and even Miriam took turns hugging her.

"Lizzie, you must return home and tell your community the truth." The seriousness of Bishop Sol's tone left no room for argument. "You need to clear KatieAnn of any wrongdoing and ask for forgiveness."

"I will. I promise."

"You need to do a lot of praying and thinking about how to mend your ways."

Lizzie nodded. "I should be able to get a ride home tomorrow."

"We can call Kathy Taylor and see if she can hook you up with the load leaving from the Annapolis market tomorrow." Clara wormed her way through the sea of people milling about. "KatieAnn, I owe you an apology. I believed the rumors I heard in Pennsylvania and told people here not to trust you. I-I ask your forgiveness."

KatieAnn was shocked speechless. Was this humble

woman in front of her the same Clara Schwartz? "Of course I forgive you." She held out her hand.

Clara grasped the extended hand and pulled KatieAnn to her in a quick hug. "It would be *wunderbaar* if you decided to stay here and make this your home."

"*Danki.*" KatieAnn managed to whisper the single word before being overcome by fresh tears.

"You *kumm* with me." Clara released KatieAnn and turned to Lizzie. "We need to talk to Kathy and get you packed. You are *wilkum* to visit again after you settle matters at home."

Lizzie nodded before facing KatieAnn again. "I'll talk to Deborah. I'm sure she'll give you your job back. I know she won't accept me, and Bea's family won't want me either, since I can't bake." Her face fell, and a dejected sigh escaped. "I can't do much else either."

"I'm sure you have talent." KatieAnn spoke kindly. "You just need to discover it and use it."

"Maybe."

⌇

KatieAnn stepped outside for a few quiet moments and a bit of fresh air. She needed to let the revelations of this evening sink in before helping with the cleanup.

The truth had set her free! She could go home to Mamm, Daed, and her family. She could bake at the Old Time Bake Shop if Deborah would take her back.

Or she could stay in Maryland and ask Bishop Sol about baking for Abby Spencer. She could talk to Luke without fear of getting him into trouble.

Luke. Had he heard about Lizzie's confession? What did he think?

KatieAnn jumped at a light touch on her arm. She'd been in such deep thought she never heard approaching footsteps. She turned to find Luke standing right beside her. Had he read her mind?

"Hello, KatieAnn." He seemed unsure what to say next.

"Hi, Luke. It's a beautiful evening. So many stars are shining down on us. And the Lord Gott placed each one there. He has them all numbered and knows about each one, just like He knows each of us."

"He knew you were innocent of any wrongdoing. I knew it, too."

"*Danki* for believing in me."

"I-I guess you're free to go home now, if that's what you want."

"*Jah*. If that's what I want." Was it?

"You could stay here. I'm sure Rebecca would be glad of that."

"*Jah*. She's my only *schweschder*. I love her and her family."

"That would be one reason to stay."

"One?"

"There could be another reason."

"What would that be?"

"You could stay because, uh, because then I could *kumm* calling on you."

"Luke Troyer, are you asking to court me?" KatieAnn shivered more from the tingling sensation racing up and down her body than from the cold.

"I am." Luke moved closer. "What do you think about that?"

"I think that would be an excellent reason for me to stay in Maryland."

Luke wrapped an arm around KatieAnn's trembling body. He bent to brush his lips across hers. "Maybe Gott had this in mind all along."

"I thought I was running away from something, but maybe I was running toward something, instead."

"To me? To a new life in Maryland?"

"To you. Here. The Lord Gott is *gut*. He has made everything work out for *gut*."

About the Author

Susan Lantz Simpson has been writing stories and poetry ever since she penned her first poem at the age of six. She has always loved the magic of words and how they can entertain and enlighten others. Her love of words and books led her to earn a degree in English/Education. She has taught students from Prekindergarten to high school and has also worked as an editor for the federal government. She also holds a degree in nursing and has worked in hospitals and in community health.

She writes inspirational stories of love and faith and has published a middle-grade novel (*Ginger and the Bully*). She was a finalist in the OCW Cascade fiction contest. She lives in Maryland and is the mother of two wonderful daughters. She is a member of ACFW and Maryland Christian Writers Group. When she isn't writing, she enjoys reading, walking, and doing needlework

Acknowledgements

Thank you to my family and friends for your continuous love and support.

Thank you to my daughters, Rachel and Holly, for believing in me and dreaming along with me.

(Rachel, you patiently listened to my ideas and ramblings, and Holly, I couldn't have done any of the tech work without your skills!)

Thank you to my mother who encouraged me from the time I was able to write. I know you are rejoicing in heaven.

Thank you to Mennonite friends, Greta Martin and Ida Gehman, for all your information.

Thank you to my friend Dana Russell and all my friends at Mt. Zion United Methodist Church for your overwhelming support and encouragement. You ladies are great!

Thank you to my wonderful agent, Julie Gwinn, for believing in me from the beginning and for all your tireless work.

Thank you to Dawn Carrington and the entire staff at Vinspire Publishing for all your efforts in turning my dream into reality.

Thank you most of all to God, giver of dreams and abilities and bestower of all blessings.

Dear Reader,

If you enjoyed reading *Plain Truth*, I would appreciate it if you would help others enjoy this book, too. Here are some of the ways you can help spread the word:

Lend it. This book is lending enabled so please share it with a friend.

Recommend it. Help other readers find this book by recommending it to friends, readers' groups, book clubs, and discussion forums.

Share it. Let other readers know you've read the book by positing a note to your social media account and/or your Goodreads account.

Review it. Please tell others why you liked this book by reviewing it on your favorite ebook site.

Everything you do to help others learn about my book is greatly appreciated!

Susan Lantz Simpson

Plan Your Next Escape! What's Your Reading Pleasure?

Whether it's captivating historical romance, intriguing mysteries, young adult romance, illustrated children's books, or uplifting love stories, Vinspire Publishing has the adventure for you!

For a complete listing of books available, visit our website at www.vinspirepublishing.com.

Like us on Facebook at www.facebook.com/VinspirePublishing

Follow us on Twitter at www.twitter.com/vinspire2004

and follow our blog for details of our upcoming releases, giveaways, author insights, and more! www.vinspirepublishingblog.com.

We are your travel guide to your next adventure!

CPSIA information can be obtained
at www.ICGtesting.com
Printed in the USA
FFHW020815130619
52961323-58588FF